Return to Madrid

Gordon L. Thomas

Gordon L. Thomas

Published by SellMy Books

A CIP catalogue record for this title is available from the British Library

ISBN 978-0-9956778-3-8

Cover picture: Francisco Pradilla Ortiz, *'The Surrender of Granada'* 1882, Palace of the Senate, Madrid

Cover design by Rohan Renard (www.RenardDesign.com)

First published 2019

Printed in the UK by CMP (UK) Ltd

SellMy Books
(contact: www.gordonlthomas.com)

About The Author

Gordon L. Thomas is retired and lives with his wife in London, England. He began his career lecturing in physics at King's College, London. He then worked in the UK Home Office as a scientist and also as an administrator. Latterly, his responsibilities were in police science and physical security. Since retiring he has become a keen writer and this is his fourth novel. For more information please visit his website www.gordonlthomas.com which you may use to contact him.

Acknowledgements

There are a number of people who I must thank for helping me with the writing of this novel. First my darling wife, Janet, to whom the book is dedicated and who gave me so much support while writing it. Janet also proofread the first manuscript and pointed out a number of errors.

Eva Peters of Twickenham Rotary Club suggested I write this story so I am deeply grateful to her.

I also thank our son, Greg, who read it critically and made a number of suggestions for improvement.

A number of others read the first draft and commented. I am therefore also grateful to fellow authors, Loretta Proctor and John Chamberlain, my good friend Chris Forkan and my sister-in-law, Karen Teuber, all of whom gave me helpful feedback.

I am also grateful to our daughter Mel Hartley, her husband Guy and Greg's wife, Sue, for their constant encouragement and for pressing me to complete this novel.

Preface

Return to Madrid is a sequel to Gordon L. Thomas's first novel, The Harpist of Madrid, which is based on the amazing life of Juan Hidalgo de Polanco, who at an early age became a harpist in the court of Philip IV, king of Spain, and who was the most famous Spanish composer of the 17th century.

Towards the end of this earlier novel, Juan Hidalgo de Polanco's son, while a student at the University of Alcalá de Henares, died in mysterious circumstances. Sixteen years after her son's passing, his mother, Francisca de Abaunza decides to investigate the death.

This novel can be read independently of The Harpist of Madrid.

To Janet

Glossary of Spanish words

calle: street, road

chuchinillo: famous dish made from suckling pig

ducat: unit of currency, 11 *reales*

iglesia: church

jumilla: type of Spanish wine made with the Monastrell grape

legua: distance of a league, 5 kilometres, about three and a half miles

libra: unit of weight, about a pound

magistral: of the master or masters

maravedí: unit of currency: 34 *maravedís* = 1 *real*

milla: about a mile

Mudejar: a Moslem who remained in Spain after the re-conquest

pie: unit of length, about a foot

plaza: a square or market square

plazuela: a small square

puta: prostitute

real: a unit of currency

tio: uncle or equivalent to 'mate'

vara: unit of distance, about a yard

zaguan: hall or hallway

Chapter 1

It is late in the September of 1685. The sun shines brightly over the whole of Madrid and hardly a cloud can be seen. But the clear night sky has given way to a chilly start to the day. The usual smells of the night soil, emptied on the streets before 6 o'clock in the morning, are barely present, masked by the cool air.

A handsome woman, who appears to be in her late fifties or possibly sixties, elegantly dressed in black and wearing a hood, is walking across the bridge over the Manzanares, the river that meanders vaguely north to south at the western edge of the town. It is still early in the morning and, apart from a few trades' people pushing carts of goods for the market or food for the shops, there is no one else to be seen. She stops at the centre of the middle span and turns south to face the river.

***

As I stand on the bridge, ready to jump to my death in the waters below, my whole life passes before me.

Juan, my husband, now dead, sitting there, strumming his harp… that moment when we first met, while Diego portrayed me… 'The Lady with a Fan'. Those first, precious moments together and alone in Juan's rooms…then, as I asked to be his lady friend…our first kiss when he took me home…my reaction to his confession of making love to a *puta*…his reaction as I told him I'd been raped by a priest…our first, fumbling intimacies…seeing each other naked…his proposal to marry me... the wedding…the birth of Juan Junior…our pride at Juan Junior's brilliance…our collapse when Juan Junior died…when I screamed and could not stop…my insanity and the years in the asylum…the miracle of my recovery…then Juan dying, not six months ago.

I miss them both so much that life has completely lost its meaning. I am ready to go. I start to cry. I climb up onto the parapet. I look down at the flowing waters below… goodbye friends… goodbye, life…

Chapter 2

That morning, Inés Manuela del Mazo climbed out of her bed earlier than usual. She stepped quietly across the bedroom floor so as not to wake her younger siblings, still sleeping soundly. She looked into the bedroom mirror as she tied her black hair up at the back and adjusted her side plaits which reached to the curve of her back. Her hair accentuated her pale, delicate ears. While her softened, round face betrayed her strong motherly instincts, she realised she was not the most beautiful of women but that didn't worry her one bit. She buttoned up her white blouse which exposed her shoulders, of which she seemed quite proud. She quickly slipped into a brown skirt.

By the time she was up, and ready to meet her friend, it was gone seven and she was beginning to become anxious. She'd told Francisca de Abaunza that she'd be at her house by 7.15 and would have to hurry if she was to be there by then. They needed to be early if they were to benefit from the bargains at the Plazuela de Selenque market. Fortunately, Francisca lived in the next road and it was an easy walk from the del Mazo's house in the Calle del Olivar.

It was almost ten past seven by the time Inés, by then wearing a heavy coat and headscarf, shut the front door, came out onto the dusty street and turned north to walk the two hundred *varas* or so to Francisca's house in the Calle de la Madalena.

Inés was forty six, fit and active. She had no trouble in walking at a fast pace to Francisca's. In fact, she enjoyed stretching herself a little. She wondered whether Francisca would be ready when she arrived. Most of the bargains had gone by 8 o'clock and they still had to walk the half *milla* or so to the market in the Plazuela. She quickened her pace a little more. There were a few other people walking the streets at that time of the morning. Two men, dressed in green sleeved jackets and wearing black tricorn hats, were approaching her. She recognised them as members of the local Holy Brotherhood and they recognised her. They

3

were walking away from the direction of the river, a *milla* or so to the west.

'Good morning, señora,' said one of the constables, the taller and thinner of the two. 'You're up bright and early! Where are you off to this morning?'

'To meet my friend who lives in the Madalena. We'll soon be on our way to the Selenque market. To pick up some early bargains!'

'Good luck, señora!' said the tall man's plump colleague.

'Thank you!' said Inés. 'I hope you've had an easy night?'

'Not too bad for a Tuesday. A few drunks and a bit of rowdiness in the Plaza Mayor but not much else.'

'Good, good! Must go! I'm late as it is!'

Inés continued along up the Calle del Olivar and turned right at the corner into Calle de la Madalena. Francisca's elegant house was along on the left. Inés knocked loudly on the door and stood there patiently, breathing just a little harder than she would have, had she not walked so quickly.

Two minutes later she was still standing there, shifting her weight impatiently from one foot to the other. 'Surely Francisca would be awake by now,' she thought. 'We need to be on our way.' She knocked again and moved towards the street to look up at Francisca's bedroom window. The curtains were open but wherever Francisca was, she needed to open that door. She knocked again. She waited and waited. In an act of pure impatience, she tried the door handle. The door swung open on its hinges.

'My God,' thought Inés. 'Now what do I do?' She wondered if someone, a street burglar or vagabond, had broken in and hurt Francisca, or, dare she even think it, had murdered her. She decided to go in.

4

'Francisca!' she shouted, as she stepped across the threshold. 'Where are you? You must be in here somewhere!' Silence. Inés walked quickly up the hall, fearing the worst. She looked into the drawing room to the right, then into the one further along the hall to the left. There was no sign of her, except that everything looked amazingly clean and tidy, as if she was expecting visitors. She walked into the kitchen. Then she saw it: a few, short, handwritten sentences on a white piece of paper. Inés picked it up and read it quickly.

My dear Inés, There is nothing in life left for me. I am going to end it all. I will always love you. Farewell, Francisca.

With great presence of mind, Inés took the note and ran out the house, closing the door behind her. Her mind raced and tears ran down her face as she half walked and half ran back to her house. Scattered thoughts sped across her mind as she went. Why was Francisca going to end her life? Why hadn't she, Inés, done something to prevent her from doing this? She felt guilty. Maybe Francisca was still alive and Inés could save her from death. Francisca needed help. Where could she be? She quickly placed the key in the lock and opened the door. She shouted out, 'Baltasar where are you? Get the horses!'

Baltasar was Inés's younger brother, one of her mother's eight children, all of whom, except Baltasar and the married María Teresa, lived in the house in the Calle del Olivar. He lived in a rented house in the Puerta Cerrada, the one in which Juan Hidalgo junior lived, prior to his death. However, the builders were doing some repairs to an internal wall so was staying at his sister's house for a few days.

He would be thirty nine in December. While he enjoyed his work as a baker in the palace kitchens, he had never succeeded in his main ambition which, like his father, was to be a portrait painter. He certainly possessed the skills. In a matter of a few minutes, he could produce, in charcoal on paper, an almost exact likeness of anyone who would pose for him.

Baltasar was tall, erect and handsome. His rounded face, much like Inés's, gave him a friendly, approachable look and he loved to talk to people. He'd stop and talk to anybody, street beggars, street entertainers, vagabonds and even the street whores whom he would occasionally tease but never partake of their services. Baltasar had great charm which enabled him to attract the ladies, to the extent that he had fathered four illegitimate daughters, all of whom lived with their mothers who were, to a minor degree, supported from Baltasar's modest income from the palace.

'What's the matter, sis? Why the panic?' shouted Baltasar from an upstairs bedroom where he was dressing and yawning at the same time. 'Thought you were going to market with Francisca.'

'Come down quickly! There's trouble with Francisca. She's left a suicide note!'

Baltasar's tone changed dramatically. 'Be right there!' A few seconds later, Baltasar was skipping noisily down the stairs, two or three steps at a time.

'Quick, look at this.' Inés handed him the note.

'She's got no reason to want to do that. I don't understand.'

'Nor do I. I thought she was coping well after Juan's death but now we know she wasn't.'

'What are we going to do?'

'Go and look for her? The bridge over the Manzanares is the most popular suicide spot. Let's go now. She may not have done it yet.'

'We'll have to move quickly. Yes, I'll get the horses. Right now. I'll just put on my coat.'

Baltasar soon appeared, holding the reins of two young horses. His was a frisky black stallion which he could barely afford to buy but had decided to anyway. Inés's was a dappled grey mare, somewhat shorter than Baltasar's mount and more docile so easy for her to handle. Inés deftly mounted her horse which almost knocked into Baltasar's as she swung it around to face Baltasar by then firmly in his saddle.

'Follow me!' said Baltasar.

'Which way is best?'

'Up to the Madalena and west to the Calle de Merced.'

'No, down to Calnario then Encomienda, surely!'

'No! Honestly, Inés, Madalena goes directly west and we'll be at the bridge in no time! Come on!'

He pulled on the reins and jabbed his heels into the stallion's side. The horse flicked his mane and galloped up the Calle del Olivar. Inés had little choice but to follow. She galloped after her brother, whom she could barely see through the cloud of dust he'd raised. He charged out of Olivar, left into Madalena and almost hit a hand pulled cart coming from the west.

'Mind where you're damned well going! You almost had me and my wagon over, you idiot!' shouted the wagoner, a stocky individual with a noticeable paunch, a red face and a dirty looking flat cap with a hole in it.

Baltasar, keeping an eye on the road ahead, raised a hand to acknowledge his error but continued apace with Inés right on his tail. They galloped along the Calle de la Madalena, past the Fuente de las Relatores and into the Calle de la Merced. Another hazard. Two wagon drivers, each travelling in opposite directions were blocking the road. Baltasar and Inés had to stop.

He pleaded with the drivers. 'Please señores, move to the side. We are trying to save a life and only have two minutes at the most!'

'Whose Christ bleeding life?'

7

'The lady's blood will be on your hands if you don't move,' said Baltasar with creditable patience and coolness.

'I'll go forward and to the side,' said the second, more sympathetic driver. His cart rumbled over the uneven, stony road and out of the way. Baltasar snapped his reins and both his horse and Inés's were soon galloping down the Calle de Merced towards the Calle de la Compania, just to the south of the Plaza Mayor.

Galloping on the roads of the city, while not actually prohibited, was regarded as dangerous and unsociable. It was generally reserved for mounted officers of the Holy Brotherhood, attempting to apprehend a criminal. So the few people on the streets at that time of the morning stopped and looked on in horror as the two of them were riding so quickly and with such abandon. Those near the middle of the road, dashed out of the way as soon as they saw the speeding riders who were leaning forward over their horses' necks to give them even more speed. A man in a pinafore, carrying a basket of bread shouted out. 'What do you think you're doing? This isn't a race track you know!' As he lost his balance, moving out of their path, he fell against a house door and just managed to hold his basket. Two loaves fell to the floor.

Not everyone disapproved. A lady in a large floppy hat, wearing a purple dress, clutching a small dog to her modest bosom and walking towards them from the direction of the river called out to them as they sped by. 'I hope you make it in time!' She could not know what 'it' could be or how much 'time' they had; or maybe she could.

They lent over as they rounded the corner into the Puerta Cerrada, then straightened up again as they passed Baltasar's house, not even glancing towards it. Other than the intrepid riders, not a living soul was present in the Cerrada so they had a clear and unimpeded ride through. They were soon entering the Plazuela del Cordon where another hazard confronted them. A troop of soldiers, probably Madrid Tercios, were marching towards them with harquebuses over their shoulders. A modest crowd of the local populace had formed and were walking alongside them, some even marching to the rhythm of the soldiers. The marching forced the two riders to stop. They had no option. Time was running out. Inés had all but given up seeing Francisca alive again and tears began to run down her face at the thought. Baltasar turned to look at Inés only to see the look of despair on her face as she stopped and stared at the mass of people confronting them.

Then, as if one of the riders had told them to do so, the soldiers veered off to the riders' left, into the Villa de Carcel and out of their way. The riders renewed their gallop. They were soon dashing down the Calle de Segoviana towards the Puerta de Puente. Seconds later, they reached the bridge over the Manzanares. As they slowed down to a canter and rode across, their eyes scanned the sides of the bridge. Their heads bowed in deep disappointment at seeing not a sign of Francisca. Inés cried openly and more tears ran down her face. Baltasar leant across and somehow managed to put an arm around her. He was almost crying, too.

They turned around, dismounted and began to walk the horses back over the bridge. Baltasar put his arm around Inés's shoulder again. She pulled out a handkerchief to wipe her eyes. She wondered whether they had made a huge error and that Francisca had gone somewhere else to end her life. Perhaps at the end of a rope in the barren waste of the Tela, where the old king used to hunt. The current monarch, Charles I, could hardly walk, let alone ride a horse. God only knew where she was.

'Who's that?' said Baltasar, as they were about halfway back across the bridge. 'It's Francisca. She's alive!' Baltasar had spotted Francisca. He could just about see her head, her face looking towards them. She was climbing down the side of the bridge and preparing for that last jump, the last move she would ever make, unless they could stop her. The two riders dismounted and left their horses standing there. They rushed towards her: Baltasar grabbed one of Francisca's arms and Inés the other.

***

9

'Go away,' I said. 'This is the end. I am jumping in!'

'No you're not,' said Inés and Baltasar together.

'We are here to save you. We cannot let you fall to your death. You have a lot to live for. If you love us, as you say in your note, you'll allow us to help you. First let's get you up,' said Inés.

It was that word 'love' that stopped me. Suddenly I realised what a fool I had been. That simple phrase that Inés had uttered, 'allow us to help you' also had a profound effect on me. I looked one last time at the waters below and couldn't jump. From that moment I knew I had to continue to live, if for no other reason than to be with these friends. I have to admit that I still had little motivation, little purpose, other than my friends, to keep me going.

Baltasar had the foresight to bring a length of rope with him, which he fetched from his horse as I clung on to the parapet with my hands and with my feet standing together on the ridge arc at a river entrance to the bridge. Inés held onto my arms but wouldn't be able to save me if my footing gave way. I was stuck in this awkward position from which I couldn't help myself back up.

'I'm going to thread this rope around your shoulders and tie it to the parapet. That will at least secure you by your arms,' said Baltasar. 'Then we'll work out how to get you up onto the road.' Somehow I managed, while retaining my footing, to lean back enough to enable Baltasar to place an end of the rope between me and the bridge. I felt quite frightened because, having changed my mind from wanting to commit suicide to wanting to survive, I was scared of falling off into the swirling water below. Baltasar quickly placed the rope through, under my arms and tied it to the parapet. How they were going to lift me out, I did not know.

By then a small group of onlookers had gathered to see me in my plight and watch my friends struggling. An old woman's eyes almost leapt from their sockets as they met mine. She was shocked into silence.

Then two large men, who looked so similar they could be twins, came forward. They each wore round brimmed hats and jackets over rough shirting material.

'Come on, *tio,* let's give you a hand to lift her out.'

'Thank you, señores,' said Baltasar. 'If you each hold one of her arms, up near the shoulder, and take up the weight of our friend down there, I'll untie the rope from the parapet. Then we'll lift her out.'

Then, possibly prompted by the first two, another two men came to help. They looked as if they could be farm labourers. Baltasar adopted the role of supervisor and Inés my comforter. 'You will have to help pull yourself up, Francisca, as these men take the rope and lift you out,' said Baltasar. Seconds later, I landed in a heap of rope and dishevelled clothing on the road. I was safe, if ashamed at what I was about to commit, had these gallant people not saved me. I burst into tears.

'Please don't cry, Francisca,' said Inés. 'You are safe now and can start again.'

I hugged and thanked her, Baltasar and the four strong men who had helped me out of my predicament. I felt very strange and still tearful. If Baltasar and Inés had not found my suicide note in time and rightly guessed that I would throw myself from this bridge into the river, pounding the rocks below, my body would have been smashed to pieces in the torrent. It was almost as if I had died and been brought back to life by some miracle of nature. In a way, that's exactly what it was. I couldn't put my gratitude into words. I vowed at that very moment, never to attempt anything as destructive and stupid again.

The small gathering of onlookers and these kind men who helped Inés and Baltasar rescue me soon dispersed and the three of us were left there in the middle of the bridge. Inés spoke first. 'Let's go back to my place,' she said.

'I agree,' I said, a little sheepishly.

'Climb up behind me on the horse,' said Baltasar. So that's what I did.

We walked the horses back to the Calle del Olivar. By that time of the morning, there were many more people on the streets of Madrid and our pace was limited by their scurrying to and fro, about their daily business. Not many words were exchanged on that gentle ride but Inés several times cast a loving smile in my direction and I responded similarly.

It wasn't long before that quiet journey ended and the three of us were sitting at the table in Inés's kitchen. Most of her brothers and sisters had left the house to go to their work or college so, apart from Geraldo, the youngest who was still sleeping, the house was empty.

'I'm going to work,' said Baltasar. 'Have a good day, ladies!' He headed for the front door and closed it behind him as he left for the palace kitchens.

'Well, here we are!' said Inés, attempting to start a conversation with me and pointing to the chairs around the table. We each sat adjacent to the same corner.

'I'm so sorry, Inés. I should never have done such a thing.' I burst into tears again and Inés stood up to comfort me. She wiped my tears in her pinafore. 'I promise I'll never do it again. It was so selfish of me.'

'Don't cry, Francisca. I'm glad you are thinking like that. Tell me frankly: what made you do it?'

'I felt so low. I had lost my true love Juan and was, to be honest, barely coping without him. And of course, Juan junior had died either by suicide, an illness or at the hands of another. The deaths of these loves of my life just got the better of me and I wanted to end it all. I'm sorry, Inés. I should have spoken to you instead of leaving that pathetic note and gone off to the river. It was an awful thing to do. I gave no thought to my friends, you in particular, and became completely overcome by the wish to die. That's all there is to it.'

'Just one more question, Francisca. Yesterday you and I had arranged to meet at your house at 7.15. When did you decide to do it? Before we made that arrangement or after?'

'I know what you are saying Inés and I understand the question. I had been feeling very low for days but tried not to show it. I woke at about 6 o'clock this morning. That's when I decided to do it. I got dressed and went to the river. Thank God you found the note! I'll be grateful to you for ever.'

'I understand, Francisca,' she said as she stood and put her arm around me again. I managed not to cry. 'It's no good just living for your friends. You need a different reason. I don't know what but something other than me and my family. You have other friends as well, of course.'

'I'm sure I'll find something. I'll think about it, Inés.'

'I will too but better if it's an idea of yours! I'm not letting you sleep in your house tonight, so let's go there and pack a few things to bring back so you can stay here, maybe for a few days. Oh, and we must lock your door!'

Chapter 3

The first night I spent in Inés's house profoundly affected me. I spent most of it awake and thinking. I couldn't believe I had survived my abortive attempt at suicide, not because I had failed in the sense of half doing it, that is jumping into the river and becoming seriously injured, but because I had been persuaded not to jump by that word 'love' and Inés and her brother's wish to help me. But there I was, lying there, looking up from a bed in a room which María Teresa, Inés's second youngest sister, slept before she got married. I was alive and grateful, grateful beyond measure, for what these two people had done for me that day. I silently offered my thanks to God for bringing these two wonderful friends to my rescue.

This was not the first time that Inés had played such an important role in my life. A number of years before, I was incarcerated in the Misericordia asylum. It was just after Juan junior had died, of whatever cause, and, as a direct result of his death, I had gone insane. This change in my life took place when I was on my way home from the Shod Carmen soup kitchen one afternoon. I called into the San Ginés church to pray to God for the soul of Juan junior. I was kneeling in a pew when I heard this loud voice in my head. The voice of Aura, one of the goddess Diana's nymphs, was telling me with great compulsion and urgency to set fire to the church. I knew her well as Aura became the goddess of the air in the second opera written by Juan Hidalgo, my late husband. I told her I could not set fire to the place. She raised her voice to an even louder pitch and told me that the only way I could avenge the death of my son was to set alight to this church.

I insisted that I could do no such thing. Then she said that she would arrange for a lightning strike to kill me if I didn't. So I had no choice. I tore up a prayer book, took a candle from the altar and set the pages alight underneath the pew in which I had been praying. I was sure I could feel Aura blowing the flames and helping the fire to establish

14

itself. Soon an almighty conflagration was burning the pews and threatening the rest of the church. I walked out of the smoke filled building right into the hands of the local Holy Brotherhood who arrested me and took me to the asylum.

They chained me to the wall and kept me in that hideous place for years. It was disgusting. It was impossible to escape from the stench of human excrement and the screaming of those poor souls who were much worse than me. Juan came to see me every day I was there. He still loved me, even in my insanity. Sometimes I was naked. One time I had smeared myself with my own shit. That day, as in many others, Inés came too. They both helped me clean myself up.

Then one day, after nearly seven years in this segment of hell, Juan and Inés came to see me. Inés had this extraordinary dream, or so I learned afterwards. She dreamt that she had brought into the asylum a medal that Pope Innocent X had given her grandfather, Diego Velázquez, on one of his visits to Italy. When I touched the medal, I became instantly cured. That is exactly what happened. Whether it was the way the light shone on the medal or whether it was a true miracle, from that moment, I was cured. My insanity had vanished from my head. Only weeks later I came home, never to go to that place again.

While lying in that bed in Inés's house, contemplating this incident from my past, I saw again that flash of light from the medal. The whole room, at least in my dream, for that is what it must have been, suddenly became an incandescent white. Every surface, every item in it, the dressing table, the wardrobe, the walls, the floor and the ceiling, even the curtains became bathed in this intense light. That shining moment was the beginning of a new dawn, a new chapter in my life, even though, in reality, nothing but total darkness could have enveloped me. I realised at that precise moment my new mission in life. I would re-investigate the death of my beloved son. That would be my new purpose, my aim, and I would not yield until I had succeeded in achieving it. I would establish beyond doubt whether he had died of natural causes, taken his own life or had been killed by another.

***

'Good morning, Francisca,' whispered Inés, as she approached my bed at about 8 o'clock in the morning. I had slept a wonderful night's sleep after not quite literally seeing the light and setting my new aim in life. 'Here's a glass of water,' she said as she placed it on the bedside table and then crept over to the window to open the curtains. She wasn't sure whether she had woken me or not.

'You are kind,' I said, as I rubbed the sleep from my eyes and yawned, making it obvious that I was awake.

'Take your time, Francisca. I'll put some breakfast on the kitchen table and you can come down when you so wish.'

Once I was properly awake, I couldn't wait to get dressed and tell Inés what I had decided. I was soon ready. I made the bed, picked up the glass of water and made my way down the stairs.

'Here I am,' I said, smiling to Inés, as I stepped into her homely, large kitchen. A large round table, surrounded by six chairs, dominated its centre and a fire in the hearth gave the room a comfortable glow.

Inés came towards me and planted a kiss firmly on my lips. 'It's wonderful to see you looking so much better than yesterday, Francisca. Pull out a chair and sit down. Shall I toast you some bread? There's a bowl of olives and some tomatoes. You can pour yourself an orange juice, if you wish.'

'I'll say, yes to all of that, Inés. You are kind.'

'Did you sleep well? Sometimes it's difficult in a strange bed!'

'I must tell you, Inés. I had the most incredible night.' I explained that I laid there thinking about her kindness and generosity and that the day before wasn't the first time she had had a major effect on my life. I mentioned the light from her grandfather's medal, if that's what it was,

16

that cured my insanity. I told her about my dream and the intensity of the light. Then I told her that I had set a new mission for my life.

'What is it Francisca? Tell me! Tell me now!'

'I am going to find out how Juan junior died. I'm determined! I'm going to do it, if it's the last thing I ever do.'

'Well, Francisca. I'm surprised... and pleased,' she said, but in a less than enthusiastic tone. 'Have you thought how you might go about solving this mystery?'

'I will go to Juan's college, the College of the King at the University of Alcalá de Henares. Then I'll find his professors. I know the departments they worked in then and I can't imagine they will have moved far from Alcalá. Other than visiting other universities, academics tend to stay in the same place for their whole careers.'

'What do you think they'll tell you that they didn't tell the investigating authorities? And that was... what sixteen years ago?'

'I don't know exactly... But I hope that they will give me information they might have feared to give before. I don't know. I can only go there and see.'

'Have you any specific plans? When will you go?'

'It's all fresh in my mind at the moment, so I have no plans as such. I need to make some so I'll probably go in about a week. I need to make arrangements to secure my house and have it looked after. It will soon be the autumn vacation so it will be good to go there when there are few students. I will ride my horse there and stay in a hotel. I don't know how long it will all take but I will stay there for two weeks, unless I get nowhere at all. When Juan and I went to see Juan junior as a student studying there we stayed in a tavern really close to the college. It was called The Inn of the King. I'll stay there, if I can.'

'Umm,' muttered Inés, as if in deep thought. 'You've thought it through quite well. I can see some problems. Identifying those professors to begin with. It's an interesting challenge but you must keep it in perspective. You have other things in your life as well, Francisca.'

'You are right, Inés. I have my wonderful friends, mainly you and Baltasar and your family. And once I have found out all I can, I will stop and carry on with life as normal but I am burning inside to do it.'

'I have an idea which might help, Francisca ... I will come with you. I cannot let you go there alone. It's not far but a lone woman of nearly seventy ... Well, you'd be vulnerable to say the least. I'll speak to José. I'm sure he'll agree...only too pleased to have some time to himself!'

'You are a marvel, Inés Manuela. I truly love you,' I said. 'But why speak to José?'

'It's only fair. We've been separated for over twenty years now but I still do quite a bit of work for him, mainly during the week. I won't be available for him, if I'm away with you.'

'I see! You do more for him than I expected.'

'Sometimes a little more than cooking and cleaning, if we both feel like it, but we won't go into that!'

'I think you just have! I trust he pays you well!' We each exploded in cheery laughter.

***

It was truly wonderful that the two of us were such good friends. This is especially true because of our differences in age. At that time, I was sixty nine and Inés twenty three years younger. We were like a mother and daughter. There wasn't much, if anything, we wouldn't discuss with each other, not only about our own lives but about others and we would freely exchange views about our country and its vicissitudes. We laughed and

18

cried together, ate and drank together and had shopped together so often that the stall holders at the market thought we were mother and daughter. We met shortly before her grandmother, Juana Velázquez died, which was only a few days after her husband, Diego Velázquez, passed away while working as chief portrait painter to the King.

Juana became my best friend shortly after Juan and I became engaged to be married. She even helped me to choose my wedding dress! Inés and her father, Juan Bautista Martinéz del Mazo, the artist who later took over Diego's post as chief portrait painter, along with Juana, were the chief mourners at Diego's funeral. It was there that we were introduced and only shortly after became such good friends. It was as if Inés had taken over where Juana had left off.

***

At about eleven in the morning, two days later, I went round to see Inés to find out whether or not José had agreed to her going and, if so, to start making detailed plans. As usual, I knocked on the door, even though I realised that she usually left it unlocked during the day and that I could freely walk straight in.

Inés opened the door. She had a nasty bruise around her eye. 'I'm going,' she said with a strong note of anger in her voice.

'What happened?' I said.

'He said I couldn't go. I said I was only asking as a matter of politeness…and I was going anyway. He came over towards me and started shouting right into my face. He said I was still his wife and that if he said "no" I couldn't go. I said I didn't care what he thought and I was his wife in name only. He stood back and punched me in the eye. I had to defend myself so kicked him as hard as I could, right in the crotch. He let out an almighty yell and fell over, banging his head on the kitchen table. I turned around and left him there!'

I was stunned. 'Inés, it's my fault! If it wasn't for me…'

'No. It's no fault of yours! You didn't hit me! He did!' She burst into tears and put her arms around my shoulders.

We were still standing on the threshold to her house. 'Let's go in,' I said, not wanting my friend's plight to be exposed to every passer-by. She relaxed our embrace so I led her into the kitchen and sat her down at the round table facing the fire.

'Let me get you something to drink, Inés.'

'There's a jug of grape juice in the cupboard,' she said, pointing over to the door.

I took a cup from the shelf and poured her a glassful. 'You don't have to come,' I said.

'Francisca, I am coming with you, bruised eye or not!' She had stopped crying by then. 'I'm sorry. I didn't mean to break down in front of you. Not after what you've been through.'

'Don't worry, Inés. I understand completely but I still can't help blaming myself... if only a bit.'

'I'm more in shock than pain. I still can't believe he was so angry and violent. He's never hit me before. He did threaten me once, when I wanted to go to see María Teresa in Toledo. She was staying at a friend's house there and wanted me to come to her birthday party. But he never went as far as striking me. A doctor as well. He should be preserving life...not punching people about!'

'I'm shocked, too. But I don't know him well. I think I've only been in his company twice.'

'I've had enough of talking about him, so let's do some journey planning!' said Inés, standing up and going to the cupboard from which I had taken the fruit juice. 'I'm hungry so let's have something to eat.'

She cut four slices from a small loaf of bread and placed them on a plate then spooned some black and green olives into a small bowl. 'Here you are Francisca. Help yourself.'

I took a slice of the bread and started to eat it. 'Nice and fresh. Get it this morning?'

'Yes from the bakers in the Calle Olmo.'

'I'd like to leave in a few days. What about you, Inés?'

'I'm with you,' she said, as she picked a couple of olives from the bowl and put them in her mouth.

'What if we head for Torrejón de Ardoz? I remember seeing an inn in the square as Juan and I passed through on the way to see Juan junior at the college.'

'Good a place as any, probably better than most and at least we'll be in a small town. I'm worried that we will be vulnerable, travelling as two women. You hear of so many highwaymen on that road, stripping and robbing anyone they can outride.'

'I've thought about that, Inés. I have an idea. You will laugh, I'm sure! What if you dress as a man? You are about the same size as Baltasar. Ask him if you can borrow some of his clothes!'

'You've got some imagination... and nerve, Francisca! I can't dress as a man! Ridiculous!'

'Why not? You can act as my son! I'll be a good mother to you,' I laughed. 'And we'll need a weapon, just in case.'

'Baltasar has one of those new flintlocks. When I ask for some clothes, I'll also try for his gun! He might even show me how to use it!'

'You agree then!'

'Of course, mother! What else could I do?'

21

Inés had thrilled me with her willingness not only to come with me to Alcalá de Henares but also to play the role of my son. She showed true friendship and at the moment of her agreement, I felt a lump form in my throat. I held back the tears.

We soon moved on to deciding about the horses. Inés would leave her dappled grey mare here and attempt to convince Baltasar to lend her his black stallion. She'd ridden it before and felt that such a powerful horse, with me on my young mare, Matilda, would allow us to outrun any attackers we might possibly meet on the way. Although Inés had probably lost José as a source of income, she confided in me that she still had a substantial amount from the will of Diego Velázquez, so she could easily afford a week or two in Alcalá. I was still enjoying a pension from the palace that I had been regularly receiving since Juan's passing so I could manage it, too.

***

The following morning, I heard a knock on my door. I wasn't expecting anybody. Several thoughts crossed my mind. Was it Baltasar who had come to tell me that Inés had been attacked and hurt by José? Could it be Inés, who had, for some reason changed her mind? I doubted the latter but could not be sure. I rushed to open it.

'Francisca! Go inside. Something to show you!' she said, clutching a large canvas bag to her chest. Her eye looked even sorer than it did the day before and was closing slightly. I wondered how she felt knocking my door. It was only a few days before that she walked in and discovered my shameful note.

'Let's go into the drawing room.'

'By the blood of Christ,' I said, as Inés carefully placed a beautiful flintlock pistol onto the table between the armchairs. She smiled triumphantly.

'He agreed!' I said.

'Yes, I knew he would! He just wanted to help us. He loved Juan junior right from those days when the both used to go to school together, even though Juan junior was quite a bit younger than him!'

'Yes, I remember it well! And what about the horse?'

'He's letting me take Caesar. I so love my brother!'

'I love him, too, Inés. He's making it so much safer for us.'

'What's more, Francisca, he's offered to look after your house while we're away. Have you a spare key I can give him when I get home?'

'Just a minute.' I went to the kitchen, fumbled through a dresser drawer and went back to the drawing room. By then Inés was standing with her hands behind her back and looking out of the window at the people walking by.

'Here it is, Inés. Give it to him with my blessing and thanks.'

'What about money, Francisca? I'm thinking of taking twenty *ducats*. What about you?'

'That sounds about right. Let's take thirty each, just to be sure. You never know!'

'Agreed! All we need is to agree a time for meeting up tomorrow.'

'Shall we make a fairly late start? We are less likely to be attacked if the road is busy. Let's leave at about ten o'clock? We can take it at a canter, most of the day.'

'I'll be here at ten, Francisca. It will be quite an adventure!' she said as she came towards me and kissed me on both cheeks. 'I'll go now and do my packing!'

***

How I ever slept that night I do not know. I don't think I did. I was so full of energy and excitement. I thought ahead to the university. How

23

would we find the professors? After all, I hadn't even met them. We'd have to make some enquiries but that was for later. How would they react to two women asking for their co-operation in investigating a death, especially as it occurred in Madrid and not at Alcalá? We'd soon find out.

I rose early and got dressed. I put on my yellow brown riding breeches: I couldn't wear a dress or skirt, not riding that distance. I packed my saddlebags, putting my money right at the bottom. I sat and eat the pieces of bread I'd saved for my breakfast. I drank the last vestiges of orange juice I'd also saved.

I sat impatiently looking out of the window for Inés. Surely, this couldn't be her. A black stallion carrying its rider approached the house. The rider was dressed in a tricorn hat, a heavy jacket and wore a black patch over the left eye. Yes, it was her. Inés looked more like a man than a lot of men! She had hidden her side plaits inside the hat. I rushed to the front door and opened it as she tied her horse to the rail outside.

'Is that you, Inés?'

She feigned a man's voice. 'No, it's one of the holy brotherhood! I've come to arrest you for the theft of a sheep!' We both laughed.

While Inés waited by the door, I took my saddlebag from the hall, walked around to the stables and saddled up Matilda. I held her reins as I guided her, snorting excitedly in anticipation of the journey ahead, around to where Inés was waiting, astride Caesar. I locked the front door, put the key in my breeches pocket, climbed into the saddle and kicked the stirrups. We were on our way.

Chapter 4

We couldn't have chosen a better day to start. The early autumn sun gave the whole of Madrid a pleasing brightness. There had been no rain for several weeks, so the horses kicked up the dust as they trod the uneven road. We made our way east, along the Calle de la Madalena towards the city gate. Although Inés and I were among the lucky ones, we could not fail to notice, as we trotted by, many examples of abject and appalling poverty, brought about, at least to some extent, by the declining wealth of our town in particular and our whole country in general.

We had to break into a fast trot as a group of beggars attempted to block our way while we passed the Church of the Holy Ascension in the Calle de Atocha. Although there were a number of people on foot, we were the only riders there. The beggars saw us from the top of the church steps and, at the shouted injunction of the apparent leader, ran down towards us, with no shoes but on their rag wrapped feet. There were at least eight of them dressed in tatters, holding out collecting pots or simply their bare hands in supplication. I pulled a four *maravedí* piece from my jacket pocket and threw it towards one of them only to be jeered and hissed at. We soon left them standing there.

'That was a close one, Francisca. Just as well you gave them something!' Inés shouted across at me.

'You can't help feeling sorry for them. They'll soon be at the Shod Carmen soup kitchen for food. I'm sure I recognised a couple of them.'

As we trotted further down the road, we saw some children who were scavenging for the odd crust of bread or a discarded piece of meat or vegetable lying on the street. Most were probably orphans but some may have been thrown out of their homes for a minor infraction or because their parents could, in these hard times, no longer afford to keep them. Several women were joining them, as if there weren't enough individuals competing for these scraps.

Such was the parlous condition in which our town found itself. With the almost complete drying up of the sources of gold and silver from the Americas and the increasing wealth of our empire on the far side of the Atlantic Ocean, our wealth had diminished and continued to do so. We could no longer afford to support battles on various fronts in Europe and, with The Treaty of Nijmegen, had even relinquished our hold on a number of our possessions in the Spanish Netherlands. These were difficult times.

We were soon passing through the Alcalá gate and onto the road to Torrejón de Ardoz.

'Glad it's so busy,' said Inés. 'Must be safer!' She had to be right. Few riders overtook us and no carriages or carts.

We pressed on for an hour or so until Inés yelled across. 'I feel like a break.'

We found a spot near some dead trees and tied up the horses. Then we sat on the dry ground to rest our legs and watch the passing traffic. We must have looked an odd couple: a woman in her later years and a much younger man in a tricorne. I took a bottle of water from my saddlebag and offered it to Inés before I took a draft myself. I suppose we had been sitting and chatting for about ten minutes when two other riders stopped alongside us. They were more obviously men than Inés!

They tied up their horses with ours and walked over towards us. Neither wore hats but each had his hair tied in a braid. One wore an old leather jacket over tight fitting riding breeches and the other, the younger, it appeared, had donned a heavy looking shirt which he wore over plain, dark blue trousers. Hardly riding clothes.

The elder spoke first. 'Good day. Where are you from and where are you heading?'

We hadn't rehearsed this. So Inés didn't know whether to speak with a low, man's voice or just speak naturally. Realising her plight, I took the initiative and spoke first.

'We're from Madrid and heading for Alcalá de Henares. What about you?'

'We are both actors, heading for the Príncipe Theatre in Madrid. We've each won parts in a play by de la Barca.'

'Oh. Which play?' I tested them.

'The Mayor of Zalamea,' said the younger, slightly thinner one.

'I play the farmer, Pedro Crespo,' said the elder.

'And I play Don Alvaro de Ataide, the army captain,' said the other.

I knew this play quite well because I remember Juan telling me about it. Calderón de la Barca had named it after a play of exactly the same name by Lope de la Vega. So I thought that, unless they were very clever in fooling us, they were genuine and therefore that we need not fear them.

'It's a well-known play,' I said. I hesitated to say more and definitely did not want to reveal that Juan knew de la Barca personally.

Inés must also have thought they were not a threat. 'Good to meet a pair of actors,' she said, without attempting to speak in a man's voice.

'It looks as if you could be an actor, too!' said the older looking one.

'I'm only dressed like this for our mutual protection,' said Inés.

'I don't blame you,' said the other. 'The roads along here can be pretty dangerous. I'm intrigued that your friend knows so much about de la Barca's plays!'

'Don't be. Her husband used to write the music for them. He and de la Barca wrote our country's first operas!'

'You must have been married to Juan Hidalgo de Polanco!' said the older one who wasn't much younger than me.

'Indeed I was. God rest his soul.'

'He was a great composer,' the older one replied. 'I was at the first performance of his second opera, "Celos Aun del Aire Matan". What an amazing work!'

'I am aware of his work, too,' said the younger.

The more senior one came up to me and shook my hand. 'I'm delighted to meet you, señora. I am honoured to meet the great man's wife. What a timely coincidence! We must make our way now. We bid the two of you a safe journey!'

The two men turned towards their horses, quickly mounted them and galloped off in the direction of Madrid.

I looked at Inés in utter astonishment. I was almost in tears to hear Juan's name mentioned in such glowing terms. I was so proud of my beloved composer. Inés looked at me.

'You must feel so good about that! Two educated men and both knew of the work of your famous husband!'

'I am surprised and proud. I shan't forget that short encounter for a very long time! Let's get back on the road.'

***

By the time we reached the outskirts of Torrejón de Ardoz, it was approaching six o'clock in the evening. The weak, early evening sun still shone upon us. We entered the village through a gate in a high wall and passed through a long, narrow street with houses each side. A horse and cart would have difficulty in negotiating the street if a similar sized vehicle was travelling in the opposite direction. This street led into a huge square with, at its far corner, an impressive church with a narrow spire climbing from the centre of its tall, elegant tower. The village looked and felt exactly as I remembered it. Little, in fact nothing I could detect, had changed in those sixteen years or so.

'Is that the inn, over there?' asked Inés, pointing to a tavern, from which a couple of staggering drunks were emerging. It was only a few steps from the church.

'That's it!' I said. 'Let's go in.'

'Please may I help you?' asked a tall, well dressed gentleman, probably the landlord, standing behind a desk, a few paces inside the door. Reddish stone slabs of various sizes, butted together and worn by constant traffic, made an interesting and unusual floor to this large drinking room, which was illuminated by the candles in a heavy looking, iron chandelier, suspended over its centre by a rusty chain. The walls were covered in a yellowish wash, which appeared darker the further up the wall we looked.

'Just a room for two for one night, dinner for two, breakfast and stabling for the horses,' I said.

'You are in luck,' said the man. 'Only one room left. It's up the stairs and to the left. It overlooks the square. Room nine.'

'How much?' said Inés, again not concealing her feminine voice.

The man's eyes opened wide as he stared intently at Inés, realising she was not the male personage that she appeared to be. Even so he didn't challenge her. 'Three *reales*, paid beforehand.'

I wondered if the man suspected us of something unsavoury with such a strong insistence on advance payment. Inés, however, didn't hesitate and in a trice had taken a small purse from out a pocket in her breeches and smacked three one *real* pieces onto the counter. He thrust a key in her hand with an ambiguous smile.

Having stabled the horses, we carried our saddlebags up to the room. Inés unlocked the door and pushed it open with her knee.

'A double bed!' I said. 'I'm not sure about sharing it!'

'In which case there's a chair over by the window,' chuckled Inés.

'I'm only joking!'

After resting our weary bodies for an hour or so on this less than comfortable bed, we changed into something more suitable for dinner. We each put on a skirt and blouse. The landlord would have trouble recognising us, especially Inés, except that she was still wearing the eye-patch.

By the time we went down to eat, there were a good couple of dozen or so men in the drinking room. Some were in groups in the booths. Others were drinking singly either at tables, standing or sitting in the booths. As we walked through to the dining area at the back, we could feel numerous eyes following us. We could understand why: it was rare to see two unaccompanied women in an inn, whether it was situated in a town the size of Madrid or in a small village like Torrejón de Ardoz. I began to wonder if it had been wise for Inés to change from her disguise. There was nothing we could have done about that.

By then the landlord, if that is what he was, had left his desk and bar area and sped across the drinking room to follow us into the dining room. 'Where would you like to sit?' he said, as he held out an arm in front of us, pointing to the empty tables. Only a couple were already occupied, all by men, all of whom looked around at the sound of the landlord's voice. Not to be intimidated, Inés looked straight at the landlord and said, 'Over there, by the window.' She pointed to a small table already set for two.

We ambled over to the table, pulled out a chair each and sat on opposite sides. I faced the door. The man stood over us and explained the choice of dishes. 'It's lamb cutlets with tomatoes and artichokes or braised beef and boiled turnips. A glass of wine is included.' We each chose the lamb. For a few moments we sat there in silence. Then Inés started an interesting line of conversation.

'Tell me, Francisca. You know as well as I do what the options are for the outcome of our enquiries over the death of Juan junior. But I'll rehearse them so we can focus on each one in turn. I'll tell you why in just a moment. First, we learn nothing... nothing at all. Second, we'll find out something totally inconclusive. In other words, something will come out but nothing that will make you feel we have solved it. Does that sound right so far, my dear friend?

'Yes, Indeed, Inés. I'm intrigued. Please continue.'

'I will but first I must tell you why I feel qualified to do so. Did I ever tell you that I too suffered the loss of a child, a child I had given birth to?'

'No Inés! I had no idea! I am shocked and saddened to hear of it.'

'So you probably didn't know I was married before I married José.'

'My God! No, Inés! You've kept that to yourself!'

'I have and I hate talking about it. But we are to talk about your son's death and I must tell you about the death of mine,' she said, with tears sliding down her face. I stood up and went around the table to hug her.

'Don't worry, Francisca. It'll do me good to tell you,' she sobbed. Then continued and I went back to my side of the table.

'When I was eighteen I married an Honofre Lifrangi. I met him while he was conducting business in Madrid. To make the story short, the Viceroy of Naples had appointed him as president of one of his advisory committees, so I had to move to Naples. I hated the thought of going because I didn't want to leave my family. But I soon settled there quite happily and after two years my son, Gerónimo was born. Soon

31

after, Honofre tragically died - he was a lot older than me - and I came back to Madrid. Even more sadly, Gerónimo developed a fever soon after I got back and he died, too. His death nearly destroyed me as Juan junior's death did to you. But that was nearly twenty five years ago and I am well recovered by now.'

'I'm astonished at your story, Inés. I can fully understand why you wanted to keep it in the back of your mind. So I can understand why you didn't tell me before, despite our long and loving friendship.'

'Thank you for being so understanding, Francisca. Yes, you are the first person I have mentioned it to, other than my family, in nigh on twenty years. But you are as good as family Francisca, and for that reason too, it is right that I share it with you. Having unburdened myself, I'll continue with my thinking then. Is that all right?' she said, looking at me in such a way that she feared that she still might cause me pain. 'Well, then there is a third group of outcomes in which we do find out the cause of Juan junior's death. The ones we have discussed. Speaking in pure conjecture, the first of this group is that Juan deliberately killed himself. If he did, you will want to know why. The second is that his death was the result of some sort of accident. Then, finally, in this group, the outcome that he was murdered.'

'All that is true, Inés. But I don't see where this is leading!'

'I'll tell you now. Frankly, as we always are with each other, I am seriously worried about how you may react to the outcome that we actually come away with. I'm especially concerned if Juan junior committed suicide.' She stood and came around the table, knelt by my side and put a tender hand in my lap.

'I want you to tell me the truth,' she said, looking up into my eyes. 'Would you contemplate doing anything similar yourself?'

I pondered for a moment before answering. I could fully understand Inés asking the question. It had been only a matter of five days or so since I had made an attempt on my own life and that was without knowing how Juan junior had met his untimely end.

'Inés, you have certainly touched a sensitive spot. To be open and honest with you, I don't know how I will react. As you know, I have a history of poor reactions to difficult situations. Had it not been for you, I could still be locked in the Misericordia asylum. But the one thing I'm certain of is that I won't ever again make an attempt on my life. I am so grateful to you and Baltasar for saving me, I could not try it again, whatever happens in the future. If I became as poor as one of those beggars outside of the Church of the Holy Ascension, I would still not do it.

'You see, I have learnt the meaning of love. You used that word when you came to rescue me on the bridge. It is a word I had not felt the meaning of since Juan died. Although we are good friends, you and Baltasar said you loved me and that is what made me want to climb back onto the bridge and live on… to live in the knowledge that I am loved and want to love in return. I just had not understood fully before. I know they say that God is love and I believe that, too. But to have the love, as I know I do, of true friends like you and Baltasar is different, more real. That is what I failed to understand before.

'Not only that, for that is so important, but you each proved your love by saying you wanted to help me and that had a deep effect on me, too. Does that answer your question, Inés?' I concluded, with a tear welling in my eye.

Inés stood and went back to her side of the table and sat down. 'My dear Francisca, you have answered that question perfectly and I truly believe your answer. I hope you do not think it bad of me to ask.'

'No. Quite the opposite. It was very courageous of you to do so, given recent events and those nearer the death of Juan junior.'

33

'I am sorry but I have further questions, Francisca.' As Inés concluded her sentence, the landlord placed a steaming plate of lamb cutlets, tomatoes and artichokes in front of each of us.

'Sorry it took so long, señoras! That should fill you. I hope you enjoy it… Oh, I'll just go for the wine.'

'So what is your next question, young lady?'

'It's a lot less emotional than the last one!' chuckled Inés and making it easier for me. 'What about the accidental death outcome. What do we do if that is the conclusion?' She then placed a piece of a cutlet and some vegetable pieces in her mouth.

'I've thought a little about that. My worry for that scenario is that someone may be trying to hide the murder of Juan junior and blaming his death on an accident. If he was murdered, obviously I'd like to know. So we need to be aware of the issue. How we would deal with it would depend on what evidence there was to support an accident.'

'And finally, what would we do if he were murdered?'

'We'd try to investigate it! You see, Inés, if it emerged that he was murdered, I think a name of a suspect would appear at the same time. From what I know of these things, admittedly and thankfully not much, if someone had evidence for murder, that evidence would surely include the name or names of the suspected murderer. If that were the case, we'd pass the name on to the authorities in Alcalá and invite them to make an arrest. Am I talking nonsense, Inés?' I then pushed my fork into a piece of cutlet I had cut off and started to eat it.

'Not a bad meal, eh? It's going down well.'

'Sorry, señoras, I almost forgot again,' said the landlord as he placed a generously full glass of red wine in front of each of us.

I raised my glass and Inés did likewise. 'Let's drink to the success of our mission, Inés,' I said. 'We can do no more than go to Alcalá de

34

Henares and find out what we can. I'm so glad you decided to come with me. My secret hope was that you would!'

***

We each slept surprisingly well, considering that neither of us had shared a bed with another for some time. I slept with Juan the night before he died, more than six months before our night in this inn and Inés hadn't actually slept with anyone since her husband, José, and her separated over eighteen months before – not that she hadn't made love with the man! I woke first and lay in the bed thinking about the next stage of our journey. We were about two thirds of the way to Alcalá de Henares and had only about two *leguas* or so to travel. Our horses would cover that at a moderate canter in no more than a few hours or so and leaving fairly soon after breakfast we should be at the inn we planned to stay at before midday. That would give us time to settle in and even to make some enquires at the university before nightfall.

Inés woke up as I was lying there. 'Good morning, Francisca. I hope you slept well. I certainly did. That red wine probably helped!'

'I'm sure it did,' I said. I leant over and planted a kiss on Inés's cheek before climbing out and stepping onto the bare floorboards.

'I hope I didn't upset you with those questions I asked you last night, my dear Francisca.'

'I was surprised, I must admit, that you started that discussion but do you know what?'

'Tell me Francisca!'

'It did me good because it helped me to see the future more clearly. And that can only be good. The best thing is that we are still great friends and love each other as such. May nothing ever change it.' I did not mention her emotional account of the death of Gerónimo.

We were soon ready to go down for breakfast. Inés decided to remain dressed as a woman for the final few *leguas* of the journey. Apparently, she had spoken to the landlord about what to wear for the last stage of tour ride and he could not see a problem. This was partly because the road was less open and likely to be busy for the rest of the way and we would be less vulnerable, or so we hoped.

We did not tarry and, within a few minutes of finishing our breakfast of fried eggs, ham and freshly baked bread, we were carrying our saddlebags out to the stables. The horses seemed to anticipate our arrival and were already flicking their tails and clacking their tongues. We saddled them up, and walked them out to the road. 'Should we ride or walk them through the streets?' asked Ines.

'We aren't short of time… so let's walk.'

We were soon out of this little town and riding towards our destination of Alcalá de Henares. Neither of us knew what to expect of this unique mission.

***

The landlord of the inn, if that was his role, was right about the road between Torrejón and Alcala de Henares. We had to take care, in quite a few places, to avoid being struck by the carts, carriages and wagons being driven between Alcalá and Torrejón de Ardoz. A constant stream of traffic confronted us. It was as if the population of Alcalá had decided to head west, probably to Madrid. We could hardly feel safer with so much traffic on the road. We decided to stop, mainly to take a drink of water from a roadside fountain. Several others had the same idea so we had to join a short queue to fill our bottles. The horses also appreciated refreshment.

We were soon on our way again. As we expected, the city came into view at about eleven o'clock we reckoned and by then the volume of traffic coming our way had diminished from the frenzy we met outside of Torrejón de Ardoz to the trickle from an emptying wine bottle. As we closed in on the city we spotted three men, apparently guards, standing outside the gate.

'What are those men doing?' asked Inés.

'I can't see from here but all will become clearer as we get closer.'

One of the men was carrying a gun. I asked Inés whether hers was easily accessible. 'Don't worry, Francisca. It's covered by this blanket, in the saddle holster. I can get it in a second, if I need to.'

When we were no more than fifty *varas* from the gate, the three men walked out into the road. One of them, a large, paunchy individual with a red face, wearing a long grey coat and a wide brimmed black hat, held up his hand to stop us.

'Good day, ladies. Two *reales* each to enter the city by the Madrid gate here and four *maravedis* for each of your horses.'

'I don't remember a charge when I came before,' I said.

'When was that?' said a dark haired individual, also dressed in a grey coat.

'About sixteen years ago.'

'Things have changed since then. They are getting so short of money in Madrid that they are charging the cities heavy taxes. It's to keep the palaces going for our ailing king!'

'What if we don't pay?' asked Inés.

'We'll have to take your names and the addresses where you will be staying and you will be sent a summons to pay a fine of a thousand *maravedis*,' said the plump one with the wide hat. The one with the gun simply stood there, pointed it skywards and said nothing.

'My view is that we pay,' I said, climbing off my horse to take my purse from the saddlebag. I gave the plump one enough to cover each of us.

'How long can we stay for that amount?' said Inés.

'Until you leave or become registered as citizens of Alcalá de Henares. Citizens don't have to pay.'

With that, the men moved to one side and let us through the Madrid gate into this less than welcoming city.

Chapter 5

We didn't remount after we'd passed through the gate and, holding on to our horses' reins, walked leisurely along the road towards the inn where we planned to stay.

'What an interesting looking place,' said Inés.

'I agree. There's not a town or city like it in Spain or anywhere else in the world. We are now walking down the Calle Cardinal Sandoval y Rojas. Have you heard of him?'

'No but I've heard of Sandoval y Rojas family, I'm sure. One of them had something to do with the royal palace.'

'Dead right. He was uncle of the disgraced First Duke of Lerma, the main adviser to King Philip the Third.'

'I thought I knew of the family.'

'Now we bear to the right down a street named after someone equally famous, the Calle Cardinal Cisneros.'

'What was he famous for then?'

'He was an incredible character. He did a number of things, including writing a Spanish version of the Bible… when the Spanish language was still developing. That was back in the fourteenth century. But he's probably most famous for starting this university, the University de Complutense.'

'How do you know all these things, Francisca? I hope you are not going to bore me with loads of useless information while we're here!'

'I only know these things through Juan junior being a student here. No. I won't bore you, Inés. I won't say another thing about the place,' I said, smiling and calling her bluff.

'No, seriously, Francisca, I am eager to learn, I promise you. José is just like you, in the historical sense only of course. Whenever we were going anywhere, he'd find out all about the history before we went. What he didn't know about Toledo wasn't worth hearing about!'

We each laughed aloud at our silly humour as we carried on along the road only to see a magnificent cathedral coming up to our right.

'Let's stop and go in here. You see, we can tie up the horses outside,' I said. 'It's the famous Iglesia Magistral. Another rarity.'

'Not now, Francisca, please. Why don't we go straight to the inn? We can visit here anytime. We'd be better off going straight there. You never know, we might miss the last rooms left if we stop to go into the cathedral.'

'I suppose you are right, Inés. We'll walk on!'

I didn't say as much to Inés, but I loved the design of this great church and its construction. The buttresses holding the walls showed a rhythmical symmetry that I'd never experienced before. They reminded me of a mass which Juan had written for the king. That too contained an enduring regularity which few could emulate. Juan had mastered such things as had the designer of this wonderful church. I was dying to go there again and show the interior to Inés.

'So where is this inn?' asked Inés.

'Not far now. It's along here on the right, about four hundred *varas* ahead. Opposite the College of the King.'

We tied our horses to the rail outside, slung our saddlebags over our shoulders and walked into the inn. It was called 'The Mad Astronomer'. The name was painted in green on a sign, over a picture of an odd looking man peering through a telescope, suspended above the door. 'That wasn't the name when I came before. I think they called it "The Inn of the King" or "The King's Head", something a lot less entertaining!' I said.

'As the guard on the gate said, things have changed in the last sixteen years. I wonder what else has changed while you've been away!'

'We'll see soon enough!'

Inés pushed the dark green door open and we went in. The floor was scattered with sawdust which smelt of stale beer and other less than pleasant odours. I could see patches of dried blood: signs of a recent fight, maybe.

We walked the few steps to a reception desk. I picked up a small hand bell and rang it. It tinkled quite loudly. No one came. I rang it again. Still no answer.

'Why is the door unlocked when there's no one here,' said Inés.

'There must be someone here somewhere. I'll go around the back and you go upstairs.'

We each tossed our saddlebags over the back of a chair and I walked through the hall to find an open door to the kitchen. The large rectangular wooden table in the centre was loaded with various items of food. A chicken, still on the spit on which it had been cooked, had been carved and the pieces of cold meat carefully arranged on a large oval platter, alongside some delicately sliced *chorizo*. Some carrots had been sliced and left on a wooden board alongside a dozen or so stems of asparagus. Someone had been working in the kitchen and been interrupted so had left the meal preparation incomplete. I walked out of the back of the inn into the garden where Juan and I had breakfasted on one of the days we had stayed there, those sixteen years before. There was no one there so I went back in.

As I reached the hall area, I heard someone creeping down the stairs. It was Inés, smiling and holding her forefinger vertically over her mouth, signalling me to remain silent. I followed her into the outer drinking room. Then she spoke. 'I walked quietly across the landing. A bedroom door was open and I could hear a groaning noise coming from inside. I peeped in and there they were. A naked woman of about thirty was sitting astride an older, half naked man. The woman was making all the noise. I turned around and came back down!'

I laughed. 'It must be the landlord and the cook. That explains the half prepared meals in the kitchen!'

'What do we do, Francisca? We can hardly wait here until they come back down.'

I hesitated. 'I don't see why not! Did they see you?'

'No. I don't think so. I was stuck to the spot for a moment… until I got over the shock… then I crept back down the stairs.'

'Let's give them a few minutes to finish, then we'll shout out! From what you heard, it shouldn't be long!'

We didn't need to call out. Within those few minutes, a middle aged man appeared, hastily tucking his shirt into his breeches. 'Oh, good morning ladies. May I help you? I am the landlord and my name is Gonzalo.'

'Yes please, señor. We are from Madrid and want to stay here for a week, maybe longer. It depends,' I said.

'Depends on what?' said Gonzalo.

'We are on a mission,' said Inés, 'and it depends how successful we are.'

'I see,' said Gonzalo, eyeing us up suspiciously. 'Well, you are in luck. Do you want a room each or do you wish to share.'

'What do you think, Inés? You decide.'

'I'm happy to share if you are.'

'In which case, may we have a double room for one week, to start with? We'll let you know whether we wish to stay longer. May we also have some lunch today and an evening meal tonight… oh, and stabling for the horses?'

'I've got just what you want, señoras. There's a room at the front overlooking the College of the King. It'll be two *reales* a night for a bed and breakfast and more for evening meals and stabling.'

'That's ridiculous. It's already cost us four *reales* to enter the town and eight *maravedís* to bring in our horses. And now you want to charge us double what we paid for night in Torrejón de Ardoz,' said Inés, her face a bright red with rage.

'What? You were charged to come through the gate?'

'That's what I said,' said Inés.

'You were tricked. There is no charge to come into Alcalá de Henares. Those crooks must have seen you coming!' he chuckled.

'I can't believe this,' I said. 'So we've been robbed by three common thieves!'

'Nothing more or less!' said Inés, still angry.

'I'm sorry, señoras. It would have been better if I'd said nothing.'

'No you did the right thing in telling us. I still can't believe we fell for it.'

'I am quite ashamed,' said the landlord. 'So bad that I will give you each a night free of charge and your stabling will be at my expense for the whole of your stay!'

'You are so generous,' said Inés. 'It wasn't you who stole our money.' She walked up to him, lifted his hand and kissed it. I'm sure she would have kissed his lips had she not witnessed him making love to that woman upstairs.

'No, I didn't trick you and steal from you but it was someone in my town. Those three are well known for taking advantage of strangers entering Alcalá. I will report them tomorrow.'

'I thank you, too, for your generosity, Gonzalo. It is not, of course, necessary but we graciously accept. Could you please show us to our room?' I said.

Gonzalo took each of our saddlebags, put them over his shoulders then escorted us up the creaky stairs, unlocked the door to our room and showed us in. Light blue curtains hung from a brass rail over the window which overlooked the busy road below. Two beds were draped in covers which were the blue of the curtains and the whole room felt warm and welcoming as the sun shone through the window.

'What a pretty room,' I said.

'I like it too,' said Inés.

'I'm glad you approve, señoras. When you are ready, please come down and we will prepare you some lunch,' said Gonzalo, placing the saddlebags on one of the beds.

We were soon downstairs enjoying, not surprisingly, a lunch of chicken breast, some bread, boiled carrots and steamed asparagus.

'What if we go over to the College of the King this afternoon and start making enquiries. We could go over and wander around? If we did, we'd get our bearings and see what's going on,' I said.

'I'm not so sure, Francisca. Wouldn't it be better to go tomorrow morning? We'd have the whole day there and probably find out just as much after relaxing today.'

I paused for a moment and wondered at first whether my great friend was protecting me in some way, perhaps hoping to delay the moment of any disappointment. But the more I thought about it, the more I realised that simply to wander around the college and locate the various departments Juan junior studied in might be a good idea. We might even see the names of the professors on their office doors and see where their other staff might be. 'No, I really want to go today, Inés. If you want to relax here, I'll go and you can have a rest!'

'No, I agree with you, Francisca. And I'll come with you! Let's go up and get out of our riding breeches!'

***

No sooner than we had finished our lunch, we closed the dark green doors of The Mad Astronomer, leaving Gonzalo in the company of his cook, and were crossing the street to the College of the King. It had gone midday by then and, given the time, there were more people than we would have expected going up and down the street. There were men pushing hand carts, some loaded with loaves of bread piled so high that, in one case, the man driving it had to hold out a hand occasionally to steady his load. Some women, wearing long white skirts, light brown blouses and with their hair tied at the neck, were carrying baskets with their contents, presumably food, covered in white muslin.

Many of the men were dressed in black academic gowns and wore large floppy caps, which half covered their eyes. The caps were of various colours, presumably representing the various faculties at the university. A number of the men were carrying rolled scrolls, each appended by a wax seal.

'It's amazing that some of these people can hardly see where they are going!' said Inés. 'Look! That one had almost walked into a horse and cart!'

We had no idea what was happening and crossed the road to the impressive entrance to the college. The polished oak, double width door was about twelve *pies* tall and enclosed by elegant decorated pilasters. The entrance was flanked symmetrically on each side by three large windows, separated by twelve to fifteen *pies*, of neat, red brickwork. Each window surround matched the entrance pilasters and appeared to be made of light grey granite. Each window of the ground floor had a similar but balconied window, situated immediately above it. Each end of the building was finished with a third story, with the same pattern of balconied windows, giving the appearance of a large book end. The overall impression was that of a building of gravity and grandeur fit to take the name of its founding king.

'It's an impressive building' said Inés.

'I won't tell you who designed it for fear of boring you!' I said.

'Don't be silly, Francisca. I said I won't be bored!'

'All right! It was Juan Gómez de Mora, who also designed the Panadería in the Madrid Plaza Mayor. Quite a famous architect.'

'You are a mine of information, Francisca! Now you will tell me who the king of the college is!'

'An easy one! Philip the Second!'

We indulged in these exchanges while standing outside the door with the streets still humming with activity.

'Well, let's go in then,' I said.

Inés pushed open the massive oak door. Despite its size, it opened with the ease of an object suspended in mid-air. Inside was a large, high ceilinged entrance hall with a man sitting to one side, behind a large desk, strewn with official papers. The man wore a maroon jacket with gold coloured buttons and had donned a white wig, of the kind worn by royal palace flunkies. As soon as he saw us, he spoke.

'Good afternoon, señoras. To whom do I owe the pleasure of their company?' was the rather formal but not unfriendly greeting.

'I am Francisca de Abaunza and this is my dear friend, Inés Manuela Martinéz del Mazo. We are here to conduct business with the heads of the departments of law, mathematics and astronomy. We have no wish to meet any one of them today but thought we might walk around the college to see where their offices might be located.'

'Would it be impolite of me to ask the nature of the business you wish to transact with the professors?'

'It's a long story but I will give it to you in brief,' I said. I explained, as Inés occasionally nodded in sympathy and agreement, that Juan junior had died while a student here and that we wanted to ask about the circumstances of his passing, despite the fact that it occurred some sixteen years before.

'I am sorry to hear about your son's death, Señora de Abaunza. I cannot say whether the professors will see you, let alone be of any help. But first let me tell you that only the law faculty is based here. There is no faculty of astronomy. That subject is dealt with in natural sciences but there is a department of mathematics. The department of natural sciences is in the College of St Pedro and St Pablo and mathematics is in the College of St Ildefonso. Is that helpful?'

'Yes, indeed it is,' I said. 'Would it be all right if we looked for the professor of law's office?'

'Not a problem señora. If you turn right at the end of this *zaguan*, follow the corridor all the way round until you reach the stairs at the back. The law faculty is at the top of the stairs around to the left. It's up there,' he said, pointing his finger up and over to his left.

'That's very kind of you,' said Inés.

'One thing I should explain is that it's graduation today, so there are honours presentation ceremonies and parties going on all over the university. But you will have no problem if you want to find the law faculty.'

'One last thing,' said Inés. 'Where are the other colleges you mentioned?'

'The College of St Pedro and St Pablo is just down the road opposite and on the right. The St Ildefonso is further down on the same side. Anyway, good luck. I must press on to sort out these papers.'

'We are so grateful,' I said.

'You can call in tomorrow if you wish and I'll escort you to the law faculty. It will look better than just turning up on your own!'

'Thank you for that, too!' I said and we made our way to the end of the *zaguan* and turned right as instructed.

As soon as we were round the corner, Inés spoke in her familiar whisper. 'What did you think of him?'

'Surprisingly helpful. After all, two women calling in, wanting to see the professors can't happen every day! He could be an ally. Did you get his name?'

'No. I looked over his papers but couldn't see a name.'

We strolled along the empty corridor and reached the bottom of the stairs to which the bewigged official at the reception desk had directed us. We could hear the distant sounds of chatter and laughter coming from the top of the stairs and smell a combination of various foods and drink, something we had half expected. We climbed the stairs to the first floor. As we approached the top, the sounds of jollity became louder. On reaching the top and stepping into the corridor, we could see a throng of students, talking and joking with each other, many with glasses of wine or beer in their hands and others holding plates of food. They were near the open doors of two offices. All were wearing academic gowns and a number were wearing blue hats, just like some we had seen on the streets. We stopped for a moment.

'What do you think, Inés? They are in our path to the Law Department.'

'Not a problem. I'm sure they won't be difficult!'

We made our way towards the celebrating students, none of whom was older than twenty one or so. One of them, a long haired, fresh faced lad spoke.

'Good afternoon, señoras. What are you doing here? Are you related to any of us who are celebrating? Would you like to join us? We are having a little graduation party!'

We couldn't believe that we were being invited to join these young people. What a privilege!

'What do you think, Inés?'

'We've only just had lunch so, speaking for myself, I'm not hungry but a cup of juice would go down well.'

'I would welcome a drink, too.'

'Yes, we'd be pleased to join you,' I said.

'Excellent,' said the boy. 'I'll introduce you to my friends. First, have a drink. What would you like?'

'Some grape juice would be fine,' I said.

Inés asked for the same and within a few minutes we were holding full glasses and engaged in conversation with these charming youngsters. I was by nearly fifty years the oldest one there but their cheerfulness and optimism made me feel young and part of the party. We asked them about the graduation ceremony which they said they had attended in the much larger College of St Ildefonso. They said they were presented with their degree certificates by the Sub-Dean of the University, a very formal individual who couldn't bring himself to smile, not even once. Those in this group were all law graduates, hoping to find well paid jobs as barristers or solicitors in Madrid, Barcelona, Toledo, Segovia or in another litigious city. They had all paid a four *maravedí* piece into a fund to pay for the food and drinks they were enjoying.

The one who invited us to join them, Alonso, asked why we were there, in the main corridor of the law department. It seemed to him, that we had wandered in aimlessly, straight off the street. I explained the reason for our presence, telling him the details of the mysterious death of Juan junior and that we wanted to investigate the circumstances. His response totally surprised both me and Inés.

'Was your son's father a well-known composer, with a name like Higuero? Something like that?'

'A very similar name. My son was Juan Hidalgo. His father was Juan Hidalgo de Polanco who was quite well known as a composer in the court of the king.'

Alonso continued. 'The case of the death of your son has long been part of the difficult history of this university, and our college in particular because he was a student at our college. It caused quite a scandal here.'

'Please tell us more,' said Inés. She could see that I was so surprised that I could hardly speak. But the significance of what the young Alonso had said soon became clear. At least we could refer to this conversation if the professors decided to deny that Juan junior had died in unusual circumstances. And Alonso hadn't yet revealed the whole story.

'It is clear from the facts that your son was poisoned. Correct?'

'Certainly,' I said, not sure how I was controlling my emotions which had been stirred by these unexpected revelations.

'Well, no one here seems to know whether he was murdered in a clever way, died of some accidental overdose of a medicine or committed suicide for reasons unknown.'

'What do you mean by "murdered in a clever way"?' said Inés.

'From what we know, your son didn't actually die here. He went home to Madrid at the end of one of the terms and died at home. So if he was murdered by poisoning, the murderer must have known that he was going back to Madrid and administered the fatal dose at such a time that it wouldn't take effect until Juan reached home.' Neither Juan nor I had thought of that before, so a new issue had already emerged, just from this gathering of students.

Another of Alonso's student friends joined in. 'I couldn't help overhearing,' he said.

'That's right, isn't it, Rodrigo?' said Alonso.

'You are talking about the mysterious death of Juan Hidalgo. God, that was a few years ago!'

'The señora here is his mother. She and her friend are here to investigate.'

'You will have a difficult job,' said Rodrigo. 'As you know, we are all lawyers and are interested in such things, especially when they happen right where we are studying law. Our conclusion, held privately of course, is that the true facts were covered up by the authorities here. I think your son was murdered. Some think otherwise.'

'Very interesting,' said Inés.

'What a conversation,' I said, by then recovered from the shock of what I was hearing and even more determined to see our investigation through. 'I suppose we ought to be going now, didn't we, Inés? Thank you so much. You are true gentlemen and thank you for the drinks!'

'Yes, we should be moving along now. We didn't explain that we are on this corridor to find out where the head of department's office is. We want to arrange a meeting with him. It's along here somewhere, according to the man on the door, downstairs.'

'Yes, said Rodrigo. Just past the corner, along on the right. Good luck with him. He's a difficult man! He won't make it any easier for you than he has for us!'

We shook hands with Alonso and Rodrigo, bid them good fortune in finding good jobs and made our way to the head of faculty's office. Inés spoke first as we were out of earshot of the students.

'I hope you feel good about all that. Useful information, I thought, Francisca. And what a surprise that we got into such a conversation!'

'I know. I'm still half in shock. But the fact that these students know about Juan's death and that it hasn't been completely lost in the past is encouraging, to say the least.'

'That's the good thing about undergraduate courses. They last three or four years, so students have plenty of opportunities to pass down the history of the college to generations coming through.'

'You are right Inés, that's just what's happened.'

We soon rounded the corner and saw emblazoned in tall black letters on a blue door, similar in colour to the students' hats, 'Professor Doctor Ignacio Andres Juárez de Lerida, Head of the Faculty of Law'. A stream of letters followed the name but neither of us could remember one of them, except the 'D', presumably for 'Doctor'. 'Here we are,' I said. 'His name is on the door of the main faculty office, so there will probably be a secretary working in there. Let's see if there's anyone there!'

Inés tried the door but it was locked. 'Shall we try this door,' asked Inés, pointing towards a door marked 'private' about ten *pies* along the same wall.

'Definitely not!' I said. 'That's almost certainly the professor's private entrance to his office. The king had one like that at the Alcázar palace. Juan told me. He'd use it to avoid people he didn't want to see. If we go in and he's there we'll wreck our chances of getting a meeting with him!'

'What do we do now?'

'Go back the way we came and go back to the inn. I'm tired!'

We made our way back around the corridor only to have to pass through the gathering of students we partied with on the way to the faculty office.

'Hello, señoras! Did you find it all right? Would you like another drink?' said the friendly Alonso as we walked through.

'I don't think so. Do you, Inés?'

'No thanks, but thank you for offering. We are on our way back to the inn now.'

'Where are you staying?'

'At The Mad Astronomer, just across the road.'

'You could do worse,' said Alonso. 'We wish you luck with your investigation.'

***

The helpful man at the college reception desk was no longer there when we passed his desk so we couldn't thank him. We made our way back up to our room in The Mad Astronomer. We each felt tired and lay down on our respective beds.

'That was utterly incredible,' I said. 'I'm so surprised and pleased that the story of Juan junior is now part of the college's unwritten mythology, if not history!'

'For your sake, so am I, Francisca. Now we have to make sure we make the most of what we heard. It could help us a lot in our work here. They key thing was the remark that the lad Rodrigo made about the cover up.'

'I agree. Let's think about that. Why would anyone here want to cover up the cause of Juan's death?'

'I don't know. What are the possibilities? One reason to hide it might be to preserve the reputation of the university. The murder of one of their students while studying here might discourage others from coming here, especially when there are other equally good universities to choose from.'

'Good point, Inés. Another reason might be to prevent the blame falling on someone they wanted to protect.'

'I like that,' said Inés.

'Let's say, just for the sake of discussing this, that one of the students involved was related to one of the lecturers or professors here. It would obviously not be in the interests of that person to reveal that his son was a killer. It would affect that person's future. Who knows?'

'And especially if that person was of great influence here. Someone who could even convince the local investigators to drop the case,' said Inés.

'You may have touched on a very significant point, Inés. We'll have to see. Let's work out how we are going to handle the meeting with Professor Juárez tomorrow, assuming he'll see us then.'

By the time we had talked our way through what we hoped would be a good meeting with the professor, it was past six o'clock in the evening and time for us to go down for some dinner.

Chapter 6

Despite a tasty meal of slow cooked mutton, shallots and mashed turnip, all helped down by a couple of glasses of a tasty *jumilla*, again I hardly slept. I was too excited at the prospect of speaking to the professor. I also felt that, if I was to lead this exploration into the death of Juan junior, I needed to control my thoughts and emotions. It would be unfair on Inés to expect her to take that role, even though she might be better equipped to do it. I decided that I must become mentally stronger and be prepared to accept, without breaking down or reacting in any embarrassing way, anything unpleasant that might be revealed about Juan junior. Those thoughts helped strengthen my determination to uncover the facts behind the mystery of his death.

'You were restless last night,' said Inés, as she sat on her bed, pulling on her stockings. 'Couldn't you sleep?'

I didn't want to reveal the range of my night thoughts so I just said, 'Really? I wasn't aware of moving about. Must have been a dream!'

***

Realising that college life doesn't normally begin until well into the morning, we arrived at the professor's outer office just after 10 o'clock. The door was closed.

'What shall we do?' said Inés.

'Knock and go in. We know what we want. A meeting with the professor.'

The secretary was sitting at a desk and wielding a quill pen, so long that the feather could have been plucked from a swan's wing. The man wore a large white wig, the powder from which scattered on his papers as he lifted his head and looked towards us. Without as much as a hint of a smile, he said, 'Good morning. Why are you here?'

'We would be grateful if we could have a meeting with Professor Juárez,' I said. 'I am the mother of Juan Hidalgo, a student here who died in mysterious circumstances, some years ago. My friend and I are investigating the facts behind his death.'

'The professor's title is Professor Doctor Juárez de Lerida, if you please.'

'I am sorry. We would wish to have a meeting with Professor Doctor Juárez de Lerida for which we would be most grateful. I've already told you the reason for our wanting to meet him.'

'Hmm… I'll have to ask him.'

The man stood, scattering yet more wig powder, and walked the four paces to the professor's office door. Without knocking, he walked straight in and closed the door behind him. He seemed to be there an age. Inés and I stood and looked at each other as we could hear a strongly raised voice, apparently the professor's, and the somewhat softer tones of the secretary, in heated argument. It sounded as if the secretary was losing. As he emerged, red faced and embarrassed, we heard from inside the shouted words, 'Tell them now', just before the secretary closed the door. Surely, the professor had refused.

The secretary settled himself back into his seat before speaking and then said, 'Yes, he'll see you. His diary is full today. So please come back at eleven tomorrow, Tuesday morning.' He then looked towards the outer door as if to tell us to go.

We walked silently around the corner, into the corridor where we met the celebrating students the day before. 'That's a good result,' I said, laughing all over my face. 'Even if he didn't want to see us!'

'Yes, they were clearly talking about ways of getting out of it but decided he would in the end! What do we do until then, Francisca?'

'We go to the Department of Natural Sciences in the San Pedro and San Pablo College and speak to the professor of astronomy and then to the San Isidro College and see if we can see the professor of mathematics.'

'What now?'

'Yes, why not?' I said, exercising my new found sense of authority and confidence.

After acknowledging the helpful man on the reception desk, just inside the college main door, we walked down the Calle San Pedro and San Paulo to the first of the colleges. We climbed the steps to the entrance and walked in. We were surprised that, unlike the College of the King, there was no reception desk but a list attached to the wall showing the locations of various departments of natural sciences.

'There it is,' said Inés. 'Astronomy is on the top floor, the third!'

'They've probably got their telescopes on the roof! Let's go straight there!'

I arrived breathless outside the department's offices. I was beginning to feel my sixty nine years after climbing this many stairs. Inés coped much better.

'You are breathing quite heavily Francisca. Shall I start asking the questions?'

'Yes, that would be very helpful, Inés.'

We walked into an office labelled 'Astronomy'. We couldn't believe what confronted us. An array of various kinds of optical instruments and clocks were arranged on three long benches that reached from one end of this laboratory to the other, a distance of at least thirty *pies*. Three young men, apparently a little older that the students of law we had met the day before, were working with these various pieces of apparatus. One was taking notes as another was looking through a telescope trained on a statue on a building opposite. The third was polishing a piece of glass with some odd looking red powder.

'Let's speak to the man taking the notes,' I said. 'He's probably the easiest to interrupt.'

'Excuse me, please,' said Inés, looking a little shy. 'I'm sorry to stop you working but may we speak to you for a moment?'

'I would welcome a good reason to stop my writing,' said the young man. 'What a pleasure to see two womenfolk in our laboratory!'

I was quite surprised by the generous welcome and smiled at the young man. Inés went on to explain the reason for our being there, summarising the circumstances of Juan junior's death.

'I don't know about your son,' said the man. 'The best thing is to ask our professor. I am a graduate student from Barcelona and have been researching here for just a year. Let me take you to the prof.'s office. Follow me.'

'That is kind,' I said. 'What is the professor's name?'

'It's Lorenzo Ramos. I'm not sure how he will be with you but we are all on informal terms with him, as you will see.'

The professor's office was at the far end of this huge laboratory. The young man knocked on the door. The instant response was a friendly 'Come in.'

'Oh, it's you, Tomé. What's the matter?' he said as we waited outside.

Nothing, Lorenzo. Just that these ladies want to talk to you about the death of a student. Apparently, he studied here about sixteen years ago.'

'You'd better ask them in.'

Within a few minutes, and after the shuffling of some chairs, Inés and I were sitting in front of the professor's desk while he peered over the brim of his glasses waiting for us to explain our presence to him. I took the lead and related the facts.

'I'm sorry to hear of your son's passing,' he said. 'I vaguely recall talk about it. I have only been working here for twelve years and so have no direct knowledge of events around that time. What I can tell you is that the professor who was head of department then is now at a university in England, Oxford in fact, and he may be returning to visit us, with his Spanish wife. I don't know whether you could come here from Madrid to see him, but he may just be able to help you. That is, if you are right and your son was a student at this college as well as at the College of the King. His name is Alan McDonnell. He is English but has Scottish origins.'

'I'm certain he studied here as well as at the other college. He told me and my husband how much he enjoyed studying here. And I'm sure he mentioned an English professor!'

'I can make a note to tell the professor about your wish to see him, if indeed he does come here.'

'Yes, please could you do so? ... I and possibly my friend will come back to see him. When will you know whether or not he'll be coming? And how long will he be staying here. I'd hate to miss him!'

'It's difficult to know whether and when he will come. But if he does it's likely to be for a period of months, a term at least. If you ask us occasionally, we can let you know how things are going.'

'We will do that,' I said, 'perhaps by letter. Would you mind if my friend Inés here came with me to see him? You would come, Inés, wouldn't you?'

'I'll definitely come back with you, Francisca,' said Inés, much to my delight.

'I would have no objection to seeing your young friend again,' said the professor, glancing at Inés. It was a strange look he gave her, which

59

prompted her to look at me, questioning the underlying meaning. He seemed to find her attractive.

That brief encounter with Professor Lorenzo Ramos gave me much encouragement. I certainly remembered Juan junior mentioning an English connection the Department of Natural Sciences enjoyed, even though I could not remember the name of the professor. We'd have to contact him about the visit, whatever happened.

'Where do we go next, Francisca? The maths department?' said Inés, as we were walking down the steps into bright sunlight, outside the entrance to Natural Sciences.

'Of course! Let's go straight there. Our luck is in now and we ought to capitalise on it!'

So we made our way to the mathematics department which, according to the receptionist at the College of the King, was a little further down the Calle San Pedro and San Pablo in the College of San Ildefonso. In a typical style, the college was built in the shape of a quadrangle with the inner offices overlooking a large open space decorated by lawns with a water fountain at its centre. The grass glowed an emerald green and contrasted markedly with the drabness of the walls of the building. We soon discovered that the Department of Mathematics was located on the second floor of the west wing so we made our way there.

It was empty, deserted. Not a soul in sight.

'What's going on?' said Inés, looking as puzzled as I was.

'I've no idea. Must be a special day of some sort. We'll have to ask someone.'

We walked around the corridor towards the northern end of the building. A long haired, older man with a walking stick stumbled around the corner.

'Let's ask him,' said Inés. 'I will if you like.'

'Fine.'

'Excuse me, señor,' said Inés, as we approached him. 'Have you any idea why the mathematics department is closed? There is no one there.'

'I am equally puzzled,' said the old man. 'My son is a lecturer here and I was expecting to meet him in his office. But it's empty and I can't see anyone either, not even a gatekeeper. Now I'm beginning to wonder if I have the right day.'

'It seems very strange to me that a whole department is closed on a term day. I know it's graduation. We came across a graduation party yesterday. But you'd expect to see somebody!' I said.

The old man accompanied us as we walked down the stairs to the outside and across the quadrangle to the Calle San Pedro. Inés and I had to walk slowly so he could, with the aid of his stick, keep up with us. When we reached the road we stopped. He introduced himself to us before he went, up the road towards the Calle de Libreros. He said his name was Manuel Lobos de Pamplona and his son was Pedro. Still baffled by the absence staff and pupils in the department, we went our separate ways.

'What shall we do now?' said Inés. 'It's early to go back to the inn.'

With the eventual approval of Inés, we decided to walk to the cathedral, the Iglesia Magistral. I had been longing to show her round this beautiful structure since she had first seen it, admittedly only the day before. As we walked along the Calle Escritorios we discussed what we had achieved so far. At least we had not been rejected from the law or astronomy departments. Quite the opposite. In the astronomy department, we had been given a warm welcome and in law a commitment, if reluctantly granted, to meet the professor. While we both felt optimistic about the events so far, there were certain oddities. It seemed as if the law professor needed time to think about how he would handle us since he had no one meeting him at the time and delayed our meeting him for a day. On the other hand, he could have been labouring over some papers or preparing a lecture. In astronomy, talk about a possible forthcoming visit by a professor from England could also have been a distraction but maybe not. We would have to wait and see.

'Let me tell you something about the cathedral while we walk there,' I said.

'Go on, but I don't want to be bored by a lot of facts.'

'It's more of a story than just facts. It is known as The Cathedral of the Child Saints. In the year of Our Lord 324, the evil Roman Emperor Diocletian killed a lot of people who refused to give up their Christianity. Here he murdered two schoolboys, Justo and Pastor. In four hundred and something a chapel was built on the site of their execution. The Pope sanctified them and in about 650 the cathedral was built in their memory. The Moors destroyed it during the conquest and it was rebuilt in a beautiful Gothic style in the last century by Cardinal Cisneros whom I mentioned yesterday as we passed it. That's all. A good story, don't you think?'

'I don't know much about the Romans but I can't believe a Roman Emperor killed two little boys. That's hideous.'

'And what makes it quite ironic and even more tragic is that only a few years later, Constantine became the first Christian Emperor.'

'Very sad, I think. Why is it called the Iglesia Magistral? Do you know, Francisca?'

'Yes, I do. It's because any priest that officiates there has to be a doctor of divinity. There is only one other Roman Catholic Cathedral in the world that has this status but I forget where it is!'

'I'm impressed that you know these things, my good friend. How do you know them? Not all from Juan junior, surely?'

'Yes! Juan junior told us, when he was studying here.'

It wasn't more than five minutes after this exchange which, thankfully, Inés found quite interesting, that we were entering the Plaza Santos Niños and could marvel at the cathedral. The main façade opened on to the *plaza*. Its austere, white stone beauty affected us as much as the richly sculpted entrance surrounds impressed us. Its tower, all of thirty *varas* high emphasised the symmetry of the structure rather than break it.

'We must climb that tower,' smiled Inés.

'It's all very well for you, my young friend. Your legs are younger than mine. I doubt I'd be able to reach the top!'

'We can only try. We needn't run up. We can always come back down again if you can't manage it! We'd be able to see the whole town from up there!'

'You win, Inés. I don't want to spoil your fun. We'll try it!'

'I'll always love you, Francisca!'

'And I you, Inés!'

The *plaza* entrance was locked so we entered through a side door next to the tower. A striking sight confronted us. A priest was giving a sermon from a raised pulpit close to the elaborate altar. His audience, probably two hundred or more students in black university gowns, all standing and clasping white caps along with a few older men, presumably their professors, also wearing gowns but theirs complemented by large white hoods, listened intently. The priest looked towards us as if to demand our silence. I carefully closed the door.

'What's going on?' whispered Inés.

'A thanksgiving service of some kind, I imagine.'

'What shall we do?'

'Just stay here for a moment.'

A minute or two later, the priest announced the title of a song or hymn. The men began to sing to the accompanying tune played on the cathedral organ. As they did so, another priest came over towards us. He was smiling and asked us if we'd like to join the singing. He explained, much to our surprise if not delight, that the Faculty of Mathematics were giving thanks for achieving the award of their degrees.

I couldn't resist a question. 'Is there a Pedro Lobos de Pamplona in the audience?'

'Indeed there is. Why do you ask? Are you related to him?'

'No, but we met his father not an hour ago at the department building. He thought he was meeting his son and was as puzzled as we were that the department was closed with not a soul in sight,' I said.

'I am the faculty priest, so I know all the students and staff by name. He is a lecturer. I'll introduce you to him at the end of the service and you can tell him about his father.'

Within another fifteen minutes the priest was leading us towards a handsome dark haired man of about thirty five. Just like other departmental staff, he wore a black gown draped with a large black hood and carried a white cap.

'Excuse me,' said the priest, 'I'd like to introduce you to these two women.'

The man's face looked blank with surprise, as if he'd seen a ghost. What he expected we did not know. We could not be a threat to him.

'These two señoras spoke to your father only an hour ago. Sorry I didn't ask your names.'

We introduced ourselves and the priest introduced us to Pedro Lobos de Pamplona.

'So how did you meet my father?' said the man, by then relaxed and smiling.

We explained that he was expecting to see his son.

'He was right, he'd come on the wrong day. He was supposed to meet me tomorrow!'

'He'll probably realise,' said Inés.

'Our surroundings here are probably not the most suitable, but do you mind if we explain why we are in Alcalá de Henares?' I said.

'Please enlighten me,' said Pedro.' We explained and concluded by saying we wanted to visit the mathematics department.

'I'm sorry to tell you that I have no recollection of the death of your son, Señora de Abaunza. I don't recall anyone by that name. All I can suggest is that you come back to the department, maybe tomorrow when we are definitely open and ask one of the professors. If you ask for me and I am not lecturing, I can accompany you, if that will help.'

Quick to see advantage in Pedro's presence at a meeting with a more senior person, Inés responded. 'What times of the day are you free tomorrow, señor?'

'From about three in the afternoon and onwards. I'd be more than pleased to help.'

'We'll make sure we are in the department by about 3.30. We are seeing the head of the law department in the morning. Where is the best place to meet you?'

'I'll make sure I'm in my office from about three onwards. It's on the second floor. Just go up the stairs from the entrance hall and it's along the corridor to the left. My name is on the door.'

'We are so grateful to you, señor,' said Inés.

We shook hands with the man and the priest and left them talking to each other.

I thought I'd make the next move. 'Come on Inés, let's have a go at climbing the tower staircase!'

Inés was happy that I'd made the suggestion and smiled widely. 'I won't go ahead of you, Francisca, I promise.'

We eventually reached the top, despite my aging knees. I was certainly less flexible than I was those sixteen years ago when Juan and I came here to see Juan junior. The view was incredible and the air seemed fresher up there than at ground level. We looked out from each of the tower's four sides. A jubilant Inés was quick to point out the College of the King and the vast complex that housed the college of San Pedro and San Pablo as well as the college of San Ildefonso where we would meet the handsome Pedro.

We left the cathedral and began to walk back to The Mad Astronomer. This was the first time since Juan's passing that I experienced any special feelings towards a man. I felt quite disgusted with myself, especially as Juan had only been dead for a little over six months. Inés could see something was troubling me. 'What's the matter, my lovely friend?'

'I'm not sure how to put this, Inés, but my heart leapt as we were speaking to that Pedro. I really took to him. I feel quite ashamed.'

Inés laughed. 'Don't worry, Francisca. It's only natural. You haven't enjoyed the touch of a man for so long now! Mind you, he's probably too young for you. I may just take to him myself!'

I did my best to put those thoughts of him out of my mind. I dwelled on memories of my wonderful Juan for the rest of the way back to the inn.

Chapter 7

We entered The Mad Astronomer and walked up to the reception desk. A woman in a light brown dress who was combing her hair with her fingers was standing behind it. We told her our names and she handed us the room key.

'Oh…and I have a letter addressed to you, Señora de Abaunza,' she said, as she turned to take a letter from a pigeonhole set in the wall behind her.

I must have looked surprised, if not fearful, as she placed an envelope, sealed with red wax, in my hand. I decided not to open it until Inés and I were in our room. We mounted the stairs at a faster rate than usual, unlocked the door and dashed in.

'I can't believe this, Inés, a letter to me. It just says my name and "Mad Astronomer" on the envelope.'

I tore the envelope open and read the letter. I was shocked and frightened at what I saw. It read simply:

'Señora de Abaunza, if you know what is good for you, you and your friend will pack your bags, mount your horses and return to Madrid. You are not welcomed here.'

It was, of course, unsigned.

I collapsed on the bed in tears. Inés put her arms around me. 'What does it say?' she said.

I handed it to her. 'Read it!' I shrieked.

'My God, Francisca. This is a very serious threat. Whoever wrote those hideous words?'

I stopped crying and regained my composure. 'We need to think about it and what we do about it,' I said, gulping at a sob.

'The obvious thought is that there is a lot more to Juan junior's death than we know about. Something someone doesn't want us to uncover,' said Inés.

'That gives me some encouragement, in an odd way. Surely, we can't be talking about suicide now. As far as I'm concerned that's good. Even if we have to think about murder. Can I see it again?'

Inés handed me the letter. 'This handwriting is very interesting, Inés. The letters are narrow and tall and slope backwards. I haven't seen anything quite like it before.'

'Hmm… I don't think I have either.'

'So who could have written it?' I said. 'And what does he think he will achieve, assuming a man wrote it. We aren't going to give up because of this, Inés, are we?'

'No, my lovely friend. Not at all. You obviously want to carry on with our mission and I'll be with you all the way.'

'Who could have written it? It sounds an obvious thing to say but someone who knows we are here and why we are here.'

'Let's go through the list of people we've met since we arrived here. We started here, at this inn. By the way, that woman on the desk was the one I saw naked making love to the landlord. I had trouble recognising her with clothes on!' We both chuckled.

'You are funny, Inés. It's good to enjoy some humour at moments as serious as this!'

'I don't remember telling anyone here about Juan junior, do you?'

'No. We didn't tell Gonzalo or his mistress, the cook and receptionist. So it's not one of the staff at the inn.'

'We told those students in the Department of Law.'

'Yes. And didn't we tell the janitor at the College of the King?' I said.

'No, definitely not.'

'We did you know. I remember him telling us that he was sorry to hear of the death of Juan junior. I remember a lump forming in my throat as he said it. It seemed so odd that someone so remote from those awful events of so long ago could say he was sorry to hear about Juan's death.'

'You are right, Francisca. I remember now you have reminded me. So the janitor is a suspect.'

'We told those students so any one of them could have written it. So could the professor of law or his secretary or even the professor we spoke to in astronomy. We even told that handsome lecturer I rather liked at the cathedral.'

'"Rather liked", my dear friend!' Inés laughed. 'The one who made you think impure thoughts! You really took to him!'

I could feel the colour rising at Inés's remarks and decided to ignore what she had said. 'Yes, he could also be a suspect.'

'Let's face it. We have told quite a number of people and they could have passed our information on to anyone.'

'So what are we going to do, Inés?'

'Go to the holy brotherhood?'

'No. I don't think so. That corrupt band of brutal thugs and robbers? How do we know that one of them isn't the author?'

'We don't but how can you suspect them. You have no facts.'

'Just a feeling I have, Inés. An old lady's instinct! But I'm probably wrong! We must carry on Inés. As long as we protect each other we should be safe, I think we should ignore it and carry on with our investigations.'

'I should burn it, Francisca, Set it alight with this candle.' Inés picked up a lit candle in its holder and went to hand it to me,

'No, Inés. I'll put it back in its torn envelope and keep it, just in case.'

***

Yet another almost sleepless night inflicted itself upon me. It was that letter. I just couldn't get it out of my head and I didn't want to wake or disturb Inés who slept soundly beside me. I really didn't know what to think. Could this be a threat on our lives? A threat of violence of some kind? There was something going on in this town that I didn't understand and I was sure Inés didn't either. I wondered if there was a conspiracy of some sort. Who would want to cover up the death of a young, innocent student? What could their motives be? Maybe it was as simple as not being found out as a murderer or being complicit in a murder. Were more than one person involved or was it just the one: the anonymous author with the odd handwriting. I suddenly thought of Baltasar's gun. At least we had that for protection.

I must have slept some of the time because I awoke with a start when Inés touched my shoulder. 'It's gone nine by the clock by the church tower, my sleepy friend. We have the meeting in the law department at eleven and we might think of how we are going to approach it.'

'I can't help wondering what he'll be like,' said Inés over breakfast in the dining room. 'I hope he doesn't shout at us like he did to his secretary when they were talking about us in his office.'

'I'd be surprised if he treated us like that. There was something about that secretary that would have made me shout! He was ridiculously formal for a start. And all that wig powder!'

'You are going to have to tell him the background as we know it and why we are here. And my advice is to show the minimum of emotion. But you won't want to appear to be interrogating him. Just asking if he can help us in some way.'

'Yes, I understand that, Inés. I'm sure you are right. We'll be polite to him and hope he treats us the same.

***

We reached the professor's outer office at about a quarter to eleven. 'What should we do, Francisca?'

'Wait here for five minutes and then go in. He can't expect us to know the exact time.'

Not a word was exchanged while we waited until I nodded at Inés and she nodded back. I opened the outer door and went in. There was no one there. We stood silently for a few minutes.

'What should we do now, Francisca?'

'Stay here. Don't let's sit. It would be rude.'

We had to admit feeling frustrated. We couldn't hear a sound from the professor's office but could not assume he wasn't in there. I whispered to Inés that we could talk, hopefully fairly naturally so he could hear us if he was in there. We chatted about the breakfast and the weather. Then the door to the outer office suddenly burst open. A man appeared, speaking as he entered.

'Those Jesus damned women will be here in… Oh, our guests have arrived,' said the man, dressed as a high court judge with a gown down to his black shoes and a distinctly off-white wig. His face looked pale as if covered by a white stocking. He was clearly embarrassed at realising we were already there. I saw this as an advantage as he might want to compensate us for his clumsy indiscretion.

'Do come into my office, señoras. We have arranged a seat each for you and one for Manuel, my secretary,' he said.

We entered a scene of almost total chaos. Unlike the outer office, which 'Manuel' kept in creditable order, the professor's was strewn with papers, open books, books piled upon other books, files of papers, the pages of which seemed to be attempting to escape to the floor, bundles of legal documents, some tied with ribbons in blue, red and purple. It was as if a hurricane had entered and blown his papers from a reasonable state into this random mess. We could see what he meant by the odd expression, 'we have arranged a seat...' It meant that they had cleared sufficient space on the cluttered floor for each of us to sit and face him across his equally paper scattered desk. We wondered how he might tutor students in this state of confusion and disarray. We concluded that he couldn't. That function, if it took place at all, had to be performed in a separate venue.

The lugubrious Manuel followed us in, clutching an ink pot, his extravagant quill pen and a leather bound notebook. Manuel took his seat slightly to the rear.

'So tell me what you want exactly. Start from the beginning.'

'I related the story of Juan junior's passing and why we were here. I managed to avoid any outward sign of emotion but at the same time wondered how anyone who worked in such abandoned conditions could possibly help us. He must have read my mind.

'Exactly how do you think I can help you?'

'Several ways, I think,' I said, trying to sound confident. 'Did you meet my son and did you know his friends? If so, we may be able to make contact with them and ask them what they know.'

'They'd have all left, not much less than sixteen years ago. I can't remember whether I knew your son or not. I've had hundreds of students through my hands since then.'

72

Then Inés made a point. 'As professor of law, could you offer any legal advice or insights into the case?'

He sat back in his chair and placed his hands on the back of his be-wigged head. Some powder dropped from it onto his shoulders. He paused as if in thought for what seemed an age but was probably less than half a minute.

'You've said something quite important, young lady. I may be able to help in that way. Do you have the report of the physician who carried out the post mortem? There may be something there that could give us a direction to travel in.'

Praise be to Inés. She had put something into his head that brought him round to sounding more constructive about helping. I glanced at her and she glanced back.

'We don't have the report but I'm sure we could retrieve it from the physician's office. With due permission, of course,' I said.

'In which case could you go back to Madrid and get it for me? I'll give it the attention it deserves and see what we can deduce.'

Despite the reign of chaos in this office, I felt that this odd character was at least making an effort to help. And our early departure to Madrid might just placate the anonymous writer of that horrible letter. 'We'll return to Madrid, probably tomorrow to fetch the post mortem report,' I said, finding the words 'post mortem' sticking in my throat.

'As soon as I receive the report, I'll start work on it,' said the professor, his eyebrows raised to emphasise his apparent commitment. 'That's all ladies. I'll see you on your return.'

His secretary took this as the cue to escort us from the office.

***

'That was quite helpful,' said Inés, as we walked back along the corridor to where we had met the partying students only two days before. As we turned the corner to the left, a familiar face was heading briskly towards us,

'Hello, señoras. Did you have your meeting with the professor?' the student Alonso said.

'We have just come from his office,' said Inés. 'He says he wants to help us.'

We paused and told him how the meeting went. He then looked along the corridor, one way and then the other. 'Come this way, if you don't mind,' said Alonso. He led us into a small office which we imagined was a tutorial room. It was unoccupied. He closed the door behind us.

'Let me warn you,' he said. 'The professor doctor is a strange man. He is mightily intelligent but he is also dangerous. He has wrecked the careers of several of his staff. Some because he thought they were a threat to his own position... and some because he didn't like them. He begins these attacks against his staff by taking them into his confidence and pretending that he will help, even promote them. Make sure he doesn't do the same to you. If there is something in the post mortem report that he feels will be more of an advantage to him than to you, you may find he won't help you. In fact, he'll do the opposite. I am telling you this because I like you and don't want to see you wasting your time here. Now let's return to the corridor. I'll go to the right and you to the left.'

I kissed him on both cheeks and thanked him and Inés shook his hand before we did exactly as he had suggested. At her comparatively young age, it would have been inappropriate for Inés to kiss the lad.

We made our way to the outside of the building and discussed our meeting with the professor on the way.

'Do you think that was a genuine offer of help or a delaying tactic?' asked Inés.

'It's difficult to tell,' I said. 'He seemed to be making a genuine offer but there are other ways he could help. For example, he could have said he'd find out about Juan junior's contemporaries and look at their records. There might be a motive for killing Juan buried in there somewhere. What he hopes to get out of the post mortem report, I fail to see. But I'm not a lawyer, so don't know how these things work. We'll just have to be patient. I'm sorry I didn't turn to you to ask about our return to Madrid. Are you happy to return tomorrow?'

'My darling friend, I am here to follow you. If you say we go tomorrow, so be it. I have no issue with that, Francisca. On the contrary, the sooner we can return with the report, the better!'

I so enjoyed my friendship with Inés, despite the wide difference in our ages. As I had only just learnt, she too had suffered the tragic death of her child, also a son. It was wonderful to have her support here in Alcalá de Henares. Nor was it simply her presence and company. She was an intelligent woman and therefore could make a significant contribution to the thinking and planning of our mission.

'Before we return, shall we make some enquiries of the mathematics department? According to the lecturer, Pedro Lobos, they won't be deserted two days in a row!' I said.

'No! I'd forgotten about him!'

'I hadn't. We must call in at his office at about three thirty.'

'Yes, but let's find some food before we go there. I'm famished!'

We were soon eating some bread, olives and tomatoes in the dining room of The Mad Astronomer. We were alone there. 'We've been here three days, Inés. Are we any nearer to solving the mystery of Juan junior's death?'

'I have a feeling we are, beautiful lady. Our presence here is having its effect. We already have the promises from law and astronomy. Our fear is that letter. But if we leave tomorrow, its writer will believe it has had its desired effect!'

I nodded agreement. 'Let's go to mathematics.'

***

We walked back down the Calle San Pedro y San Pablo to the San Ildefonso College and through into the bright green quadrangle, up the stairs to the mathematics department on the second floor. It hummed with persistent activity. Students in ordinary clothes and some in gowns were going hither and thither along the length of the corridor, as if we'd arrived at a class changeover. We wondered exactly what was happening as this was surely the vacation. We managed to avoid crashing into the students as we walked along the corridor to the left looking for Pedro's office. It bore a sign saying, 'Señor Pedro Lobos de Pamplona, lecturer'. I could feel my heart flutter, as if to miss a beat or two, and my face redden.

'Shall I knock on the door, Francisca?'

'Why not?'

We stood there a full minute waiting for a response. Inés knocked again and we waited. Still no sign of Pedro. I attempted to open the door. It was locked. My face dropped.

'That's disappointing.'

'I wonder where he is?' said Inés.

'Who knows? Let's see if we can find the head of department.'

We walked the whole of the rest of the corridor only to discover that if we'd gone back from Pedro's office, we would have walked only a dozen or so paces. There it was emblazoned on an outer door: Gregorio Estrada, Head of the Department of Mathematics. We paused outside.

'Shall we go straight in?' said Inés.

'Yes. But let's knock on the door before we do.'

'We were greeted by a loud, deep 'Come in'.

A heavily bearded man of about fifty with his hair in a braid and wearing a worn leather waistcoat sat facing us across a wide desk. Order prevailed in this, the tidiest office we had visited so far.

'May we speak to Professor Gregorio Estrada, who I believe is the head of the department?' I asked.

The man stood and held out a welcoming hand. 'I am Gregorio Estrada,' he said modestly. 'To whom do I owe the pleasure?'

He shook hands with each of us as we introduced ourselves. His smiling, open face made each of us feel confident and comfortable. Two chairs had been placed almost next to each other at the side of his desk.

'Please be seated,' he said, pointing to the chairs. Then, 'Please explain why you are here? It's very unusual for a lady to come into my office, let alone two!'

I told him about the death of Juan junior and that we were investigating the cause. I said that Juan was a keen student in his department and that we had already had some success in law and astronomy who seemed willing to help with our investigation.

'I will do my utmost to help you but you have set yourselves quite a challenge. It's a long time since your son died and much evidence, if any, will have vanished or been lost by now. I am not discouraging you, of course, but the task you face is daunting. So you are sure your son studied in this department?'

'Certain,' I said. 'He loved studying mathematics which he regarded as the key to understanding the universe.'

'You have an elegant way of expressing it,' he said. 'But many of us mathematicians also think that! I can't say I remember your son's name but we have, as you might imagine, highly accurate records of all those who have attended this department from its very inception. Unfortunately, the records are not in my office but along this corridor a few doors. If you'd like to wait here a few moments, I'll soon be back.' He stood and smiled at us as he closed the door behind him.

'What a nice man,' said Inés. 'Do you think he is married?'

'Why are you asking?'

'If you can take a fancy to Pedro, I can at least take a fancy to Gregorio!'

'You are a tease, Inés, but I love you dearly.'

While we waited we talked about our journey back and how long we might take to get the post mortem report. Then whether we could persuade Baltasar to return to Alcalá. His presence would surely discourage the anonymous letter writer from causing any trouble. The professor then appeared, walked over to his desk and sat down. He looked distinctly unhappy.

'My dear señoras, the news I have for you is not good. We have no record of a Juan Hidalgo attending this department.'

I just managed not to shed a tear but could feel the corners of my mouth drop. I struggled to produce any words.

'Impossible,' I said quietly. 'He loved studying here. He regularly said as much. He talked about the motion of the planets and how mathematics helped him understand them.'

'That would have been taught in astronomy, señora.'

'Yes, but you surely would have covered the mathematics.'

'You are right on that count,' he said. 'But I'm just reporting what our records reveal.'

'I'm astonished,' I said. 'I find it impossible to believe.' By then I felt quite angry, knowing full well that Juan junior studied here. He had said as much many times and how he enjoyed studying mathematics.

'This means that I cannot be of help to you, señoras, even though I wish I could. Is there anything else I can help you with?' he said, holding his hands out towards us.

'It seems not,' said Inés. 'I think we should go now.'

'Thank you, professor,' I said. 'It was good to meet you and thank you for doing your best.' I saw no point in annoying him with some remark we might later regret.

He stood, came around the desk, shook hands with each of us in turn, walked to the door and bade us goodbye as we left his office.

As we walked along the corridor towards the stairs, Inés spoke first.

'There is something wrong here, Francisca. I know there is. Some mistake. It can't be true.'

'I know. Let's head for Pedro's office and see if he's returned. We'll tell him what's happened,' I said, feeling dejected and bitterly disappointed.

We reached the lecturer's office and, once again, knocked on the door. There was no reply. We waited a few moments, knocked again. Still no answer. Both thoroughly surprised and miserable, we decided to return to The Mad Astronomer.

'Señoras, señoras, please wait!'

We looked around, half expecting to see the professor, but it was Pedro who was shouting at us.

'I'm so sorry that I missed you earlier. Come into my office! How did you get on?'

He closed the door behind us and pointed at two chairs. I could hold off no longer and burst into tears. Inés came over and put her arm around my shoulders.

'Whatever is the matter, Francisca isn't it? Have I remembered your name?'

'Yes, you have. Your head of department, Professor Gregorio Estrada, denies that my son studied here. That means terrible things for me. If true, it means that my son was lying to me and my husband about studying here. That cannot be true. He wouldn't lie to us. Why would he?'

'There is something wrong somewhere,' said Pedro. 'We must investigate further. I'll see what I can do? Perhaps the professor has made a mistake.'

We bade our farewells to Pedro after saying we would return.

***

Inés and I went back to the hotel. I had difficulty containing my anger at the professor who, though apparently kind and thoughtful, had by his findings, if that is what they truly were, implied that Juan junior had lied to me and my beloved Juan. Inés could not believe it either. We thought that the professor could be hiding something from us. Did he know more about Juan junior's death than he wanted to show? Denying that Juan was a student there could, he might think, deflect us from investigating what might have happened while Juan was studying in his department. There could be no doubt that he had studied there. Juan was constantly telling us how much he enjoyed it. If the professor was lying, Pedro could not have known it. Otherwise, he surely wouldn't have made the offer to help. That was the re-assuring conclusion we both reached.

Chapter 8

We trotted into an unwelcoming Madrid which was shrouded in a cool autumn mist. Even the horses seemed to regret entering the city. We stopped outside of my house and dismounted.

'My dear friend, are you sure you want to stay alone or would you prefer to come back with me?' Inés could not be sure, despite my assurances, that I wouldn't do something to end my life.

'I would prefer to stay home, Inés. There is much to do, despite being away for less than a week. I need to think about how I'm going to approach the Royal Physician. I almost cry every time I think of the words "post mortem", let alone say them.'

Inés, bless her, gave me a gentle hug. 'I fully understand, Francisca, my sweet friend. I think we should go to the palace tomorrow to ask about the report. There's nothing stopping us and I want to come with you. Would you mind or would you prefer to go alone?'

'It would be nice if you came, too. You are such a good friend! Shall we meet at ten, by the cathedral clock, at your house? We can walk there, if you wish. I doubt that we will be able to see the physician there and then, but we may be able to get an appointment.'

***

That night was the first I had spent alone since the cowardly and unforgivable attempt I had made on my own life. I felt surprisingly calm and at one with myself, now that I had embarked on this mission, this challenge, to solve the mystery of Juan junior's death. Inés had been my saviour in more ways than one and before I climbed into my bed that night, I got down on my knees and gave thanks to the Almighty Father for giving me this treasured friend. Without her and Baltasar I would be dead and buried in a suicide's grave. Tears came to my eyes as I uttered a quiet 'amen'.

I lay there in silent contemplation of where this mission had taken us. Although we appeared to be no nearer the solution, we had achieved something by raising the issue of Juan junior's passing with the academic authorities at the University of Alcalá de Henares. Crucially, we had also received offers of help, even if they were conditional, as made clear by the professor of law who demanded the post-mortem report. The astronomy offer, of meeting the Scottish professor was different. It was still unclear as to whether the foreign professor would actually leave England and possibly less clear whether he would bring his wife. I was most heartened by the lecturer Pedro who said he would help us. I was astonished at the feelings I felt towards this handsome man. Such feelings frightened me and I tried to dismiss them. An older woman like me just shouldn't have them, most would think. Then I remembered that letter. I did my best to forget it, eventually succeeded and fell asleep.

***

I arrived at Inés's just before the clock chimed. 'What amazing timing, Francisca, you must have known how long it would take to walk to my house. You must have counted the steps, one a second!'

'You are teasing me again, Inés, but I love you despite your chiding!'

'So what shall we do? You've walked so we have no choice but to go by foot. A drink first?'

'I think not, Inés but thank you. Let's make our way there.'

We walked most of the way, arm-in-arm, just like a mother and daughter. It was at times like this I realised just how lucky I was to have my own house in this city where poverty, hunger and deprivation left many living lives in back alleys, under hedges in parks or in church yards. As we passed the junction of Calle de los Relatores and Calle de Atoche we were accosted by a mixed group of children, all in rags, one with an emaciated dog on a string lead, and three carrying begging bowls which they rattled as we tried to pass. I took a four *maravedí* piece from my purse and tossed it into the bowl held by a matted haired girl of about eight. Her bare faced response startled me.

'That all you can afford, you rich bitch! Go and shit yourself.'

Inés looked at me and I glanced back. We each quickened our pace, in case these unfortunates attempted to attack us. I realised, not for the first time, that Juan, my husband, had left me comfortably off, even to the extent of ensuring I received a generous pension from the palace. Such thoughts made me utterly ashamed that I was about to throw it all away while standing on the parapet of that bridge. I couldn't feel anything but guilt. How long would these feelings last, I wondered. I was becoming quite sick of them.

'What are you thinking about, Francisca?'

'Oh nothing! I just feel a bit nervous about approaching the physician.'

'Don't worry. He surely cannot refuse us.'

'You're more optimistic than me.'

We entered the Plaza del Palacio after about half an hour's walk. The contrast there with some of the sights we had seen on the way would have been surprising had we not seen it before. We stood and watched the action for a minute or two. People were coming in and out of the main, central entrance of this beautiful, symmetrical, if austere, building. The identical towers, one at each end, seemed to enclose the main structure like a pair of gigantic, stone bookends. We could guess where some of these people were heading and why. Some, with wigs and gowns, were obviously lawyers. There was a small detachment of soldiers marching across the square, heading for the stable block in the western corner. There were men in tricorne hats and short coats, possibly administrators, carrying scrolls of paper, one with about ten, all in a bundle, each tied in a bow with purple ribbon. There were others too whose dress said nothing about them, ordinary people like us, going on unimagined business or even using the square as an intermediate step to another destination.

'Shall we go straight in?' I said.

'Why not?'

The tall, oaken doors were open to each side. They seemed to devour us. Our footsteps echoed in the throat of the entrance hall. I'd last made these steps some six months ago when I'd tried in vain, after Juan's passing, to discover whether Juan junior had, like his father and grandfather before him, been a special agent for the king, that is, whether he had been a spy. The answer was no answer. So I expected a negative response to a request for a document as sensitive as a post mortem report. Then where would we be? My face must have displayed my pessimism.

We joined a queue of other enquirers. There must have been ten or twelve of us, a motley if well-ordered gathering. We stood before a high desk, defended by two uniformed guards, one with a white wig and matching epaulettes on a dark blue, knee length jacket, the other, presumably the first guard's junior in similar garb but bare of epaulettes. One side of the desk acted as the station for several men in white shirts who escorted the enquirers into the depths of the palace or showed them back to the entrance, if they were refused admission. We queued for at least twenty minutes while reasons were given, rejected or accepted for entry.

'Yes, ladies? You next? What do you want?' said the one with the epaulettes.

'Well…umm…,' I uttered.

'Out with it woman. Ain't got all day!'

84

I rapidly composed myself. 'I need to see the Royal Physician. He undertook a post-mortem on my son, sixteen years ago and I need to borrow the report.'

'You'll be lucky. No one walks out of 'ere with one of our documents,' he said, giving himself a share in every paper there.

'Who decides?' said Inés.

'In your case the Physician.'

'In which case we'd like an appointment to see him, please,' I added.

He turned to half face one of the white-shirted escorts. 'Take these women to room 17 in the West Wing,' he said, almost snarling.

The man led the way and we followed. I had to half run to keep up. Inés found it easier. The corridors were barely lit by candles distributed along the walls. They were arranged with such meanness, the space halfway between them was almost totally dark. The escort unlocked the door to room 17. He opened it and held it so we could enter. We did and he went, closing the door behind us. The light coming through the waist high window gave the tiny room an unexpected cheeriness. We were almost blinded by the shock of light. Beneath the window stood another desk, this one shorter than the one in the palace entrance hall. The chair behind it faced into the room which was scattered with chairs for the use of those to be interviewed by the person sitting at the desk. We sat down and waited, but for no more than five minutes. The door burst open and in came a short, chubby man dressed in black. His clean shaven face bore a half smile.

'Good morning, ladies,' he said, as he walked in, lifted the tails on his coat and sat at the desk in front of us. 'Perhaps you'd like to sit a little closer. If so, by all means move your chairs.'

We shuffled the chairs forward a few *pies*. 'I understand you wish to see the Royal Physician. Could you please explain your request?'

85

I related the whole story, starting from Juan junior's time at Alcalá de Henares, his death, the post mortem, my mission to investigate the cause of his death and the law professor's wish to see the post mortem report.

The man put his hands behind his head, as if pondering our request. Then, with his eyes closed, he asked the question. 'Why does this professor want to see the report?'

Inés helped as I thought about the question. 'He wants to know if there is anything in the report that could help him investigate Juan junior's death. For instance, the names of anyone at the university who may know about the death; anything in the cause given by the Royal Physician which may give the professor a clue as to where to begin.'

Still with his eyes closed he gave us his decision. 'In normal circumstances, I would refuse your request but you have what I regard as a genuine need to borrow the report. There are obvious problems, the main one being that your son's death occurred so long ago... but I'm sure your law professor is aware of that and will be taking that into account, don't you think?'

'I'm sure he will,' I said.

'So I will ask the Royal Physician if he is prepared to lend you his report.'

'Will we see him?' said Inés.

'Only if he wishes to see you,' he said, by then with his eyes open and his hands on the desk in front of him. 'Otherwise he will, if he agrees, authorise me to hand over the report to you.'

'How long will this take?' I asked, by then smiling and more optimistic.

'I'm not sure exactly. I shall write him a memorandum explaining your request. I'll tell him that there is a degree of urgency and we'll just

86

have to see what he says. He will of course have to locate the report before he can give it to you. I suggest that you come back in three days. I'll give you a note to give the guards on reception when you return. They will admit you without further questioning.'

He reached under the desk to retrieve a pot of ink and a quill pen. He scribbled a short note on a piece of paper, waved it in the air to dry and gave it to me.

'I'll see you in three days then,' he said. He pulled a chain which hung from the ceiling behind him. A moment later, a different, white shirted escort took us back to the palace entrance.

***

'What did you make of that?' said Inés, as we began walking back across the *plaza* in the direction of her house.

'Hard to say. I think all this is procedural. They have to filter out the genuine requests from the spurious. I feel better about it, now we have passed the test. All we need is a positive response from the physician and we can return to Alcalá.'

***

Those three days passed slowly. I spent much of the time cleaning the house and generally tidying up. On the second day, I remembered that the threatening, anonymous letter was still in my saddlebag, exactly where I had put it when we were about to leave Alcalá. Prompted by intuition, I decided to hide it. Over the years of our marriage, Juan had collected various items of pewter which decorated a plate shelf mounted near the ceiling of our kitchen. I folded the letter and placed it deep inside the largest of his almost black pots.

I woke with a start on the morning of the third day. I had dreamt that the Royal Physician found not the report but its ashes in a sealed envelope, exactly where he expected the report to be in his files. It all seemed so real. Surely it could not be true. That report had become the key to the investigation. I soon realised that a dream has no connection with reality and prepared myself some breakfast.

Just as I was finishing, I heard a loud knock on my door. I wasn't expecting anyone so hesitated for a few moments before I went to open it.

'My God, it's you, Inés. You look pale. What's happened?'

'It's Baltasar. He's had an accident. He cut his hand in the palace kitchen and has lost a lot of blood. The palace admitted him to the General Hospital. I've just returned from there. He's delirious and I don't know what to do!' She put her arm around me and started to sob.

'I'm sure he'll be fine, Inés. He is in the right place. What did they say about him?'

'They say he's probably strong enough to survive and they've put on a tourniquet to stop the bleeding. He looks terrible.'

'Inés, I'll go alone to the palace. You go back to the hospital to be with Baltasar.'

'I shall take your advice, Francisca. Do you mind if I go now?'

'Inés, go!' I hugged her, wished her well and asked her to give Baltasar a kiss from me.

***

That afternoon I walked back to the palace. The square seemed even busier than last time. It looked as if preparations were being made for a parade of some kind. Several carriages were standing outside and grooms were harnessing horses to the shafts. I walked around them to the entrance and joined the queue. When it came to my turn, I handed the note our plump interviewer had given me to the guard with the epaulettes, the same one as before. He read it and handed it to an escort who kept it and took me back to room 17. It felt different being there alone waiting for attention. I waited much longer this time, upwards of a quarter of an hour. I was becoming quite anxious, an anxiety I could not share. Then the door opened and an official, dressed in a similar long black jacket to the one we met previously, appeared. By then I was sitting in one of the chairs. He motioned me to sit in front of the familiar desk as he sat behind it.

'Good afternoon, Señora de Abaunza,' he said, sounding remote and official. 'My name is Guzman. I have some news for you about a post-mortem report you wish to borrow. The Royal Physician has agreed to lend it to you on two conditions. The first is that you show us your certificate of birth. The second is that you provide a surety of 250 *ducats* against the loss of the said document.'

'There is a problem with my birth certificate. It was lost when my family moved from Viscaya to Madrid in 1628. I was eleven then. Nor am I sure about finding 250 *ducats*. I'll have to raise a loan but let me worry about that,' I said, surprised at myself for dealing with him with such assurance.

'Hmm..,' he muttered. 'Do you have any other means by which you can prove your identification?'

'Not exactly but there is a record of the marriage between me and my late husband, Juan Hidalgo de Polanco, at the church of San Justo, you know, in the Calle de San Miguel. Would the Physician accept that as proof?'

'Wait here. I'll go and ask him,' was the surprise reply. It was helpful and meant that I probably wouldn't have to wait and come back another day.

I stood and wandered around the room while waiting. I looked out of the window into the palace courtyard. There were a number of small tents there, open to one side. They looked like market stalls. People were buying various objects from the owners. Whatever they were selling they were small things like trinkets of some sort, too small for me to see from where I stood. The door opened just as I had this thought.

89

'There is no need to sit, señora,' said Señor Guzman, 'if you are more comfortable standing.'

'I was just wondering what was happening out there'

'There is a sale of jewellery. Jewellers from the Platería come here occasionally and sell their wares. Too expensive for the likes of me. Anyway, I spoke to the Physician and he is content for you to provide a proof of your marriage to Don Juan Hidalgo de Polanco. He wants you to go to the church of San Justo and obtain a sworn document, signed by two of the priests to the effect that you were married there and the date, etcetera, along with the names of any witnesses. He will accept that as proof of who you say you are.'

My excitement welled up inside me. I could have kissed him! 'I'm so grateful, Señor Guzman. I shall go there straight away.'

'A little slower, señora. The church officials may want some documentary indication of who you are. Obviously not a birth certificate but a letter addressed to you or something from your bank with your name and address on it. I'm sure you will remember the date of your marriage. It is the man who forgets! So you should go home first.'

'You are right, señor. I'll do that. I'll probably have time before evensong.'

'You will also need to bring the surety, preferably in cash.'

I hadn't forgotten that and needed to work out how I would raise it. It was a lot of money, more than my Juan earned in a year.

'The last time I came, the official gave me a note to take so I didn't have to be interviewed before I came in. Could you please do the same?'

'Just a little patience, please señora. I am just about to write you something.'

He shook hands with me as he handed me a fresh note. 'Good luck, Señora de Abaunza. If you do exactly as I've asked we can hand you the document you need on your return to the palace.'

***

I can't remember walking so fast, not even in those days when I wanted to get home quickly from my work at the Shod Carmen soup kitchen to see my beloved Juan. I thought on the way about calling to see Inés but decided not to do so until I had been to San Justo.

On reaching home, I went into the study and soon found a letter from the bank addressed to me. I then walked to the church. I passed the same group of begging children, still by the Calle de los Relatores, which had been so unpleasant when Inés and I had seen them, just three days before.

'It's her again, that bitch who dumped a shitty four *maravedí* on us on Monday,' said the same girl.

'If everybody who passed here gave you four *maravedís* you'd be very well off,' I said, passing them at a good pace.

They all turned and hissed at me. They did nothing else only because the street was quite busy at that time of the afternoon. I continued along the Calle Merced, into the Plaza Major. I could not believe my ears. A small group of musicians was accompanying a singer. I had to stop to listen:

'....*Love and know of me*

That I love until not to know

That I love well

Him who loves me...'

Tears began to form in my eyes and ran down my cheeks. This was a song for which Juan had composed the tunes and I had written the words. We wrote it for the king some forty years before. I hadn't heard it for twenty years or more. What a wonderful surprise! I wiped my tears away and pressed on. I was soon walking up the Calle San Miguel towards the main entrance to the church and walked in. Apart from a lady kneeling in prayer in one of the pews at the front, I could see nobody. I stepped towards the aisle and bowed towards the altar. As I looked up, I saw a priest walk into the transept. I walked towards him.

'Good evening, padre. Could you help me please?' He was a tall, slim individual, about ten or so years younger than me. His face expressed no emotion but looked as if he laughed quite a lot.

'What is it, señora? Come into my office,' he said, pointing towards a closed door. My mind went uncontrollably back to the priest who raped me after my mother died, nearly fifty years before. I shuddered at the invitation and hesitated.

'Would you rather speak here?'

'No, padre. I'll come into your office.'

We went in and he closed the door. Much to my relief he didn't lock it. We sat in chairs almost directly facing each other.

He leant towards me and looked straight into my eyes. 'I think I recognise you, señora.'

'A good start I thought. Maybe he officiated in some way at our marriage.' Then the death blow.

'Aren't you the woman who set alight to the San Ginés church, about fifteen years ago?'

I felt dreadful. I couldn't deny it. I bowed my head in shame. I couldn't speak. It is remarkable how the misdeeds of your past can catch up with you at the worst time in the future.

'You are probably thinking that in that knowledge I could not help you. If so you would be wrong. My job as a servant of God is to help all who need my help, whatever the wrongs of their past.'

'You are a kind man, padre. How do you recognise me when I don't recognise you?'

'I was serving in San Ginés at that time. I helped put out the fire. You were delirious talking about some ancient goddess. You could only be described as mad.'

'You are right, father. You witnessed the biggest regret of my life.'

'But you shouldn't regret doing something you had no control over.'

I could not believe that he showed such understanding. I had met many priests in my life but none as generous and sympathetic as this one, a true man of God.

'Tell me, señora. How can I help you?'

I told him my name, related the story up to that point and asked if he and a colleague could provide the certification the Royal Physician had requested. He said he would help if he could and took me to the registry where the church records are held. I had never seen such a well organised collection of documents. The hundreds of volumes of records were neatly arranged in year order on wide shelves, mounted on the wall. The priest worked his way along a particular shelf until he came to the volume with the year marking 1636 to 1639. He carefully slid it outwards from its place, put it on a table and started to turn the pages.

'You see, they go back to the twelfth century. When the church was founded. Here we are,' he said. 'The twenty first of September, 1639. Abaunza, isn't it? Married to Don Juan Hidalgo de Polanco. My goodness, he's the famous composer isn't he? The one who wrote the requiem mass for our late king. Oh, and those operas!'

93

'The very same,' I said with pride but holding back a tear.

'And here are the witnesses. So all we need now is a letter signed by me and another prelate. I'm afraid I am alone here for the rest of the day but tomorrow the bishop is visiting San Justo and he I'm sure will provide the second signature. He will be here to celebrate matins so if you come back tomorrow, around midday, I will give you the letter.'

'I cannot thank you enough, padre,' I said ,as I bowed to him and took his hand.

'Until tomorrow then,' he said with a broad smile as I turned to leave.

***

I couldn't wait to tell Inés about my day's labours. I didn't know whether she would be home or still at the hospital or whether Baltasar was well enough to be sent home. I went straight to Inés's. She took several minutes to come to the door. She looked ill.

'What's the matter, Inés? How is Baltasar?'

She started to cry. 'I think he is going to die, Francisca. He hardly recognised me when I saw him. He's just lying there staring into the distance. I've been with him all day. Well, until an hour ago when they asked me to leave. His hand is swollen up. It's the size of a boar's head. His fingers are twice as thick as normal. Something has got into the wound. He is bad, Francisca. Really bad. They were talking about cutting off his hand if it doesn't soon improve.'

'Holy Lord Jesus, Inés. What should we do?'

'I'm going back tomorrow. They say I will have to give permission if they are to operate. I'm so worried. How will he react if he survives? I'll have to tell him I agreed that it should be sawn off.' Tears streamed down her face.

'It won't come to that, Inés. He'll be better by the morning, I'm sure. Let me come in and make you a drink. You look as if you need one.'

I went to her larder, took a large jar of grape juice from a shelf and poured some into a mug. 'Get this down you, Inés. It's quite cool where it's been next to the wall.'

She drank it and whether I imagined it or not, I don't know, but the colour soon returned to her face.

'Listen, Inés. There's no reason for me to go home. I'll stay with you tonight. Up to now, you've comforted me but now it's for me to comfort you.'

'I accept your kind offer, Francisca. It will be good for you to stay. Talking to you will take my mind off Baltasar. And you have to tell me how you got on at the palace. I'm sorry I didn't ask before.'

By then it was about six o'clock in the evening. The daylight was beginning to fade. I volunteered to make us a meal so, with Inés chatting to me, I prepared a light dinner of *chorizo* and chicken, cooked in olive oil. While in Inés's kitchen I told her all about my amazing day. I surprised her with the revelation that the priest recognised me as the woman who set fire to the San Ginés church. I said the kind man would be asking the bishop to sign the identification document the following day and I would collect it then.

'And what about the 250 *ducats*. How are you going to find that? It's a lot of money.'

'I have some money at home. It's under my bed but I'm not sure how much. We were well off after Juan's mother gave us most of the proceeds of the sale of her love sleeve business but we spent much of that to pay for the damage I'd caused to the San Ginés church. I'll check under the bed tomorrow. I may have 250 ducats. I may not.'

As we sat in Inés's kitchen, eating our meal and sipping a glass each of a white wine Inés brought from her larder, the conversation turned in a direction that shocked me.

'I know I am in an emotional state, Francisca, but there is something I need to bring out into the open with you. A few months back you asked me if I wanted to borrow the manuscript that Juan had written about his life. You wrote the last chapter. I'm very angry about what you say in it about Baltasar. It's a mountain of lies. You say that he became a famous portrait painter and travelled around Europe painting portraits of European royalty. Whatever made you say that? You know as well as I do that he is a baker in the palace kitchens.'

'Some things you write are hard to explain,' I said, stumbling over my own words. 'I love Baltasar as much as I love you. I've always been ambitious for my friends and that includes Baltasar. You and he saved my life when I was at my lowest point. When I wrote that paragraph, I realised he wanted to be a portrait painter and follow in his father's footsteps into the post of court painter to the king. He is a very talented artist, Inés, and I still believe he could achieve that post, if he really wanted it. So when I wrote those words, I gave him a similar post of a travelling portrait painter, something I thought he could achieve even easier than working for the king. I didn't want to refer to him in a lowly position in the king's bakery, even if I think he will escape it into greater things. Please understand that. You know I wouldn't want to upset you or Baltasar.' I took another sip of the wine and wondered what Inés's reaction would be.

'So you think Baltasar is in a lowly position, do you? What audacity,' she shouted. 'And what about you? Who are you but the widow of a famous man?' She also took a sip of wine but threw the glass into the fireplace. It smashed into a hundred pieces.

Her actions stunned me, almost into silence. 'I don't know what to say, Inés. Please forgive me. If I had thought my words would have offended you, I'd never have written them. Maybe, I should have said nothing about Baltasar. The book will never be published anyway. It's a private story which will never be read by anyone else.'

'I was so angry when I read those words, two days ago, I seriously thought of abandoning you as a friend and leaving you to investigate Juan junior's death on your own. I'm still undecided.'

'In which case, Inés, I'll go home now.' I started to sob, stood up from the table and went towards the door into the hall. I half expected her to follow me to ask me to change my mind but she didn't.

***

I felt sad walking up the Calle Oliver towards my house in the Madalena. At the street corner, I stopped to wipe the tears from my eyes. I had brought all this on myself. How stupid of me to write an exaggerated picture of poor Baltasar, especially as it was almost inevitable that Inés would read it. I cursed myself. But, much to my own relief, I felt quite resilient. I had no intention of letting this setback with Inés put me off my mission to investigate the death of Juan junior. I had made good progress that day without Inés at my side and I felt quite proud of the fact. I would go to Alcalá alone if necessary, despite the threat of the anonymous letter.

Inés was a good person and had been through a many trials in her life. Two marriages and the death of a child of the first one had made her more mature than her years. I suppose that is why we had become such good friends after her grandmother, Juana Pacheco, had died no more than a week after her husband, Diego Velázquez, had passed away. I didn't want to lose her as a friend but, if that was to be the result of our dispute, then so be it.

I unlocked my front door and walked in. I made my way straight to my bedroom and pulled a small box out from under the bed. Kneeling on the floor, I tipped the contents onto the mat and started counting my money. I counted it twice with the same result: 163 *ducats* and 4 *reales*. But for about twelve *ducats,* which I hadn't spent in Alcalá, that was my total worth in cash. I wondered about borrowing some from other friends or family. Juan's mother was still alive, bless her, and well into her nineties. I used to visit her about once a fortnight and felt she would help. My friends Balthasar, the estate agent, and his wife Vitoria might be willing. They say that you should never borrow from friends or relatives unless you are prepared for them to become your enemies, so these were not attractive options. 'I know,' I thought, 'I'll go to the bank and ask for a loan. I would repay it as soon as the palace refunded the surety on the post-mortem report.'

I slept well that night, knowing I had a plan.

Chapter 9

I woke early the following morning and started my packing, ready to ride back to Alcalá, that day or the day after, depending how I felt. By the time I had had breakfast, tidied the place and tidied myself it was time to go to the San Justo church to collect the certificate that would secure the post-mortem document. And go to my bank and ask for a loan. I put 150 ducats into a bag which I could carry over my shoulder and set off.

My house was only a twenty *varas* or so from the junction of Calle de la Madalena and Calle del Oliver. I crossed the road and started walking towards the Calle Merced. As I was about ten *varas* from the Calle de los Relatores, I heard the urgent shouting of my name.

'Francisca, Francisca, stop! Wait for me!' Inés was shouting as loudly as she could. I stopped. She ran up to me, put her arms around me and held me tight.

'I am so, so sorry, Francisca. Please forgive me for what I said yesterday. I was wrong to shout at you like that. I've been awake all night thinking about it and I now plead with you to forgive me!'

'I've already forgiven you, my dear friend. You are having such a difficult time with Baltasar and I'm sure this affected what you said.'

'It doesn't matter what you say about him in your book… or rather Juan's book… Francisca. As you say, it won't be published in our lifetime so it just doesn't matter and you say good things anyway. I just don't know what I was thinking about.'

By then, still hugging, we had moved awkwardly from the middle of the road and stopped by the Puente de los Relatores, one of the most delightful fountains in our town.

'Please, please don't worry, Inés. Of course I forgive you. I should never have said those false words so I am more wrong than you are!'

At that point we broke out of our hug, looked into each other's eyes and burst into tears. Tears of relief that we had each retained our best friend. In a minute or two we each wiped our eyes in our handkerchiefs.

I spoke first. 'So back to more important matters, how is Baltasar? Any news on him?'

'I am on my way to the hospital now, Francisca.'

'Please give him my best wishes and love. I hope he's better today.'

'Of course. I suppose you are going to San Justo.'

'Yes and I'm going to my bank to ask for a loan to cover the 250 *ducats*. I have about 150 so need more.'

'I shall provide it, Francisca. It can come from my grandfather's estate. It is the least I can do. I shall organise it, my dear friend. Leave it to me!'

At that point we agreed to meet at my house at four o'clock that afternoon. By then, Inés would have the latest news on Baltasar and, with luck and a fair wind, I would be in possession of the crucial paper from San Justo.

***

I crossed myself at the rear of the church. I heard a scampering of feet as the priest, whom I met the day before, ran from one of the aisles. He stopped in front of me.

'I have good news, Señora de Abaunza. Come to my office. I have the document for you!'

I could have hugged and kissed him, I was so pleased.

'The disappointment is that it is not signed by the bishop. He had a more pressing engagement and could not visit us. Another colleague here has signed it for me and we've included the names of your witnesses. I

100

have made an additional note to say that I knew you personally and that we met for the first time some fifteen years ago. I haven't for reasons of discretion said how we met.'

He handed me the document which took the form of a scroll, tied with ecclesiastical purple ribbon, which bore the seal of the bishop of San Justo.

'Take it señora and may it have the effect that you so dearly want. I think it will.'

I thanked him again, shook his hand and, with the scroll in my shoulder bag, returned home.

Several hours after I'd arrived, there was a loud knock on my front door. It sounded like a man's knock. In these unexpected circumstances the mind turns to negative possibilities. Had Inés been hurt in some way? Had she sent someone to tell me of Baltasar's passing? So it was with some trepidation that I went to the door and opened it.

'By the good Lord Jesus, it's you, Baltasar. You are better! Wonderful!' I said.

He and Inés were standing next to each other on my threshold grinning at me like a pair of Venetian clowns.

'As you can see, I am as good as mended now, Francisca.'

'What was the miracle cure? You were as good as dead yesterday!'

'The doctors took a big risk and tried something they'd not tried for years. They bathed my hand and arm in hot, salted brandy. The vapour from it made me quite drowsy, I can tell you, not that I remember much. When I woke up this morning the swelling had almost completely gone. I felt five hundred times better, well enough to walk home. Admittedly, I'm not home yet but it's only a few *varas* from here!'

All three of us laughed. We were all delighted that Baltasar had made such a speedy recovery, especially as he had been so bad the day before.

'The hospital told him not to do too much for a couple of days. Then he can get on with life, as normal,' said Inés. 'So he is going to see his bosses at the palace tomorrow and ask for relief to accompany us to Alcalá.'

'They won't agree to that, surely. Only the bosses themselves have time off. The likes of us have to work every day!'

'Maybe, Francisca, but I'm going to tell them about your mission, the threatening letter and that you and Inés need protection, for a time. They can only refuse. I don't think they will because there are too many of us working in the kitchen at the moment and, if I volunteer to go unpaid, they will be too pleased to get rid of me! But before I do, must ask your permission, Francisca, to tell them why we are going to Alcalá.'

'You have it, Baltasar! You are marvellous!'

***

I felt much safer knowing that Baltasar was almost certainly coming with us. Inés more than made up for her argument with me about Baltasar by borrowing 200 *ducats* from the estate of Diego Velázquez to cover the surety and to provide a substantial excess. She was quite surprised that the executors were so cooperative but I was not: she was the main beneficiary of Señor Veláquez's will so the monies were in effect hers anyway. Two days after Inés' and my reconciliation, for that is what it was, I made my lone way to the Alcázar Palace, armed with the statement of my identity from San Justo's wonderful priest and 250 *ducats* in gold coin, which I carried there in a small sack over my shoulder. Within twenty minutes, I almost ran from the palace with the post-mortem document, before they changed their minds.

Baltasar told us that he'd never seen the master baker as cheerful as when he said he needed temporary relief from kitchen duties. The palace treasury had barely enough cash to pay the senior officials and could usefully distribute the money that Baltasar would otherwise have been paid. What joy: a man to guard and support us.

***

We prepared ourselves to leave and two days later, in the middle of the afternoon, appeared at the Madrid gate into Alcalá de Henares.

I immediately recognised the three men standing outside. One of them, clumsily wielding a handgun, stepped into the road to stop us.

'Good afternoon, señores. Two *reales* each to enter the town and four *maravedís* for each of your horses,' said the man with a gun.

'Ignore them,' I said. 'They are the vagabonds, thieves who robbed us last time.'

'Just pay up or you'll get a taste of this,' said the gunman, pointing it into the air and waving it about.

Just as he finished his sentence a gunshot exploded into our ears and a cloud of dust rose from near the man's feet. 'Just get out of our way,' said Baltasar, pointing his gun at the man's head. The man dropped to the ground in an untidy heap. We trotted through the portals. His two colleagues just stared at us.

A few steps in, I turned to Baltasar. 'That scared them,' I said.

'I wondered why he didn't try to fire back,' he said. 'His gun couldn't have been ready. I have the other one of the pair on the other side of my saddle so could have dealt with him!'

That potentially dangerous incident told me much about Baltasar. He acted with calmness and speed in adversity and did not take advantage of having the upper hand with the street robbers. He could have killed the man with a single shot but chose only to raise a dust cloud on the ground in front of him. And he could have discharged his matching pistol but decided against it. These qualities would serve us well while engaged on this difficult challenge.

We made our way towards The Mad Astronomer. To our side stood a gnarled and ancient stone boundary.

'Do you know what's behind that wall?' I said.

'No idea,' said Baltasar. 'I know we are only six *leguas* from Madrid, but I've never been here before. And I was not impressed by the welcome outside!'

'It will improve, I promise you,' said Inés.

'This is the outer wall to the famous Archbishop's Palace. It was first a fortress built by the Moors to keep us Christians out. Then in the *reconquista* it became a temporary home for the Archbishops of Toledo to protect them from the Moors!'

'You aren't indulging us in your boring history are you, Francisca?'

'Keep going, Francisca! I'm interested, even if Inés isn't!'

'Well, many Spanish kings lived there for various times, including Isabella and Ferdinand. Their daughter, Catherine of Aragon the future Queen of England was born there. So was Ferdinand the First, Holy Roman Emperor who was a son of the mad queen Joanna. It is famous for being the first meeting place of Isabella and Christopher Columbus…'

'You are a valuable source of knowledge, Francisca. Is there more?'

'Yes but, as Inés says, I mustn't be tedious about it!'

'Go on Francisca, I'm only teasing you.'

By then we were walking the horses past the Plaza Palacio. 'That building to the left of the palace is the Convent of San Bernardo. It was founded by Cardinal Bernardo de Sandoval y Rojas an uncle of the infamous Duke of Lerma.'

'What a beautiful building,' said Inés. 'It looks very important, right next to the palace! Didn't you mention the Cardinal the last time we rode these streets. They named the road after him.'

'Well remembered, Inés,' I said.

'It seems strange that the Cardinal was made a saint, especially as he was the Inquisitor General!' she said.

'I'm not surprised,' said Baltasar. 'The Inquisition was and is supported by the Popes. They call themselves Christians, but delight in burning heretics at the stake. How many have they put to death now?'

***

We tied our horses to the rail outside the inn. Baltasar pushed the green door open and we walked in with our saddlebags over our shoulders. The familiar smell of stale beer and other less identifiable, equally pungent smells struck our nostrils, despite what appeared to be fresh, quite deep sawdust on the floor. The place appeared and sounded empty, even though four o'clock was approaching.

'Don't say Gonzalo is upstairs again, making love to the cook!' said Inés.

I giggled.

'No!' said Baltasar. 'Is he the landlord? Is that what they were doing?'

'Yes. Inés crept up the stairs and saw them at it!'

'I'll go this time!' said Baltasar, laughing with his whole face.

'No. I suggest we wait here at the desk…Oh, there's the bell. Let's ring it!' I said, picking up the small bell and tinkling it as loudly as I could.

The ebullient Gonzalo appeared from the kitchen, rubbing his hands together to remove some flour. 'Señores, how can I help you?' he said. Then recognising Inés and me, 'It's good to see you, ladies. Welcome back!'

Within moments we had settled the rates with Gonzalo, who allocated a double room to me and Inés and a single to Baltasar. By good fortune, we could have the same room as we stayed in before, with Baltasar just along the corridor from us. 'It will seem like home,' said Inés.

That night over dinner we discussed our tactics in dealing with the law professor.

'Should I come, too, or should you and Inés go alone?' said Baltasar.

'We all go. There is strength in numbers,' I said.

'I agree,' said Inés.

'In which case, I agree, too. I shall not go armed, except by my wit!' said Baltasar.

'Should we make an appointment to see him or just hope he can see us?' I said.

'Hope he is available when we go into his outer office,' said Inés. 'His secretary can make an appointment for us if he's not free then.'

'Do we need to see him?' said Baltasar. 'Couldn't we just leave the post mortem report with his secretary?'

'No,' I said emphatically. 'We need to see what he intends to do with it. I was left unsure when we last saw him.'

'Me, too,' said Inés.

***

At just after 10 o'clock in the morning, all three of us arrived at the professor's office door. We stopped outside. I felt quite nervous and not optimistic about this encounter.

'Do we just knock and wait for a response?' said Baltasar.

'Just that,' I said. Baltasar knocked firmly.

'Come in,' was the welcomed reply.

'Good morning,' I said. 'My name is…'

'Get to the point. I recognise you, of course,' said the secretary, flicking back his head and simultaneously scattering wig powder over his jacket and the floor. 'You have a report for Professor Doctor Juárez de Lerida, I believe.'

'Yes, I have the report and I have to ask the professor to sign for its delivery. May we see him?'

'I'll ask him.' He stood, scattering more wig powder, walked straight into the professor's office and closed the door behind him. He seemed to be in there an age. Eventually he emerged with a stern look on his face.

'Yes, go in.'

I took the lead, followed by Inés, then Baltasar and finally the secretary who closed the door behind us.

'I'm delighted to see you again,' said the smiling professor, whether he meant it or not. 'I understand you have a document for me, the post mortem report. And you want me to sign for it!' he chuckled. 'Why the formality?'

'I had to pay the Alcázar Palace a substantial surety to obtain it. So I'm being very careful about its handling. I cannot afford to lose the surety.'

'Do you have a receipt I can sign?'

I removed an envelope from my bag and took from it a small piece of paper on which I had written the words:

'This is to acknowledge the receipt of a post mortem report concerning the death on the 11th of July in the year 1669 of Juan Hidalgo de Polanco, a student of the College of the King, Alcalá de Henares, signed.....................and dated......'

I handed it to the professor who looked at it closely, even holding it up to the light, as if to look for a watermark.

'Hmm...' he muttered. 'This signifies a lack of trust.'

'I don't think so,' said Baltasar, stepping in quickly with an explanation which was better than mine. 'Señora de Abaunza has a duty to the palace to account for the exact whereabouts of the document at any point in time. If she is in possession of a signed receipt she can show it to any official who wants to see it. Is that clear?'

'You've persuaded me. I'll sign.' He dipped a long quill pen into a pot of black ink and scratched his signature and the date on the bottom of the paper. He left it to dry. I handed him the report.

'May I ask what your plan may be in taking the investigation further forward? How are you going to use the information in the report?' I said, confidently.

'I have been thinking about that,' he said. 'It critically depends on what it contains. We have to bear in mind that your son died some sixteen years ago, so what it says may be of limited value to me. The job of the pathologist, in this case the Royal Physician, was to determine the time and cause of death. I will need more information. That is why I am asking you now to go to the Holy Brotherhood here and ask for their report of the investigation.'

'Why didn't you ask for that before, Professor Doctor Juárez de Lerida? We could have brought you both documents at the same time,' I said, in frustration and furious at the man's time wasting. It wasn't often I showed my anger in raising my voice but I just couldn't help myself.

'I have a request professor, if you don't mind,' said Baltasar, stepping in immediately after me. 'You are the professor of law and will have greater influence with the local brotherhood here than any of us. They have no idea who we are and have no credibility with them. May I therefore suggest that you write and give us a letter that we can pass to the authorities here asking for the report? Could you do that here and now please? We don't mind delivering it if you tell us to whom.'

'I'll do that. Please wait outside,' he said with reluctance but possibly recognizing his unwarranted prevarication.

Baltasar's ability to help in this mission was becoming clearer by the hour. By being firm, demanding and respectful, he had persuaded the professor to write a letter, even though our preference was for the professor to work with the post mortem report, at least as far as he could go with it. Within a few minutes the professor appeared in his outer office and handed Baltasar an envelope, sealed at its rear with red wax. He had addressed it to: *The Captain of the Holy Brotherhood, Calle Carmen Calzado, Alcalá de Henares.*

'As soon as I receive the report, we will begin the investigation,' said the professor, in such a flat tone that none of us believed he wanted to help. We could only retrieve the report and see what he did with it. Each of us felt it might not be very much. After the professor had indulged us a round of handshakes and nods of his head, we left his office, not uttering a word until we reached the road outside. The letter remained in Baltasar's manly grip.

'That was a surprise,' said Inés. 'Why didn't he just use the report we brought him from Madrid?' Inés avoided using the words, 'post mortem' to protect my feelings.

'I just don't know,' I said. 'He seems to be playing with us. For whatever reason he doesn't seem to want to help us at all, even though his words sound as if he does.'

'Well, what do we do now?' said Inés.

'What's stopping us going to the office of the brotherhood now?' I said. 'The sooner we can deliver the letter, the sooner we can make progress. And I know the way there.'

Ten minutes later we were approaching the brotherhood's quite modest office. A picture of chaos confronted us. A crowd of about fifty people had gathered outside. They were facing the building and chanting loudly. Some were holding banners. Several constables, each wearing a tricorne hat and a green sleeved coat, were confronting this mob and holding them back from forcibly entering the building. One constable raised a baton and brought it down heavily on the shoulder of a bearded man who then attempted to grab the baton from the constable's grasp. A large woman in a white dress and wearing a bonnet confronted another constable and tried to pull him over. It was as if a minor battle was raging. Several people were standing away from the crowd and looking on.

'What's going on here?' said Baltasar to one of the bystanders.

'The holy brotherhood are holding one of the lecturers from the university on a charge of treason. All he's done is to say he's against the monarchy. These people want him released and are trying to break into their office. They may well succeed!'

'We'll never get through that crowd,' I said. 'Not without risking our lives. Let's just go back to The Mad Astronomer. We can try again tomorrow.'

'Agreed,' said Baltasar and Inés, in unison.

We sat in the drinking area in the inn and discussed what was happening at the brotherhood's office. 'I don't understand it,' said Inés. 'After over a century of rule over a united Spain, why would anyone want to change from having the king as head of our country?'

'Many,' said Baltasar. 'Charles the Second is incompetent as well as incontinent.'

Inés and I chuckled.

'He is a disaster as a monarch,' said Baltasar. 'And it shows in the running of the palace as well as the country. His mother, Marianna was the true ruler. Not that she was much good, relying so much on Nithard for advice. Now that she's been exiled and John of Austria has become Prime Minister, things are even worse. So it's not surprising, at least to some, that there is reaction against our monarchy.'

'My Juan was always a supporter of the king, even when the old king died and Mariana became Regent,' I said.

'Yes, but Juan was always loyal. The king made him what he was, so he had to be grateful. Loyalty is part of it,' said Inés.

'I don't agree with that,' I said, with more than a hint of sharpness. 'Juan was a composer in his own right and would have written great music, whether or not the king was his patron. I'm not surprised either. When we came to Alcalá when Juan junior was studying here, we could detect feelings against the monarchy. They've become worse if what we saw was an example.'

'It's not a problem we will solve,' said Baltasar. 'We'll just have to hope we can deliver the professor's letter tomorrow.'

***

That night, as I laid in bed with my hands behind my head, I felt frustrated by the lack of progress on my mission. I was no nearer unravelling the cause of Juan Junior's death that I was the day Inés and I rode to Alcalá de Henares for the first time, almost three weeks before. Perhaps I was being impatient. Perhaps I was expecting too much of those like the professor of law, the mathematicians and the astronomers who had offered to help us. I drifted into my slumbers not knowing really what to think.

I woke with a start. Inés was moving my hand which by then was over my face.

'Wake up, Francisca, we must go down for breakfast soon or we'll be too late!'

Within an hour all three of us were outside the Office of the Holy Brotherhood. The mob had dispersed and the area outside was back to normal, except that one tired looking man was standing outside holding a placard which read simply: *'Long live the King.'* We hoped the mob of the day before didn't appear and confront him. We each looked at the other.

'Do we go straight in, all three of us? Why don't you and Inés go in?' said Baltasar.

'No,' said Inés. 'You and Francisca.'

Baltasar and I entered. One lonely constable sat behind a desk with his head leaning against the wall, as if sleeping. We stopped in front of him. He didn't stir. He was sleeping. Baltasar knocked on the desk, not too firmly but making sufficient noise to wake him. He sat upright, causing his tricorne to fall to the floor behind him. He stood, picked it up and put it back on his head.

'Good morning,' said Baltasar, smiling at the awkwardness of the encounter. 'We are here to deliver a letter to the Captain of the Holy Brotherhood, señor.'

'Give it here,' the man said, looking embarrassed. I handed it to him.

'Anything else you want?' he said.

'That's a difficult question to answer,' I said. I explained the reason we were in Alcalá de Henares and that the professor of law had offered to help. I said what the letter was about and asked how long it would take to deliver the investigation report to the professor. I offered to deliver it in person.

'Can't really help you, señora. First we need to find the report. That won't be easy. Then we need to decide whether there's anything in it we would not want the public to know about. It's only then we could decide whether to release it. You did the right thing though, asking the professor to write this letter. Our Captain knows him and goes to him for legal advice.'

That was reassuring. At least we had not apparently created a problem by involving the professor. If the relationship between him and the local captain was bad, that could have seriously delayed the release of the report or denied it completely.

'How long do you think this will take?' said Baltasar.

'Don't know. Haven't got a clue. Depends on what else the Captain's got his mind. These illegal demonstrations against the monarchy won't be helping him. I'd say three weeks, if not longer. Come back a week today and ask again. Don't expect to get the report though. Refer to the letter from Professor Doctor Juárez de Lerida. I imagine it carries yesterday's date from what you've told me. Whoever's on duty here, you must give him the date of the letter. Otherwise, it won't be found in our files.'

We bade the officer good day and went outside where Inés was waiting for us.

'That was quite quick,' she said. 'No queue then?'

We told Inés about our exchange with the desk officer. 'So we could be here another three weeks just waiting for the report,' said Inés.

'That's right,' I said.

'Let's give it a week and see what happens,' said Baltasar.

***

That week passed very slowly. We were trapped between the professor's office and the office of the brotherhood like a boar trapped between two groups of hunters.

'What about going to see your contacts at the Department of Astronomy?' said Baltasar.

'Not much point,' I said. 'It's only been a little over a week since we heard about the professor from England's visit. I said I'd write to the professor of astronomy to ask whether he was coming or not. Yes, I'll write to him. We can deliver the letter by hand. That will give us something to do!'

'So we are stuck then,' said Inés. 'What are we going to do for a week?'

'All I can suggest is that we visit some of these beautiful places in Acalá de Henares. There are plenty of them and each has a history of its own. We haven't yet shown Baltasar the Iglesia Magistral, the Convent of our Lady of Hope, the other colleges of the University, especially the beautiful façade of the College of Saint Ildefonso, or the beautiful parks and squares in the town.'

'Let's do that, Francisca. What do you think, Inés?'

'All right, as long as Francisca doesn't bore us too much with the history!'

A week of doing not very much in the confines of this small town, interesting as it was, hardly inspired us. In fact, it put considerable strain on our relationships, especially that between Baltasar and Inés. Although Baltasar meant no ill, Inés reacted badly to Baltasar's chiding, usually over trivialities that caused him some amusement but served only to irritate Inés. She even walked out of dinner one night after Baltasar accused her of eating too much. He bore the appetite of a horse so could hardly criticise her.

Each of us was getting quite tense in anticipating what we would learn when we returned to the Office of the Holy Brotherhood.

'I think they will give us the report,' I said, more in hope than genuine optimism.

'I don't,' said Baltasar.

'There's only one way to find out,' said Inés.

Exactly a week after our first meeting at the brotherhood we returned. Inés said she couldn't bear the tension of waiting outside again so all three of us went in. We were about the sixth group in a queue of various individuals with complaints, accusations, payments of fines and other miscellaneous reasons for being there. After waiting patiently and silently for about half an hour we arrived at the desk. Baltasar explained to the different officer from the one before why we were there and what we wanted.

'Just a moment, I'll have to go and check,' said the officer. While he was away, several other groups of people and a few individuals joined the queue behind us. Some started tutting and hissing.

'It's not our fault,' said Baltasar, having turned around to address them. 'We had to be patient and you'll have to be, too!'

Eventually the officer returned. 'No. The letter has not been dealt with yet. Come back in a week's time. Maybe you'll get what you want then.'

'Only "maybe"?' I said, sounding more impatient than I meant to be.

'That's what I said,' he uttered and turned to the next in the queue behind us. Heads lowered in our disappointment, we went outside.

'This is becoming a nuisance,' said Inés, as we started to walk back to The Mad Astronomer.

'I agree,' I said. 'I don't know what to suggest. We've exhausted the interesting things to see in Alcalá but I don't want to go back to Madrid.'

'I think I may have to,' said Baltasar, stepping quickly to one side to avoid some horse droppings. 'I know there's a banquet in a few days' time and I think I should be there.'

This came as something of a shock but I could understand Baltasar's reluctance to stay while we floundered in this state of no progress. Then an even bigger surprise.

'I hate to tell you this, Francisca, but I think I'll go back with Baltasar.'

'But you said…'

'I know, my lovely friend. But I have a family and they will be missing me. Let me go for a couple of weeks and I'll come back and help you,' she said as we were approaching the inn. 'But I want to be sure you are safe, Francisca. So I want you to write me a note, a short letter, telling me you are all right. You must write every day. If I don't receive a letter, I shall immediately come back to help you. But that anonymous letter has had no effect and I believe that the danger has passed.'

'I'm not so sure, but I fully agree that you and Baltasar should return to Madrid,' I said, when I didn't mean it at all and was bitterly disappointed with the two of them. I wondered whether Inés was still harbouring bad feelings over what I'd said about Baltasar in Juan's book, even though she was quite distraught and apparently sincere when she said she forgave me.

'We'll pack now and try to get back to Madrid before nightfall,' said Baltasar.

'Damn the pair of you!' I thought. 'They can't wait to go.'

Inés handed me the pistol while she was packing her saddlebag. 'You might want this, Francisca. Take it. I won't need it while I'm with Baltasar.'

I kissed each of them goodbye before they mounted their horses and walked them towards the Madrid Gate. They turned to wave and I waved back to them. I didn't expect to be alone at that moment. It would have been nicer if they'd at least have seen the day out and left the following morning. I regretted cursing them less than an hour before. The fact was that Inés was my best friend and I loved her intensely.

Chapter 10

I locked the door. I spent the rest of the day in my room, a strange and unexpected situation, being alone with my thoughts. I had to trust in my ability to find the cause of Juan Junior's death. I owed it to the two loves of my life, now passed. I shed a tear. I knew I could not achieve it alone but I knew how to engage people to help me. Already some had come to my aid. The Astronomy Department enjoyed the highest place in the band of my optimism, followed by the lawyers. The Mathematics Department, while I held embarrassing thoughts about the young Pedro, had to be the most disappointing, rejecting even the suggestion that my Juan had studied in their midst. They were wrong but would not admit it. While I thought of doing so, I wrote a brief letter to Inés that I would give to Gonzalo in the morning to put into the post.

I felt apprehensive about going down to dinner. While Baltasar and Inés were there, the thought of feeling shy or self-conscious hadn't entered my mind but there alone I felt quite different. I stumbled on the solution: I would change into a dress, tie up my hair and splash on a little perfume. I would hold my head high and my back straight as I walked into that dining room. I didn't care about the sawdust on the floor or the smell of stale beer and things. I pushed the door open only to be glared at by ten or more pairs of eyes suddenly staring in my direction. I walked in and made my way to a table near the window. I felt so confident I surprised myself. Juan would have been proud of this lonely figure on her mission, in this strange place.

Gonzalo walked over and stood by my side. 'What would you like, señora? I know you are alone of course but you will be safe here while I am taking the orders.'

'What are the choices?'

'We have braised Aragonese lamb, duck from the Mazanares or a very nice *chuchinillo* from Segovia. Your choice. But I recommend the *chuchinillo*.'

'I'll have the lamb,' I said, 'and a glass of *jumilla*, preferably from Murcia.'

'But where else, señora?'

'That's settled then!'

'It will take fifteen minutes, señora. We are busy tonight and there is only one chef in the kitchen.'

'I can imagine which one,' I thought, inwardly chuckling to myself.

I sat there, trying to listen in to the discussions around me. Most of the voices were quiet and discreet, except for those of one couple who spoke so loudly it seemed as if they were deaf. Then I heard a voice approaching from an angle behind me and arriving in front of me.

'Good evening, señora. You appear to be alone. Would you object if I joined you for dinner?'

How could I resist such a charming request? The stranger was at least twenty years younger than me, tall, wearing a brown leather jacket and his hair cut short. His sharp features gave him the look of an educated, possibly academic gentleman, quite in keeping with whom you might meet in this famous university town.

'It will be my pleasure, señor. Do sit down.' I stretched out my arm towards the seat opposite at this table for two.

He sat just as Gonzalo appeared to take his order. 'Ah, Señor Mojaro, let me take your order.' Gonzalo reeled off the night's choices.

'I'll have what the señora here is having. All right?'

'Of course, señor?'

119

'And the *jumilla*?'

'Yes, if that's what the señora has chosen.'

It wasn't long before this studious looking gentleman and I had introduced ourselves to each other and were deep in conversation.

'It seems strange that a lone woman is here in this rather unusual town, Francisca. Would you care to enlighten me?'

'Not before you tell me why you are here, Sancho. You appear to be a single man, after all!'

'I am here on business.'

'And what might your business be?'

'I supply materials to the colleges. The paper, ink, quill pens, chalk, charcoal, laboratory equipment, maps, globes, chemicals, samples of various kinds. I even sell them books, textbooks, notebooks, religious books, books about Greek mythology and the works of the poets.'

'What about clothing, gowns and caps for example?'

'No. Other companies supply clothing.'

'So where are you based?'

'I have an office in Toledo. And I have suppliers all around Madrid. It's a successful business,' he said, stressing the word 'successful'.

'Surely, you don't work alone?'

'No. I have a staff in Toledo and in the university towns I deal with.'

'Universities?'

'Yes, Salamanca and Valencia but I serve colleges in various other towns.'

'I've never really thought about where universities get the things they need from. How do they know about you?'

Inevitably, he asked what an unaccompanied woman like me was doing in this town. He seemed such a nice man that I gave him the full story. At times I was almost in tears and he acted with great sympathy, especially when I told him about Juan junior's death and its catastrophic effect on my sanity.

'So you were confined in a lunatic asylum. For how long?'

'Seven years. It was awful. I thought I'd never be free to live with my beloved Juan again. He was the example of kindness. He would visit me every day. Most times he would come alone but sometimes he would bring one of my friends. I remember one day when Juan and my friend Inés came. I'd only jut smothered my naked body with my own excreta. The first thing they did was to clean me up. I was truly mad.'

I told him how I was cured by the miracle of the flash of light from the medal that the Pope Innocent X had given Diego Velázquez.

'So where are you now in your mission?'

I explained.

'There is one thing I don't understand,' he said, raising his eyebrows in disbelief.

'Tell me,' I smiled.

'The Department of Mathematics. You say they deny that Juan junior studied there.'

'Yes!'

'And you know he did?'

'I do!'

'Do you have any proof? For example, some papers your son may have produced, obviously of a mathematical nature?'

'I have some papers of his but I'd have to look for the mathematics.'

'Just a thought,' he said.

It intrigued me that I had dared to speak to this man. If Inés and Baltasar had been here then, I would not even have met him. He would not have asked me to join him for dinner. We had enjoyed a pleasant time together and I felt quite confident that I could trust him.

'Well, Francisca, thank you for allowing me to join you for dinner. Maybe we could meet for some breakfast tomorrow?'

I readily agreed that we meet in the dining room at 9 by the chimes of the cathedral clock.

***

I went to my room thinking how lucky I had been to meet this man, Sancho Mojaro. Somehow that evening's meeting gave me more confidence in my ability to pursue my mission, whether Inés and Baltasar were here with me or not. I even began to think that I could manage better without them, even though they were my most treasured friends. But I should not diminish the contributions they had each made so far, even though both had suddenly deserted me.

I looked around as I entered the breakfast room, Sancho beckoned me over to him. I didn't think twice and in moments I was pulling up the chair and sitting opposite him.

'Did you sleep well?' he asked. 'I hope so, after our conversation last night.'

'In fact I did sleep well, once I had settled down. I hope you did, too!'

'I too took a few moments to get to sleep. I was thinking about the denial you received from the mathematics department. I find it odd. I deal with them a lot and they actually seem friendly people. I have an idea and I cannot wait to tell you about it.'

'Please tell me, Sancho. I can wait no longer!'

'You should go back there and insist that your son studied there. Insist! Tell them that you have the evidence at your home …even if you don't. Tell them you want them to examine their records for the years he was there and prove to you, from the records, that he wasn't there. You never know, that might make them quite keen to help you!'

'Goodness me, Sancho, you have really made me stop and think. I didn't tell you last night that I actually met some of the mathematicians in the Iglesia Magistral when Inés and I went there, all but three weeks ago. They were praising God for their success in the examinations.'

'Did you get to know any by name?'

'Yes. One called Pedro. He was a very nice man and I met him again at the mathematics department when my friend Inés and I went to see them to ask them about Juan junior.'

'Go and see him, this Pedro. He's the most likely to help.'

It surprised me that Sancho had told me in such emphatic terms how I should deal with the mathematicians. He was instructing me. I hesitated for a few moments.

'An interesting idea, Sancho. I may well take you up on it. But I need the report of the investigation first. I can offer nothing to anyone without it.'

'It is just an idea, Francisca. I didn't mean it to sound as if I was telling you.'

We parted as soon as we finished our breakfast. Sancho said he was going to his office in the town and I went back to my room after agreeing that we would meet again that night for dinner. I sat on my bed in thought. I couldn't just sit there doing nothing. I had to do something to further my mission. I decided to make myself a nuisance at the Office of the Brotherhood. I would pester them every day until they gave me the investigation report. I left The Mad Astronomer at about 10 o'clock in the morning and began to walk there. As I was about to turn down the street where the office was situated, I could see a group of about twenty men demonstrating outside, another protest of some kind. Several were waving flags. They were not Spanish National flags nor were they flags of the monarchy. Two well-dressed individuals were holding a banner suspended between them. It read: *'Down with the king. Long live the Republic.'*

I stopped on the street corner for a few minutes wondering what to do. Suddenly, about a dozen, green jacketed constables burst out of the brotherhood's office and, without obvious provocation, set about the demonstrators, hitting them hard with wooden batons. They shouted at the demonstrators using the most violent and obscene language. One of the demonstrators fell to the ground, bleeding badly from the head. Another grabbed one of the batons and hit back at the officer from whom he snatched it. Another officer punched the retaliator in the stomach. The man fell to the ground clutching himself. Another came to his aid.

I saw no point in waiting there, so I turned turn around to go back to The Mad Astronomer. I almost walked into him. The Professor of Law was standing right behind me.

'It's you, professor. Sorry, I didn't see you!'

'Good morning, señora. I didn't expect to see you at a demonstration!'

'I came here to see if the brotherhood would release the investigation report so I could bring it to you!'

'Really? Are you sure you are nothing to do with the demonstration?'

'How could I be anything to do with it, professor? I am just an innocent bystander. Don't you accept that I've come here for the report? And nothing else!' I hope I sounded irritated at his implying I was somehow involved. How stupid of him.

'As you are so emphatic, I must accept what you say,' he said, sounding quite reluctant to be persuaded by what I'd said. 'In fact I was on my way to advise the captain here on a point of law in relation to these demonstrations. But, like you, I certainly don't want to be caught up in the violence so I shall go back to the college. I'll see you when you have the report. Once you get it, I'll start work on your case.'

He turned and went, not even bidding me good day. A grey cloud of disappointment descended upon me. This man, on seeing me here, had a clear opportunity to offer to ask the captain for the report, thus making life easier for me. But he didn't. Such was his interest in Juan junior's case. I began to wonder whether to give him the report, presuming of course, that I would obtain it. I remained shocked at his implication that I was involved in the demonstration. Dejectedly, I wandered back to The Mad Astronomer.

***

That night over dinner, I told Sancho about the demonstration and about meeting the professor of law.

'My analysis is simple, Francisca. He is either not interested in helping you because he is busy with his other work or, and this seems more likely to me, he knows more than he is prepared to admit and will frustrate and delay your investigation. You should continue with your efforts to get the report but I would think seriously about not giving it to the professor.'

'Maybe, I should read it myself,' I said. 'I think I could do so without getting upset at what it contains.'

'You might find your best allies, the astronomy department, might like to see it. It will at least have records of the people interviewed by the brotherhood. That might give them a lead.'

'I'm even more determined to get my hands on that report.'

I wrote another short note to Inés.

***

In the hope that there would not be a demonstration the following day, I made my way back to the office of the brotherhood. The demonstration had dispersed. Two torn banners and a broken flagstick, lying on the side of the road, signalled its passing. Others in front of me had also decided to come that day rather than attempt to break through the demonstration. I joined the queue. There must have been twenty of us. The man in front of me turned around. He was about forty, dressed in tatters and smelled of stale sweat and a hint of urine. One of the many street sleepers in this town, I imagined.

'What's a smart lady like you doing here? Can't imagine you've done much wrong,' he sniggered.

I paused, not quite knowing what to say. On the one hand, I didn't want to engage this stranger in conversation but on the other I didn't want to provoke any unpleasantness while standing in this queue of people who might react against me. And I certainly didn't want to give him the impression that I was an old *puta*.

'Ain't you got a tongue in your, head, woman?'

'I've come here for a report,' was all I could bring myself to admit.

'A report? What sort of report?'

'I have no intention of enquiring of your business here, señor, and would be grateful if you would refrain from asking about mine.'

'Please your bloody self.' He turned to face the direction of the queue.

I was relieved at his response. In fact, I felt quite pleased with myself in managing to deflect him. As the queue moved forward, I could feel a certain tension between me and this man who, when it was his turn to be dealt with at the reception desk, exaggeratedly leant forward towards the constable behind the desk, almost doubling himself over it, in a deliberate attempt to avoid my listening to the awkward dialogue which took place. My reaction was to move back slightly so as to avoid overhearing the animated, lengthy exchange. I was becoming more and more nervous about how I would ask about the report. The man eventually left, dissatisfied with the constable and making his feelings clear to those in the queue as well as the constable. Then the constable beckoned me.

'Yes, señora?'

I explained. My nerves gave in to a hesitating disjointedness.

'Just a minute,' he said. He got up from the desk and disappeared into the office behind him.

I could not believe what I saw when, not more than two minutes later, he returned. He was carrying an envelope.

'Here you are, señora,' he said, handing it to me over the counter. Then looking towards the man behind me in the queue, 'Next one please.'

'Thank you! Thank you! I'm so grateful!' I said. He ignored me. I just had not expected this overwhelming result. Perhaps the professor of law had said something to the head man. I almost ran out of the office, in a combined state of shock and elation. Walking up the Calle Carmen Calzado, I became calmer and started to think about what I should do with this sacrosanct document, which could hold the key to the cause of Juan junior's death. Should I take Sancho's advice and read it myself

127

before giving it to the astronomers. No. I would follow my instincts and initial plan and give it to the professor of law. So I made my way to the Department of Law, clutching the document in my hand.

I soon reached the College of the King, easily pushed open the massive oak door and entered.

'Ah, señora. We have met before, I think,' said the same marooned jacketed, white wigged janitor who had greeted Inés and me when we first came to the college over three weeks before.

'Yes, señor. I remember your friendly greeting, then,' I said, returning his engaging smile.

'You and your friend were investigating the unfortunate death of your boy. Have you made any progress?'

'Yes and no. We have managed to retrieve some crucial documents about his death. We have given Professor Doctor Juárez a copy of the post mortem report and I now want to give him this which is the report of the brotherhood's investigation into my son's death. I am so excited! I've just been given it by the captain's office!'

I have good news for you, señora. I know the professor is in. I spoke to him as he passed me, about an hour ago.'

I thanked the man for telling me and skipped up the stairs towards the professor's office on the first floor. I knocked on the door of the outer office and waited. No reply. I waited a full minute more and knocked again.

'Come in,' bellowed a voice from within. I entered.

'Professor, it's you!'

'Whom else did you expect?'

'I thought I would meet your secretary first.'

'In which case, I am sorry to disappoint you,' he said with a stern look on his face.

'Far from it, professor. I cannot say how pleased I am to see you. I have the copy of the brotherhood's report on their investigation. Here.' With my outstretched arm, I offered it to him.

'Thank you, señora. I am most grateful. You have obtained it in shorter time than I expected.'

'I was surprised to get it so soon. Only a few days more than a week!'

'I'll look at it as soon as I can, along with the post mortem report. I'm not sure when I can start but within a week or two, I imagine. Is there anything else for now?' He fixed his stare on the door, hinting that I should leave. But I needed to ask him a question.

'Yes, there is something else. How are we to make contact with each other when you have something to tell me?'

'Where are you staying in Alcalá de Henares?'

'In the inn of The Mad Astronomer.'

'Oh, that den of sin,' he said, much to my surprise. I had no idea why he should refer to it in such terms.

'I have no evidence of that,' I said, remembering well the encounter that Inés had witnessed between Gonzalo and the cook.

'I will write to you, Señora de Abaunza. As soon as I have anything to say. Certainly within two weeks.'

By then he was holding the door open and explicitly inviting my departure. As I walked down the stairs, again I could feel nothing but disappointment. Despite his apparent early interest in Juan junior's case, the professor seemed to want to delay any thinking he might do for as long as possible. I thought then that Sancho might well be right: I should have taken the report, taken it back to my room and read it before taking it to the astronomers. Now too late.

The thought of Sancho made me think about his idea of challenging the mathematicians about Juan studying in their department so, as the day was still young, I decided to go there. I would first go to Pedro's office and see if he could help.

I was soon standing outside of the office with the familiar sign on the door: Señor Pedro Lobos de Pamplona, lecturer. I knocked.

'Come in please.'

I recognised his voice, smiled to myself and walked in.

'Señora Francisca de Abaunza, I believe. I've been thinking of you.'

I could hardly confess my embarrassing thoughts about him, to take him to my bed. No! I must not even let it enter my mind.

'Really?' I said.

'Yes. Do you remember that when you came here before with your young friend,' he said, 'I said I'd try to help you? To see if we had a record of your son studying here?'

'Yes, I do remember.'

'Well, I've taken some action and put an official request to our records department. Any day now I'm expecting a reply.'

I went up to him and hugged him. I couldn't help myself. He would, anyway, not expect a woman in her late sixties to be trying to seduce him. I let out a tear or two.

'No need to get upset, señora. I am just trying to help!'

'Those are tears of joy, Pedro,' I said. 'You are the first person in this town to take any action to help me and I'm delighted. I hope you don't mind me using your first name.'

'Not at all as long as I can use yours, Francisca. Anyway, have a seat and we can talk about your son's case.'

'Haven't you any lectures to deliver?'

'Not now, no.'

I told him about everything that had happened since I last saw him.

'I can understand your disappointment that your friends have gone back to Madrid,' he said, 'but you have to admit that they couldn't have done much more whether they'd been here or not. And you wouldn't have met Sancho Mojaro. You seem to have great confidence in that man. But I would be careful, if I were you. Don't forget the threat in that letter.'

'You don't think he could be its author, do you?'

'I don't know. Someone wrote it and wanted you out of Alcalá. You are still here so the threat could still be valid.'

'But so much time has passed. That letter was written more than three weeks ago and nothing has happened to me!'

'Maybe your Sancho is totally reliable and a true ally. I'm just suggesting you take care.'

'I'll take care, Pedro. I promise you.'

'Good! And you've done well to get those reports. My only doubt is that they are with the professor of law. From what you've said, he won't be doing much with them! I suppose we'll have to wait and see!'

The most striking thing Pedro said was that word 'we'. It immediately identified him with my mission and that gave me the wonderful feeling of having someone at the university on my side.

'I know you mean to help, Pedro. Otherwise you wouldn't have asked the records people about my Juan.'

'I can't promise anything, Francisca, because I have a job to do here. But I don't spend all my time in the mathematics department and I'll try to help you.'

I hugged him again. Before I left this friendly and helpful man, I asked him when he could tell me about the result of the records people's enquiries. He suggested that he would see me at The Mad Astronomer in two days' time. Much to my delight, he said we could meet for dinner.

***

I wondered whether I should spend the two days in going back to Madrid. After all, the town was not that far away. I could check that all was well at my house and that it had not been broken into. There were plenty of thieves more than willing to enter a property they noticed had been empty for some time. Then I remembered that Inés had said she would pass by occasionally to see that all was safe and sound. So I decided that I'd stay in Alcalá and take my sadly neglected horse, Matilda, out for a ride or two.

I couldn't remember a period of time going so slowly. I began to wish I'd gone back to Madrid. The loneliness made it worse. Sancho had gone back to Toledo and had business elsewhere so couldn't tell me when he would return.

Chapter 11

It was about midday. Not an especially pleasant one. It was cloudy and quite bleak outside. I lit the candle on my dressing table, just to give the room a modicum of brightness and to make me feel a little more cheery, not that I felt especially bad or sorry for myself. It was just that the investigation had stalled and that I was powerless to move it along. I had decided against a breakfast and, not yet dressed, but clad in little more than my dressing gown, was selecting what to wear that day. A firm knock on the door startled me into dropping my yellow blouse onto the bed.

'There's a gentleman to see you, señora. He's downstairs in the drinking area,' said Gonzalo, as I opened the door in response to this unexpected interruption.

'A gentleman? Who could it be? Did he give his name?'

'No, señora. Just said he wanted to see you. Youngish fellow. About thirty five, I'd say.'

'Tell him I'll be down in about five minutes.'

'Very well, señora.'

My heart missed several beats. It had to be Pedro with news from the records department. It then started to beat faster as I speculated on what he would have to say. I should not be too optimistic. News so far had not been good and it would be surprising if he had discovered anything that contradicted what the department had said before. Or could it be Sancho, having returned from his business trip to … I had forgotten where…Toledo, Segovia? I admitted to myself that I preferred it to be Pedro. I ruled out anyone else so I could yet be taken unawares.

I quickly rubbed a wet flannel over my face, dried myself and splashed on the minimum of perfume. I buttoned up the yellow blouse and quickly pulled myself into a skirt. Bare legged, I slid into a pair of shoes and dashed out of the room, locking the door as I went.

I opened the door to the drinking room. That early in the day, not that many were there, all men. All four of a gathering of older individuals were laughing and chatting. I heard the words 'she' and 'her' so imagined they were relating the story of some woman or other. Two others were having a drink while standing and talking to each other at the bar. Some three or four more were standing or sitting next to tables. Some wore round, stiff brimmed hats, others were bareheaded, some with long hair in braids, others short cropped. I recognised none of them, except one of the older men whom I had seen when I was having breakfast a few days before with Sancho. I walked through the room into the reception area and opened the door onto the Calle de Libreros. I looked up and down the street but saw no one I knew. So I walked back into the bar area towards the door to the stairs.

'Excuse me, señora,' said one of the men standing alone. 'Are you Francisca de Abaunza of Madrid?'

'Yes, I am.'

'I'm from the Office of the Holy Brotherhood,' said the swarthy looking gentleman with no hat and short hair. 'I'm afraid I have bad news for you. I've come to retrieve the report you collected two days ago. Unfortunately, we gave you the wrong one. I do apologise.'

I could not believe what I was hearing. What incompetence. My heart sank like an olive stone in a glass of water. So progress on that front had been purely illusory. I shrugged at him with my hands in the air. 'I don't have it. It's with Professor Doctor Juárez in the Department of Law at the College of the King, just across the road from here. And where is the actual report on my son?'

'We are searching our archives as we speak now, señora. You will have to collect the one we gave you in error. You signed for it so it's your responsibility.'

'I signed for nothing. Your man at the desk simply handed it to me…in an envelope. You can recover it yourself from the professor. You made the error, not me,' I said, my face burning with rage.

'I understand, señora. I'll go now.'

'And give the correct one to the professor, please!'

'Thank you, señora.'

The man turned and went. I could not remember feeling more disappointed and angry at the same time. I could have cried but didn't. I went back to my room and laid on the bed. Having recovered from the shock of the brotherhood's mistake, I felt quite pleased with the way I'd dealt with the young official. I didn't know whether he was a constable himself or not. I didn't really care. But I'd got my own way in not having to go to the professor. If I had to explain the mistake to him, that could have counted against me. The brotherhood's man having to do it himself, left me in a good position, at least I thought so then.

***

It was getting quite late when another knock on the door broke me from my slumbers. I quickly slid off the bed and straightened my hair with my hands.

'Yes, who is it?'

'Gonzalo, Señora de Abaunza. There is another man to see you. He says he knows you. His name is Pedro.'

I opened the door and smiled, looking Gonzalo straight in the eye. 'That's excellent news, Gonzalo. Could you please tell Pedro I'll be down in three minutes?'

'A pleasure, señora!'

As I combed my hair and straightened my skirt, I couldn't help wondering what Gonzalo thought of these men calling on me. For certain, I would not be explaining, but it made me smile, all the same. And what news would Pedro bring? Surely I could not be unlucky twice in one day!

'Thank you for coming to see me, Pedro. I'm so pleased to see you, whatever your news!'

'Let's make our way into the dining room, Francisca. I've asked the landlord to reserve a table.'

'I've had a difficult day, but I'm sure everything is about to change!' I suddenly felt a little embarrassed at my tone of voice. I blushed a little at the thought. After all this young man must be at least thirty years my junior.

We sat at the table I'd used before at the far end. I could wait no longer so asked him direct. 'So, what is your news, Pedro?'

'I have a surprise for you, Francisca. The records department have discovered that there is no doubt at all that your son was a student in the mathematics department!'

I got up from the table, went round and gave Pedro a kiss and a hug. 'I'm so pleased, Pedro! I cannot tell you how thrilled I am!'

I sat back down again and sobbed a little. 'I'm sorry, Pedro, but I'm quite overwhelmed by your news,' I said, wiping away my tears with a handkerchief. 'So what happened? And how did the change of view come about?'

'Very simple. The papers on Juan were filed under the wrong year, so when I asked them to look again, I suggested they check the files for up to two years before his entry date and for the two years after. They were filed in the year after!'

'I'm so glad I didn't give up on you!'

'So am I, Francisca! But that is not my only news. I reported this new result to our head of department, Professor Gregorio Estrada. He has offered to help you, as best he can. He sends his apologies for the error in the records and has asked me to say that this is his way of making amends. He asked me if I could assist your investigation. Needless to say, I readily agreed! I'm not sure what I can contribute but we will work together!'

'My God, Pedro! Am I dreaming? I cannot believe what you have said. Pedro, you are the best thing that's happened to me since I left Madrid! I am delighted that you are there to help me.' I put my handkerchief to my eye to wipe away yet another tear…a tear of joy.

'It could be a lengthy operation, Francisca. But I think I should start with the report of the brotherhood's investigation into your son's death.'

'There is a serious problem with the report, Pedro.' I told him about the surprise visit earlier that day of the man from their office.

'Sounds like you sent him away acutely embarrassed. So they still have the report?'

'Yes, unless they have found it by now and taken it to the law department.'

'So what do you think we should do about it?'

'I think we will have to be patient for a few days but there's nothing wrong with working out our tactics for continuing our investigation!'

Over the next hour or so, and over a meal which Gonzalo served us, we decided how we would take matters forward. I expressed my worries at the error the brotherhood had made over Juan junior's investigation report. I wondered if they would ever find it. Pedro was less concerned. He assured me that they would be so embarrassed over their error, they would stop at nothing to retrieve it. At the first opportunity, I would bring the report back from the law professor and give it to Pedro. He would read it and make what he could of it before he and I met again to see if the report itself showed any failures or obvious omissions that we could follow up. In the meantime, I would speak to the professor in the astronomy department whose colleague was due to visit from England.

'Who should we tell about your involvement, Pedro? I'd like to let Inés and Baltasar know.'

'Yes, but no one else. Not even your friend the supplier of materials to the University. And you can tell them strictly on the basis that they tell nobody else. I think you said you send them a short note every day. Best not to mention it in your letter.'

'I agree to all that, Pedro.'

We hugged each other as we parted and promised to meet in a few days' time, after I'd been to the law department to relieve the professor of the report.

Despite my excitement, I still managed, before going to my bed, to spend a moment writing a short letter to Inés. It just told her I was coping well, even though progress was slow. I slept well that night, especially after my delight at renewing my relationship, professional as it was, with the ever helpful Pedro.

***

No one could have been as surprised as I was to see Sancho sitting at a breakfast table. I imagined he might still be in Toledo or wherever he said his business would take him. As my eyes struck his, he looked over and beckoned me towards him. I saw no reason to refuse.

'Do join me, Francisca. We need to spend some time telling each other what has happened in the time I've been away. What progress have you made? Any sign of your friends from Madrid? Have they returned? Did you take up my suggestion of going to see the mathematicians?'

'Yes and you must tell me about what you have been doing. I thought you'd be away for longer,' I said, as he stood and pulled out a chair for me to sit next to him.

'I am back earlier than I thought, mainly because I have to arrange the delivery of a large order we have taken from one of the ecclesiastical colleges here. I've spent most of my time on the road and only a short time in Toledo. So how have you fared?'

I had to think carefully about what to tell Sancho. I felt I could trust him enough to be quite open to him but I also had to ensure that I protected Pedro's position. I told him about the brotherhood's mistake over the report of their investigation; that the mathematics department had admitted that they had made an error and that Juan junior had in fact studied there. I also said they had offered to help in some way.

'Well, Francisca. Seems to me that you've made one step backwards and one step forwards. So where is the brotherhood's report now?'

'Yesterday they were claiming to be actively searching for it. I can't imagine they've found it yet! I've asked them to take it straight to the law department.'

'A mistake, Francisca. You should have asked to see it yourself first!'

'I'm not sure I could cope with it in any objective way. It is better in the hands of those with no vested interest.'

'And what about Inés and Baltasar?'

'They are still in Madrid but quite honestly, I think I'm managing quite well on my own.'

'You shouldn't spend too much time alone Francisca. In fact, I have an idea for you. I have a female colleague who lives here in the Calle Ramon, off the Calle Major. She's a very nice lady and I've told her all about you. She's a little older than me and helps me with my business here. She has invited us both around her house for dinner tonight! Her name is Carmella. What do you think? Have you other plans?'

139

For a moment, I didn't know what to think. Could I trust this man to that extent? And what about his friend? It could be a trap. I hadn't forgotten that letter. Then I realise that I was being silly. This man had shown me just how trustworthy he was. He'd even suggested new ideas for helping my investigation along.

'Yes, Sancho. I'll come. It will be a nice change to escape from the walls of The Mad Astronomer for a few hours.'

'That's settled then, Francisca. I'll let Carmella know. You can be my chaperone! What if I meet you in the reception area at about 7 o'clock?'

***

I was really excited at the thought of being a guest at a dinner. I hardly knew what to do with myself. I decided to go for a walk. I wouldn't go near any of the university departments but I'd look at some of the places in Alcalá that I was less familiar with. There were a number of convents in the south west of the town so I made my way to the furthest of them, the Convent of Santa Catalina of Sienna. As I approached, I could see a small group of nuns standing outside enjoying a little autumn sun. I asked one of them about the convent.

'We are very lucky, señora. It used to be a Renaissance palace constructed in the middle of the last century. We moved here in the fifteen nineties. It is beautiful inside. Come and have a look, if you are interested.'

I couldn't resist such a tempting and friendly invitation. The interior of this former palace impressed me. The owner, Carlos de Mendoza, must have spent a king's ransom on the ornate interior. Gold leaf glowed on the highly decorated ceilings, marble statues stood guard at the bottom of the extravagant staircase.

'We are quite embarrassed by the level of luxury but we eat very modestly and our rooms are all but little cells,' said the nun who had invited me in.

'It's wonderful,' I said. 'I wouldn't be embarrassed at all. I'd just enjoy the inherited luxury!'

'Come into the kitchen. This is a little more fitting!'

There were several nuns working in this large room. The smell of a rich broth drifted through the air, as one of them stirred a large cauldron which sat on the hearth. Pots and pans, many of copper, some of pewter, were suspended from racks that could be dropped down from the ceiling by pulleys. The nun was right. The kitchen had no fancy embellishments, which was not surprising considering the lord and master would spend little time in there and nor would his guests.

I walked with my hosts to the elaborate front door, thanked them for this welcomed diversion and made my way to the Convent of the Agustinas, to follow up their recommendation of viewing that rather different construction.

I didn't stop for lunch on the way back from the convents. I still felt awkward going into eating places as an unaccompanied woman, even though many women students seemed much less inhibited than me. They were of course some fifty years younger.

I rested for a few hours once I was back in the anonymity of my room at the inn. I didn't sleep, such was my excitement at going out to this woman's house for a meal. I spent a few minutes thinking about what to wear, not that I had much choice. I'd wear a skirt and blouse with a scarf and my long coat. I made my way downstairs just before what I imagined to be seven o'clock, to be greeted by the ever smiling Sancho.

'You look enchanting, Francisca. And that perfume is a delight!'

'I'm glad you are pleased. I didn't want to overdo it, especially as another lady's guest!'

'If you are ready, let's go. It's only a short walk from here to the Calle Ramon.'

We set off, not quite arm-in-arm but Sancho was sufficient a gentleman to insist on walking on the outside of me, just a little further into the road. I felt good in the company of this kind and considerate individual, despite not knowing a great deal about him. Perhaps I would find out more once any sort of conversation started at Carmella's house. Equally, I was dying to meet her and tried to imagine what she looked like while on this short walk.

We arrived at Carmella's front door not five minutes after leaving the inn. Her house was closer than I had imagined. By then it was dark. Sancho knocked on the door and we waited but for less than a minute.

'It's you, Sancho, and your new friend at The Mad Astronomer. Do come in!'

Carmella and I shook hands and Sancho gently kissed her on both cheeks. She guided us along a candle lit hall into a drawing room furnished with two sofas which faced each other in front of an open fire. It all seemed very homely and welcoming.

'Let me get you a drink,' said Carmella. 'Do you prefer a red or white wine, Francisca? I think Sancho would prefer a red.'

I then felt an excruciating pain as something very hard hit me on the head. I collapsed in a heap on the floor. That was the very last thing I remember about that night.

***

I had no idea where I was, what time it could be or even what day it was. I opened my eyes and looked around. I couldn't see anything but total darkness. It felt as if I was inside some sort of dungeon. I was terrified, shocked and betrayed by a man I thought I could trust. And this Carmella had been his accomplice. What a stupid fool I had been. He was the man behind the anonymous letter. There could be no doubt. I was so glad I had kept it. If I ever got out of here I would show it to the brotherhood.

I couldn't move. They had tied me up. My feet were bound together so tightly the pain tracked up my legs. They had tied my hands behind my back. Why hadn't they killed me or were they waiting for some special moment. Surely, they weren't going to ransom me?

I vaguely remember a dream or was it a reality of being carried in the back of a wagon from somewhere to somewhere else. Could they have moved me from the house in Calle Ramon to somewhere more forbidding? I didn't know what to think. I was in a state of utter confusion and fear. I shouted out at the top of my voice, 'Help me! Help me! I'm in here!' No reply.

There was no echo; no reverberation. They had confined me to a room somewhere. It had to be in Alcalá, surely but where? Should I attempt to move, to slide across the floor? But I could be on a ledge and could hurt myself if I fell. Or was lying on something cold, a stone floor probably. I realised I was dressed. In the same clothes that I'd worn to the Calle Ramon. I was sure they hadn't perpetrated some obscene act on me. At least I couldn't feel as if I'd been assaulted, other than the pain at the top of my head where they hit me and knocked me unconscious. I couldn't move my hands so I couldn't even feel a lump or bruise if I had one.

I let out some tears, both in anger and in fright. I was in serious danger. If they were going to perpetuate my life, one of them would surely come into this place and give me food and water. I had no choice but to await my fate. I felt fear of an intensity I'd never experienced before. Where would this end?

Chapter 12

'I'm getting quite worried, Baltasar,' said Inés, as she poured her brother a cup of juice for his breakfast. 'I haven't received a letter from Francisca for two days now. What should we do?'

'Wait until tomorrow. If we haven't heard from her by lunchtime, we'll head for Alcalá to see what's going on. Do you have any clues from her letters?'

'Nothing. All she's sent are short notes saying she's all right and wishing us the best.'

'Umm…not mentioning any problem, then?'

'No, but how could she know if there was a problem in the making? Today, I shall prepare for the worst. I have a horrible feeling that something has happened to her. That letter warning her to go. Whoever wrote it has done something to her. God knows what. I'll get the saddlebags ready while you are at the palace. If you can find out whether they can spare you for a few days that would be useful. If not I'll go alone.'

'There is not much on in the kitchens at the moment, Inés. They'll be only too glad to see the back of me!'

Inés prepared for the journey to Alcalá. She didn't know how long they would be gone but packed sufficient clothing for a week. As usual, she bought some fresh, clean water from the water seller in the Calle Atoche. She paid him to fill two large flasks they would put in the saddlebags.

Tomorrow came. Inés kept peering from the window, hoping to see the man from the postal service. 'Here he comes!' she thought as he slowly rode his horse down the Calle Oliver. 'Please let him bring a letter,' she silently prayed. The rider rode straight passed, not even stopping at one of the adjacent houses.

'Oh my God,' she uttered. 'So we go to Alcalá. Please God, let Francisca be alive and well.' She was suddenly engulfed by a cloud of guilt. How could she and Baltasar have left Francisca, an old lady, to fend for herself in Alcalá? It was excusable to let Baltasar return... but for both of them to leave was a sin. Especially, knowing she had been the subject of that threatening letter.

***

One day of fast riding later, Baltasar and Inés were tying up their sweating horses outside The Mad Astronomer. They walked in and rang the bell on the reception desk, the one Inés and Francisca had rung on their first visit together.

'Welcome back to our modest inn,' said a smiling Gonzalo, as he appeared from the direction of the kitchen.

'We've no time for gratuitous greetings,' said Baltasar to the unsuspecting landlord. 'We are here to find out where Francisca de Abaunza, one of your clients could be. We understand she is no longer staying here.'

'She left in the company of a man called Sancho Mojaro. They left here at about 7 in the evening, three nights ago. Señora de Abaunza's room is exactly as she left it. I've no idea where she is. Her horse is still in the stables.'

'Why didn't you report the fact that she has gone missing?' said Baltasar.

'How could I know she is missing, if indeed she is? For all I knew, she could have gone away with Señor Mojaro for a few days.'

'Who is this man?' said Inés. 'Does he stay here?'

'I can't possibly tell you. Much as I welcome you back to the inn, I am unable to give you private information about my clients.'

'As you know, we are close friends of Señora de Abaunza. That being so, could you please let us see what state her room is in? I will pay any outstanding dues,' said Baltasar.

'Of course, señor. Let me take you there now.'

They followed Gonzalo up the stairs to Francisca's room. He unlocked the door and held it open so they could enter.

'Has the bed been made?' asked Inés.

'Not since your friend left.'

'Interesting. Here are some creases in the counterpane, as if she had an afternoon nap before she left with this man,' said Inés, who had a sudden thought. She sped over to the chest of drawers and pulled open the one at the bottom. 'Here it is!' she said. 'Your gun, Baltasar. She couldn't have thought she was in danger otherwise she'd have taken it with her.' She gave it to Baltasar who concealed it in his coat.

The two of them looked closer at items in the room but failed to find anything to arouse suspicion.

'Seen enough?' said Gonzalo.

'Yes, thank you,' said Inés.

They followed Gonzalo down the stairs into the drinking area.

'May we book a couple of rooms for a few days?' asked Baltasar.

'You are lucky. I have only two left. Each on the first floor.'

'Fine,' said Inés. 'We'll leave them for now. We need to think about what we do next.'

'I'll leave you here,' said Gonzalo, who quickly left as if he couldn't wait to get away from them.

***

'What do we do now?' said Inés.

'Simple. We go straight to the holy brotherhood and report Francisca as a missing person.'

'Yes, I agree… but we should also take our own initiative and make our own enquiries.'

'What do you mean?'

'Let's assume she is still alive and in Alcalá de Henares. I can't imagine there are more than a few thousand people in this town. Many are students. We prepare a description of Francisca and go knocking on doors and asking people in the street if they have seen her and where. We also find any derelict buildings and look inside them.'

'Did you say you visited some professors at the colleges, Inés? Should we ask them to help?'

'A good idea, Baltasar! We'll do that, too!'

Feeling guilty at the situation they believe they have created for their friend, Inés and Baltasar made their way to the Office of the Holy Brotherhood. By then it was quite dark. They joined a short queue of others waiting there. Baltasar spoke first. The official manning the desk asked for evidence that Francisca was missing. The two hesitated for a moment until Inés told him about the absence of the expected letters from Francisca. She explained that the letters were prompted by the anonymous letter which was sent to Francisca a few weeks before. The man surprised them both by saying he knew Francisca. He said he had an embarrassing meeting with her only four days earlier when he had to tell her she had been given the wrong investigation report. He explained that he gave the correct report to the professor of law that very day. He asked

147

why they hadn't reported the anonymous letter before. They said they had all dismissed it as the words of some madman. He said the brotherhood would need to see the letter. Neither Baltasar nor Inés knew where it was. They were comforted by the officer assuring them that the brotherhood would do everything in their power to find Francisca.

***

Having fallen asleep in tears, I was woken by shards of light suddenly shining across the floor where I lay. The door to this horrible place was opening. I could hear the sound of footsteps. A female voice rang out.

'Wake up woman. I've brought you some food.'

'How can you expect me to eat with my hands tied behind my back?'

The woman, wearing a mask over her eyes and upper face, was carrying a tray upon which she had balanced a lit candle in a holder. Its flickering light gave me the chance to look briefly around the room in which they had confined me. It was a large but almost empty cellar of some sort. Some wooden boxes stood against the far wall, probably old wine boxes. The floor was scattered with pieces of rubbish, mainly odd bits of paper but also some discarded clothing. I noticed a lady's dirty underskirt amongst it.

She placed the tray on a table, not far from me. It was hard to see any of her features in the candlelight. I guessed her voice was that of a fifty year old. I didn't recognise it.

'I will untie your hands,' said the woman. 'Just be patient.'

I didn't see the point in holding back. 'Be patient? What audacity. I've been trussed up here all night waiting for one of you evil swine to untie me.'

'Careful what you say. You are in no position to make demands of me. Anymore of that abuse and I'll take the tray away and leave you to starve.'

'And I thought I could trust you people, especially your Sancho Mojaro who turns out to be a liar and a cheat. How wrong could I have been?'

'You were given long enough to get out of this town. You are not welcome here. If you'd had any sense you would have gone when we warned you to go. You are causing all sorts of trouble, if only you knew what.'

Our disjointed conversation continued for a full five minutes while the masked woman gave me some food and some water.

'I'm surprised you didn't kill me if you were that concerned about my actions. Why didn't you?' I said, coolly and quite surprising myself that I could be so calm in this perilous situation.

'We haven't decided what to do with you yet.'

As the woman was about to take the plate from my hand, I thought hard about throwing it at the wall. Not a good idea. The woman may make life even more difficult if I did anything that destructive. I thought I may as well collaborate unless these people made my life completely intolerable and just quietly think about how I might escape.

'So how long do you plan to keep me here? Someone is sure to find me.'

'As I said, we are deciding what we should do with you. Now put your hands together and behind your back. I have to tie you up.'

The woman showed all her strength in re-tying my hands. I tried to resist but she overcame me. She was younger and stronger. She picked up the tray and made her way towards the door.

'I'll be back later today,' she said.

'Why not untie my feet? I can't go anywhere with my hands tied behind my back in this locked room.'

'I'll think about your question and let you know later.'

I felt slightly better now that I knew I was in contact with my kidnappers, or at least one of them. There were at least three: the man who called himself Sancho Mojaro, the woman Carmella, if that was her name, and the second woman, the one in the mask. They must have known I was about to discover something important about the death of my son. Otherwise, why would they want to hide me away? The answer lay in what they were trying to conceal. Surely, their guilt. What were their plans for me? They must have some idea? Would I arrive in a bundle on the streets of Madrid at the dead of night? Or be found in a sack, drowned in the Manzanares? Only they knew or perhaps they didn't know either.

***

Inés and Baltasar were sitting at a breakfast table at The Mad Astronomer. 'We need to plan our day,' said Baltasar. 'What should we do first?'

'Simple. We go to the professor of law and explain to him what has happened. He might have some idea where Francisca could be.'

'If you remember, I argued with him about going to the brotherhood last time we were there. He doesn't like me.'

'I remember it well! Afterwards we go to the mathematics department. They denied all knowledge of Juan Junior. We see what their position is now.'

'Then we go to astronomy?'

'Yes, then we start asking people if they have seen anyone who looks like Francisca.'

'I have an idea, Inés. I inherited some of our father's talents as an artist, not many of course, but enough to draw a reasonable portrait of her. We could show it to people on the streets.'

Inés went over and hugged him. 'You are a genius Baltasar! What a clever idea! We could show it to the brotherhood, too!'

'No, I have an even better idea…I'll draw another portrait for them as well!'

Inés persuaded a somewhat reluctant Gonzalo to let her take some paper, a pen and some ink for Baltasar to use for the portraits. Within an hour's working on the breakfast table, Baltasar had produced two pictures which were uncannily like her and all but identical. He'd even captured that slightly wistful expression that she had when not thinking of anything in particular. Inés remembered that look from her grandfather's portrait of her, 'The lady with a fan'.

'My God, Baltasar! Father couldn't have done any better! He'd be proud of you!'

'See if you can get an envelope out of Gonzalo that we can put them in. Then we'll go.'

Rather than visit the law department they decided that it would be better to deliver a copy first to the brotherhood. The officers could familiarise themselves with it and display it in a window or on the enquiry desk.

The officer on the desk knew nothing about Francisca's plight.

'But we came and reported her yesterday as a missing person,' said Baltasar.

'That's as maybe but I haven't heard about it. Just a minute, I'll look in yesterday's records.' Within a few moments of disappearing into the back room, he emerged smiling.

'Yes, it's in there. So what can I do for you now?'

151

'Please take this portrait of our friend who is missing. Someone may recognise her and know where she is.'

'I'm grateful, señor. What a nice picture. Drawn by a good artist! We'll make sure our street patrol officers see it and we'll put it on display.'

Baltasar and Inés made their way back along the street to the College of the King. They were later than they intended but by 11 o'clock were discussing, with the law professor's bewigged secretary, a possible meeting.

'I'm afraid the professor is lecturing this morning. He will be returning at about 1 p.m. You can wait here for him if you wish.'

The thought of passing upwards of two hours in the talc flicking presence of this oddity of a man did not seem attractive.

'No, if you don't mind, we'll return at 1 o'clock,' said Baltasar, noting Inés's sideways glance and taking command.

They went from there to the mathematics department and knocked on the door of Professor Gregorio Estrada's office. The friendly professor welcomed them with a smile and invited them to sit in front of his desk.

'How can I help you?'

Inés explained what had happened. Baltasar showed Francisca's portrait to the professor. 'Of course I remember,' said the professor. 'In fact I have appointed one of my staff to help her to investigate her son's passing. He is Pedro Lobos de Pamplona. He is an excellent fellow and is just the kind of man to help.'

'I've met him,' said Inés.

'Really?'

'Yes, first in the Iglesia Majestral when the students were celebrating their success in the examinations…and again when Francisca and I came to the department to ask whether Juan junior had studied here. If you remember, you told us then that he hadn't and after seeing you, we went to Pedro's office.'

'I'll take you to him now, assuming he's there. By the way, I didn't tell you that we have found records that prove that your friend Francisca's son definitely studied in my department!'

'Excellent news!' said Baltasar.

Professor Estrada led Inés and Baltasar the dozen paces to Pedro's office and walked straight in. 'Pedro, I have some visitors for you. They are friends of Francisca de Abaunza, who has apparently gone missing.'

'What? I was speaking to her only what three or four days ago. What's happened?' he said, with strained anxiety in his voice and his eyebrows raised.

Inés related the story and told them about Sancho Mojaro.

'I warned her about that man. So he or one of his collaborators wrote the anonymous letter.' He told them that he had promised he would meet Francisca in a few days' time and that in the meantime he would see what he could do to help the investigation. He said he wanted to see the brotherhood's report on the case.

Baltasar came up with an interesting thought. 'Did Francisca describe this Sancho to you? Is he tall or short? How old is he?'

'She didn't actually describe him but she said he told her he supplied paper, ink and other products to universities. The one thing I have discovered is that no one called Sancho Mojaro supplies anything to our department.'

'When did you discover that?' said Inés.

'Yesterday morning. I went around to The Mad Astronomer to tell her but she wasn't there and the landlord didn't know where she was. If he did know, he wasn't telling.'

'I'm getting quite suspicious of that Gonzalo,' said Baltasar. 'He became quite defensive when we asked him about Mojaro. By the time you went to see Francisca, she would have not have been seen at the inn for at least three days. So he just told you she wasn't there?'

'No more and no less,' said Pedro.

'He knows more than he's telling,' said Inés

***

About five hours or so later, the door of my prison cell opened in a burst of light. The same masked woman appeared carrying the tray. At least it sounded like her. I wasn't especially hungry or thirsty but I really needed to use a chamber pot.

'I've brought you a cooked meal,' said the woman in a friendly tone. Let me untie you so you can eat.'

'I'm not very interested in eating. I need a pot more than anything. I haven't been since yesterday before you kidnapped me.'

'There's a pot outside. I'll get it.'

My immediate needs were about to pose some problems for the woman. She had to untie my legs and my arms, otherwise I would not be able to manage to do what I needed to do. The woman must have thought about the problem because she came up with an elegant solution.

'I'll untie you,' she said. 'But I'm going to keep a rope tied to your leg so if you try to attack me or escape, I'll simply pull on the rope to prevent you.'

It wasn't long before I'd finished and wiped myself with a cloth the woman brought me. I hoped she was at least as embarrassed as I was at having to do it in her presence.

'Do you want any food or don't you?' she said.

'What I really want is to know where all this is leading. What are you going to do with me? Why is it you want me out of Alcalá?'

'You know I can't tell you that. If you don't want any food, I'll take it away. At least have some of this fruit juice?'

'How do I know it's not been poisoned?'

'I'll show you,' said the woman, taking a gulp from the cup.

I drank the rest. The woman tied me up again and left. A long, dark night loomed ahead of me.

***

Baltasar and Inés explained to the mathematicians that they had a planned meeting with the professor of law.

'I wonder if he has yet received the true version of the report into Juan junior's death,' said Pedro. 'The sooner we can see a copy here, the sooner we may be able to make some sense of what actually happened.'

'He's definitely received the report,' said Inés. 'An official at the Office of the Brotherhood said he personally delivered it to him earlier today.'

'In which case do you think you could ask him for it? I need to see it,' said Pedro.

'Better still, I'll write a note to him asking him to give it to you,' said the professor. 'He owes me a very big favour and just won't be able to refuse. I'll go back go back to my office and write the letter.'

'He's a wonderful man,' my boss, said Pedro. 'If there is anything mathematically possible that we can do to solve the mystery of Juan junior's passing, then we will do it, I can assure you.'

A few minutes later, Professor Estrada appeared clutching a cream coloured envelope, the rear of which had been sealed in blue wax. 'Just give this to Professor Doctor Juarez de Lerida and ask him politely to open it. I'm sure he will cooperate!' he said.

***

Baltasar and Inés arrived back at the professor of law's office as the cathedral clock chimed one o'clock. The professor was enraged about something that had happened earlier and was expressing his fury at the bewigged secretary.

'No, I'm not going to apologise,' he said at the top of his voice. 'He was in the wrong not me.'

'He then noticed Inés and Baltasar. 'Excuse me. What do you want?'

Baltasar spoke in the politest of terms. 'Please, Professor Dr Juarez de Lerida. Perhaps you will remember us? My sister Inés and I visited you a few weeks back along with our friend Francisca de Abaunza to seek your help in solving the mystery of her son's death.'

'Of course I remember. I've just received the brotherhood's report of their investigation. I haven't had a moment to spare to look at it and I don't know when I will.'

'I wonder if we could ask a special favour,' said Inés. 'It's best explained by giving you this letter which is from Professor Estrada, head of mathematics.'

'You do get round our colleges! Hand me the letter,' he said, still angry from his previous encounter.

He opened it roughly and urgently and quickly read it. 'So he wants to take over our part of the investigation. We'll he's welcomed to it. It will be a relief for me and my colleagues not to have to do it! By the way, why isn't Señora de Abaunza with you?'

'We believe she's been kidnapped, professor. We cannot be completely sure but she has disappeared from The Mad Astronomer. She's been missing for three days.'

'I see,' said the professor. 'I'll just get the report.' He vanished into his inner office and, obviously knowing exactly where he could put his hands on it, emerged moments later with an envelope which clearly contained a thick set of documents. He handed it to Baltasar.

'Thank you, professor. We'll take no more of your time.'

'What a result, Baltasar!' Inés said, as they walked along the corridor from the professor's office. 'We have the report. Shall we take it straight to the mathematics department?'

'Yes, we'll do that. What do you make of his remark about Francisca's disappearance… "I see"?'

'I found it astonishing, not to say upsetting! He already knew that Francisca had been kidnapped. He's another who knows a lot more that he wants to reveal.'

***

I lay there in total darkness, scared and trembling. I could not give in to these people. I had to survive. I thought of my Juan and knew that he would want me to escape from this place. And I had vowed to see my mission through to the end. I had to know what or who was behind the death of our son. I started seriously wondering how I could escape. I had all the time I needed to think of something. Somehow, I had to trick the woman into untying me or hold my hands in such a way that when she tied them up again, I could move them in the rope sufficiently to wriggle out of it or to be able to untie it myself. I would then have to overpower this woman, my gaoler, and knock her into unconsciousness and tie her up so I could break away.

The routine of the masked woman coming twice a day to feed me and to ensure I was comfortable continued for three days. I would strike on the following day, assuming I was alive and still there.

***

'That's just what I need,' said Pedro, as Baltasar handed him the envelope containing the brotherhood's report. 'Let me just check that it is the correct document. Yes, it's fine. I'll start reading it as soon as I can. Probably tomorrow. I do hope Francisca is safe and well and I hope you find her soon.'

'Yes, we are still very concerned about her. For the rest of the day we will be asking people on the streets if they have seen her. Baltasar's drawing of her will help, I'm sure,' said Inés.

The two of them, true to their word, trawled the streets of the town. They must have asked two hundred people about Francisca. They interrupted conversations, spoke to individuals, to women pushing their babies in wooden wheeled prams, to men delivering merchandise in carts who had stopped outside of shops. The walked the length of the Calle Santiago, the Calle Major and into the Calle Libreros, the Calle Escritorios and the Calle de los Colegios. They walked the side streets and alleyways. No one they spoke to admitted seeing Francisca, not in the last three days.

Then they stopped a woman in the Calle San Juan, not far from the cathedral. The woman tried to avoid them and was acting strangely. She was carrying a metal tray with an unlit candle, a cup and a plate on it.

'Please can you tell us whether you have seen this woman?' said Inés, showing her Baltasar's drawing. 'She is a friend of ours and has gone missing?'

'Never seen her before in my life,' said the woman, who looked shocked at the sight of the portrait, turned away from them and sped off down the Calle Major.

By the time the sun was beginning to set, the two of them were exhausted and started to make their way back to The Mad Astronomer. 'That was a strange reaction from the woman carrying the tray,' said Baltasar.

'Why would anyone be carrying a tray with a plate and candle on it?' said Inés. 'I'm mystified. Did you see where she went?'

'No. She disappeared down the Calle Major in the same way we are heading.'

'Could she be one of Francisca's captors?'

'I doubt it. There any number of reasons for carrying a tray. She may be going to get some food from someone or has taken some food to someone, an old lady perhaps who can't cope on her own.'

'Or she could have come from giving food to Francisca?'

'You are speculating, Inés! She said she hadn't seen Francisca and we have to accept that.'

'All right... but I'm not so sure!'

Over dinner that night, Inés and Baltasar worked out their plan for the following day. They would continue to question people on the streets but before they started they would visit the Department of Astronomy to ask the staff there if they had seen Francisca. They would also try to identify any derelict buildings or empty houses they could explore. Several incidents had troubled them. The landlord Gonzalo's attitude made them suspicious. They thought he knew more about Francisca's disappearance than he was saying.

'Why don't we challenge him?' said Inés.

'That would be difficult. We can hardly accuse him of lying to us. We've no evidence, only suspicion. But it gives me another idea. We could tell the brotherhood about our suspicions and see what they make of them.'

'Good thought,' said Inés. 'We could tell them about our other doubts, including the attitude of the professor of law.'

'Interesting point.'

And about the lady with the tray!'

'You are joking I think! We'll call in to see them tomorrow!'

***

I don't remember sleeping much that night. I just could not get warm lying there, trussed up on the cold floor. In a way, I was quite elated at the thought of escaping and I had a plan. The candle light crossing the floor as the door opened provided a kind of dawn. The masked woman appeared with her tray.

'Good morning,' her usual greeting.

'Good morning,' my usual reply.

'I have some news for you. Tomorrow morning, early, we are moving you to another location. I can't tell you where except that it will be outside of Alcalá.' My heart leapt. My motivation to escape that day became even stronger. The thought of them taking me somewhere else both frightened and inspired me.

'Why can't you tell me where? I'm surprised you haven't released me onto the street so I can go back to Madrid. I'm hardly going to stay around Alcalá after the way you've treated me.'

As usual, she had brought me a breakfast of bread, this time with some olives, and a cup of grape juice. I took my time eating and carefully concealed the stones from the olives. The previous day, I had manoeuvred myself around the floor and, in the darkness, found various small stones. I had made a small pile of them right next to where I lay. After I'd eaten, I quietly filled my hands with stones and the olive pips. She couldn't possibly see what I was doing.

'I suppose you want to tie me up again.'

I offered her my two hands placed together. As before, she tied the rope across the centre of my hands and around the wrists. She them pulled tight and tied me.

'Do you want to use the pot?'

'Not now but please bring it and some cloth this afternoon.'

'I will,' she said, picked up the tray and left.

Within about half an hour I had managed to ease the stones out of my hands and onto the floor. After another half an hour of struggling, I undid the rope. I was elated. I was free! Free, but trapped in this underground, dark, damp smelling dungeon.

A few minutes later, after a rest, I untied my legs. I managed to stand but almost fell in doing so. I felt my way over towards the door. Just a tiny breath of light emerged from beneath it. I tried to remember whether the masked woman sounded if she was descending steps before she opened the door or whether she walked along some passageway or other. I concluded that I would have noticed if she came down any steps. It would sound louder and more distinctive. So the little speck of light I could see was probably from a door or window, further along this passage. I would have to make sure I could use her candle when I made my escape.

I decided to lie on the floor, before she came, and pretend all was normal. I'd loosely wrap a rope around my feet and make it look as if my hands were tied. About four hours later, the door opened in a burst of candle light. She came in.

161

'I really need the pot,' I said.

She put the tray, with the candle on top, onto the floor. 'I'll get it.'

She had left the chamber pot just outside the door. She brought it in and put it next to me. She bent over to untie my feet. As she did so, I stepped out of the rope. I picked the pot up by the handle and used all my strength to smash it as hard as I possibly could, right into her face. The pot made a noisy crack as it smashed to pieces

'You God hating bitch! You've made me bleed. I can hardly see! My eyes are full of blood. Help me!'

I carefully took the candle and placed it on the floor. By then she was kneeling with her head in her hands. I could show no mercy. I stood and kicked the plate of food from the tray. I picked it up. It was made of metal. Wonderful! I hit her as hard as I could with the edge of it, right on the side of the head. She collapsed on the floor. I just could not believe I could do this to another human being, let alone a woman. But it was a simple case of her survival or mine. I quickly tied her hands behind her back and tied her feet. She was bleeding badly. It was time for me to go.

Chapter 13

Inés and Baltasar walked to the astronomy department. It was not far from the inn and quite pleasant in the weak autumn sun. 'I hardly slept last night, Baltasar. Thinking of Francisca. We really let her down, you know, leaving her on her own. It was an act of cruelty.'

'It's no good looking backwards, Inés. We are here doing our best to find her. We can do no more. I never did understand why you came back to Madrid with me. I had to get back to work but you could have stayed.'

'You are just making me feel worse, Baltasar. You can be really nasty when you want to. I wanted to come back to make sure the family were all right. A good reason, I think.'

'Sorry, Inés, I didn't mean to upset you.'

The little disagreement over, or as over as it was going to be, the two of them were walking down the Calle San Pedro and San Paulo and almost at the building in which the astronomers were located. Inés remembered it was on the third floor. Both breathless, they arrived at Professor Ramos's office. He was delighted to see them.

'I recognize you, señora. But not you señor!'

'This is my sister, Inés. She came to see you with her best friend Francisca.'

They told him the story of Francisca's disappearance, the probable connection with the anonymous letter and the man Sancho Mojaro. The professor sounded equally concerned and said he had not seen her since the visit Inés and Francisca had made together. As he said, there was nothing he could do but said he would keep an eye out for her and ask any of his students and colleagues if they had seen her. He also said he was hoping to hear from the English professor in a few days about whether he was coming to Spain and when. They thanked him for his concern and left.

'He sounds a very genuine person,' said Baltasar to Inés.

'I agree. He sounded just as concerned about Francisca as we are. And he will tell his colleagues, I'm sure. Where to now? Shall we go to the brotherhood's office, and tell them about our suspicions?'

'All right. I reluctantly agree!'

***

I carefully picked up the lit candle by the holder and opened the door. It led into a corridor and I could just make out some faint light coming from a corner about ten *varas* away. Surprisingly, the masked woman had left the key in the door so I locked her in and put the key in my coat pocket. I then crept along the corridor towards the source of the light. Much to my horror, I heard voices coming from around the corner. I stopped. They were men's voices and they were coming towards me. This was the end. I'd have to surrender. Then one of them spoke.

'Who is that?'

I just could not bring myself to speak.

Another of the men spoke. 'This is the Alcalá Holy Brotherhood. You are under arrest. Come out whoever you are.'

I could not remember being more relieved. I felt overjoyed. The brotherhood had found me, even though they didn't know it yet.

'I am Francisca de Abaunza. I have been held prisoner here for four days and I've just escaped.'

The men were still not sure. I could have been one of the kidnappers trying to trick them.

164

'Come slowly towards us and hold the candle up so we can see your face.'

I did as instructed.

'It's her all right. I recognize her from the drawing,' said one of them.

One of them took my hand and they led me out of the place, around that corner where the light was coming in, up a flight of stairs into another large room then out of a door into the autumn sun. The intensity of the light almost blinded me. I put my hands over my eyes.

'Are you all right?' said the officer wearing the tricorne.

'I just feel blinded by the light but otherwise I'm all right. I've tied up one of my kidnappers, a woman, and locked her in the room where they held me.'

'We are going to take you back to our office so you can sit down and make yourself comfortable,' said the officer without the hat. 'We'll worry about your kidnapper later.'

'I broke a chamber pot on her face and she is bleeding badly.'

The two constables walked me back to their office. I turned around to look at the building where my captors had imprisoned me. It looked like a derelict warehouse and was in the Calle San Juan, not far from the archbishop's palace.

My legs felt stiff as we started so I could move only quite slowly. The officers were generous with their patience and told me not to hurry. Then I had another astonishing surprise. As we approached the corner of the Calle Carmen Calzado and the Calle Major, with one of the officers on each side of me, I could see two familiar figures approaching. Inés and Baltasar were waving and shouting with joy at seeing that I was alive and presumably well.

Inés and I simply burst into tears and stood at the side of the road and hugged each other. Baltasar embraced both of us. It was a heady reunion.

'I'm so sorry we left you here, Francisca. Please forgive us! My God, you are in a state. Look at your clothes. It looks as if you've been rolling around on a dirty floor.'

'As far as I'm concerned there is nothing for me to forgive. If anything, it is me who should be asking for forgiveness for being tricked by a man into going to dine with him. There was no dinner only a hit on the head and four days in an underground dungeon until I escaped… and these constables got me out of the place! And, yes, I have been rolling around on a floor, the floor of that horrible place where they kept me.'

We hugged each other again among renewed tears.

***

The Holy Brotherhood wanted to interview me so the two officers led me into a room in their building. They invited Inés and Baltasar to join me and explained that they might want to question them, too. The officers, the one with the tricorne, still perched on his head and the bareheaded one, sat on their side of the desk while the three of us sat on the other.

'I'm afraid this has to be a formal interview,' said the one with the tricorne. I am Sergeant Felipe Ortiz and my colleague here is Officer Mateo López who will make a record of this discussion.' The three of us gave our full names.

'Could you please start, Señora de Abaunza,' said Sergeant Ortiz, 'by telling us why you are here in Alcalá de Henares.'

Baltasar made an unwelcome and loud interjection. 'You already know that officer. We have been dealing with you about the death of her son.'

'I would be grateful if you don't interrupt,' said Sergeant Ortiz with a sharp edge to his voice. Baltasar meekly apologized.

I began by telling them why I was there. They wanted a detailed account of when we left Madrid, why we had returned, where we had stayed in Alcalá, when we returned, why Baltasar and Inés had returned to Madrid, what prompted them to return to Alcalá and what exactly they had been doing since their return. They asked me to tell them how I had met this Señor Sancho Mojaro, how many times I had seen him, exactly what kind of relationship I had with him. They asked me to describe him and whether he had any distinguishing features such as a scar or odd inflection in his voice. I could only tell them what he looked like and that his accent was that of a person who was a native to this part of Spain. I said he sounded well educated. I told them what this Sancho had said about his work as a supplier of various items to universities.

At that point, Baltasar asked if he could speak. Sergeant Ortiz asked him to go ahead. 'When Inés and I visited the mathematics department yesterday, one of the staff there told us that he had found that no one of that name supplied his department.'

'Thank you. That's useful to know.'

He then asked me to describe the events around my abduction. I told them about the invitation to dinner with the so called Carmella. I described her as best I could.

'Could you take us to the house where you went for dinner with these people? Was it dark when you went? Exactly what happened when you arrived there?'

I described the sequence of events from the invitation until I was hit hard on the head as I walked from the front door into the lounge. I said I could certainly take them to the house.

'We'll go there after this interview,' said Sergeant Ortiz, whom I was beginning to admire for the thorough way he was conducting this meeting. He was being fair, objective and thorough.

He then asked me to do my best to describe how I ended up in the warehouse where I had been hidden. I explained that I had no recollection of how I had arrived there except that I felt I had been taken tied up in a wagon or on a cart. He asked me to go through the daily events where I was confined, how often my captors visited me, how often they fed me and what they said. He asked me to describe the woman in the mask or at least do my best to do so.

'I hope you haven't left her in that room,' I said.

'No. We took the key you gave us and have been there to arrest her. Some of our officers are interviewing her as we speak. Her face isn't as bad as it might have appeared to you. There was a lot of blood but no permanent damage.'

In a way, I felt quite relieved. I would have felt bad if I had caused her serious injury.

'May I ask a question?' I said.

'Please do, señora,'

'How did you know I was being held captive in that building?'

'It is a matter of observation and questioning of events. Yesterday, one of our colleagues noticed a woman going into that building. She appeared to be carrying food. To our knowledge that building is unoccupied save for the odd beggar sleeping in the doorway. You had been reported missing and we wondered if she was going there to give food to you. We knew what you looked like from Señor del Mazo's portrait of you. So Officer López and I followed her this morning. Need I say more?'

'I told you, Baltasar! We saw what was probably the same woman yesterday and were on our way to tell you about her, weren't we Baltasar?'

'Yes and about our other suspicions.'

'So you drew a portrait of me, Baltasar? Very clever!'

'Two, in fact!' said Inés. 'We have been carrying one and asking people in the streets if they have seen you and when! A woman carrying a tray aroused our suspicions when she seemed to recognize your portrait and dash off down the road.'

'Could you please tell us of your other suspicions?' said Sergeant Ortiz.

Baltasar told him about Gonzalo at the inn and the professor of law and why Inés and he had doubts about them. Sergeant Ortiz thanked him but made no further comment.

'Before you take us to the house where you were taken on the pretext of being entertained to dinner, I would like you, Señora de Abaunza, to come with me to another room. Just to prepare you, we'd like you to confirm or otherwise the identity of the woman whom we allege held you captive,' said Sergeant Ortiz.

I indicated my willingness and we went, leaving Inés and Baltasar with his colleague, Officer López. Sergeant Ortiz lead the way downstairs into a corridor of what appeared to be cells used to keep prisoners. An odd smell, a little like rotting food, pervaded the air.

'Which one is it?' said the sergeant to a large bellied bald gentleman, obviously the gaoler.

'This one 'ere, guv'nor,' the man said as he put a key into a heavy lock and turned it with a clunk. He opened the door.

'Do you recognize that woman?' said Sergeant Ortiz, with no sign of feeling.

I looked in.

'That's the fucking bitch who smashed my face in with a piss pot! The woman who locked me in the warehouse!' she shouted. The tone of the woman's voice and her accusations startled me but I tried to show no sign of reaction. She could do me no harm: they had chained her to the wall by her feet and arms.

'Yes, that's the one. I recognize her voice and her lower face. Her mask covered the rest of it.'

The gaoler closed the door with a metallic crash, which reverberated through the corridor, and locked it. Sergeant Ortiz led me back up to Inés and Baltasar.

'Thank you, Señora,' he said, as he opened the door to the room which we were in before. He went to sit behind the desk again.

'This anonymous letter we referred to earlier. Where is it now? It could be a central piece of evidence.'

'I hid it in my house in Madrid.'

'Could you, or you, Baltasar, retrieve it for us?'

'I'll return to Madrid and get it,' said Baltasar.

'Excellent. All I need now is for you, Señora de Abaunza, to take me and Mateo to the house where you were taken for dinner by this character, Sancho. It's on your way back to The Mad Astronomer, so you would have to go near there on your way back to the inn,' said Sergeant Ortiz, respecting the state of my legs and assuring me there would hardly be any additional walking. 'And I'd then like to see the room you were staying in at The Mad Astronomer.'

'Why would you want to see that?' said Inés.

'With the kidnapping of Señora de Abaunza, a major crime was committed in our town. It is our job to solve it. Since the last place that the señora occupied before her abduction was that room, it is our duty to examine it.'

'According to Gonzalo, it has been left as it was before the abduction,' said Baltasar.

'That will help,' said Sergeant Ortiz.

***

We left the Office of the Holy Brotherhood, accompanied by Sergeant Ortiz and Officer López. By then I was quite tired and could still only walk slowly. We stopped outside of the house in the Calle Ramon. 'Are you sure this is the one, señora?'

'Certain,' I said.

'Let's carry on to the inn,' said Sergeant Ortiz. He led the way and we all followed.

Gonzalo was visibly shocked as he saw the five of us waiting by the reception desk. He looked at me as if I was a ghost from the recent past. He said nothing. He could see from their jackets that we were accompanied by two law officers but waited for one of us to speak first.

Sergeant Ortiz spoke. 'I gather you are the landlord here.'

'I am indeed.'

'Do you recognize this woman?' pointing to me.

'Yes. She is Francisca de Abaunza, one of my clients. She has been staying elsewhere for a number of days, I gather.'

'Right and wrong at the same time. She was kidnapped from this inn four days ago by a certain Sancho Mojaro. Are you familiar with that name?'

'Yes, he dines and has breakfast here occasionally but does not stay.'

'Other than serving his needs here, have you ever had any other dealings with him?'

'None, officer.'

'Could you give Señora de Abaunza the key to her room? I am going to examine it with my colleague here,' he said, nodding towards Officer López.

All five of us went up the stairs to my room. I opened the door. 'Do you mind if I go in first,' said Sergeant Ortiz.

'Please do,' I said.

He walked slowly around the room. He opened the wardrobe and looked in, then closed the door. He opened each drawer to the chest of drawers then closed them. He then emerged onto the landing.

'I'd like you to go in and see if anything has been disturbed while you've not been here,' he said.

I looked around the room, opened and closed the drawers in turn. 'There is a gun missing!' I said in a loud voice. 'Baltasar lent me his gun and it's no longer where I put it.'

'We took it,' shouted Inés from outside. 'When we asked to look in your room when we returned from Madrid.'

'Did you take anything else?' said Sergeant Ortiz.

'No,' said Baltasar.

'I think I've seen all I want to see,' said Sergeant Ortiz. 'Thank you for all your help, the three of you. I assume you will continue to stay here. We will contact you if we need to speak to you again. If you move, please let us know. The sooner you can recover that letter, Señor Martinéz del Mazo, the better. Thank you again.' The two officers shook our hands and went, leaving the three of us on the landing.

***

We agreed to meet for dinner that night. I arranged with Gonzalo to have a bath. I just couldn't wait to cleanse my body of the filth from that confinement. Despite the tiny space in the bath and the small volume of water I could use, brought to me by Gonzalo's friendly cook, I allowed myself to soak until the water became almost cold. I stepped out feeling a new woman, as I towelled myself down, and much refreshed.

The dinner was an emotional time for each of us. Inés simply could not stop her flow of tears or saying she was sorry in leaving me in Alcalá to go back to Madrid.

'Please, Inés, there is nothing to be sorry for. You did nothing wrong. I think we, especially us women, are full of emotion over my escape from captivity. What I didn't tell you was that the woman with the mask told me I would be moved to a place outside Alcalá early the following morning. So my incentive to escape became suddenly much higher!'

'Maybe you should have mentioned that to Sergeant Ortiz, Francisca.'

'I suppose I should have but my mind was flying at random in that room they interviewed us. We'll mention it another time.'

'The important question is how are they going to capture the so called Sancho Mojaro? Who is he and what is his connection with the death of Juan junior?' said Baltasar.

'If we knew that we'd have solved the mystery,' I said. 'I'm sure that there is a lot more to Juan junior's death than appears on the surface. Otherwise, why was I kidnapped and held in that horrible place? I know I am part of this story and sometimes find it hard to be objective but something strange is happening here and I think the Brotherhood realise that, too.'

'I agree,' said Baltasar, 'and I am involved but less so than you, so can be more objective.'

'Is it worth trying to speculate?' said Inés.

'Probably not,' said Baltasar. 'We should concentrate on facts alone.'

'I'm less sure,' said Inés. 'If we have some ideas about what is happening, or what happened all those sixteen years ago, that could help our investigations.'

'I spent some time thinking about this while being held captive. The key lies in the letter. Sergeant Ortiz agrees. I don't know what it will tell them but I am not a brotherhood officer. Like you, I suspect the law professor and Gonzalo.'

'Felipe Ortiz is smart and he'll come up with something, I'm sure, Francisca,' said Inés.

***

We concluded our discussion at breakfast the following morning. By then Inés had taken control of her tears and we were all feeling better now that I had come safely through my ordeal.

'Turning to practical things, if we all agree, I'll go back to Francisca's house and get the anonymous letter.'

'I think you should go now,' said Inés. 'Agreed, Francisca?'

'Definitely.'

'I'll saddle up my horse and then I'm on my way! Just tell me where it is exactly, Francisca, and give me the key!'

Inés and I stood by the tethering rail outside the inn and waved Baltasar on his way. We then went into the drinking area and sat at a table to work out how we could take the investigation forward.

'The one thing we have to realise, Inés, is that we are carrying on with looking into Juan junior's death. There may be a connection between that sad event and my kidnapping but it is the kidnapping that the brotherhood are investigating, not Juan junior's passing.'

'I see that Francisca, but we may find that in solving the kidnapping they may solve the riddle of your son's death. That would be quite a result.'

'I agree. All I'm saying is that we do all we can to look into Juan junior's death. Do you agree, Inés?'

'Of course. So what do you think we do next?'

'It would be good to know when the English professor and his wife are coming to Alcalá.'

'Francisca, I haven't told you this. When Baltasar and I went to see Professor Ramos yesterday to tell him about your disappearance, he said he was expecting to hear any day now about the visit and when they would arrive! And another thing, while I think about it. Your friend Pedro has got the brotherhood's report into Juan junior's death and will have started looking at it by now!'

'All that is good news, Inés. How do you know that Pedro has the report?'

Inés told me about the letter written by Professor Gregorio Estrada to the professor of law and how she and Baltasar retrieved the report, only two days before.

'We'll have to be patient and see what Pedro comes up with,' I said. 'All we can do is wait.'

'There is one thing I'd really like to do, Francisca,' said Inés.

'Really?'

'When Baltasar and I went to see Professor Estrada and Pedro, Pedro seemed very concerned about your disappearance. He wasn't exactly in tears but he seemed very worried. I think we should go to see him and tell him you are all right. He said he warned you about that Sancho individual and was quite upset to find you hadn't heeded him.'

'You are right. He did warn me. I agree. Let's go to see him.'

We could see no reason not to go there that morning. We agreed to meet by the reception desk after we had gone to our rooms and prepared ourselves for the visit. It wasn't far to walk but it was much colder and darker than the day before and looked as if we were due for rain. So we would need our winter coats. I really liked Pedro a lot so put on a splash of my perfume. We chatted as we went to the department. After my bath, a good meal and good night's sleep in a comfortable bed, my legs felt much more able to walk so we managed it at a comfortable pace. We went straight to Pedro's office and knocked on the door, not knowing whether he'd be there or not.

'Come in,' was the welcomed reply.

'You go in first and see what he says.'

'Francisca, you are all right! They found you. I'm so pleased to see you! Come here! I want to give you a hug.'

He hugged and hugged me. I wondered when he would let me go. Surely this man of thirty or so couldn't feel as attracted to me, a much older woman, as much as I felt attracted to him.

'It's so good to see you, too, Pedro,' I said, quite breathlessly after his squeezing.

'So tell me what happened to you. I'm dying to know!'

I took him through the whole chronicle of events from the last time I saw him, through the kidnapping, my escape and rescue by the brotherhood.

'Those men are more competent than they seem. Sounds as if your man, Sergeant Ortiz, is very good. He will discover who this man Sancho is and his accomplices. I'm sure Inés will have told you that I now have the correct report on the brotherhood's investigation into Juan junior's death. With the blessing of Professor Estrada, I started to read it yesterday. There is a lot of detail in it, mainly records of statements made by staff at the colleges and statements made by the students.'

'Do you remember any of the students' names?'

'Not off hand… but I can find them, if you wish.'

'Not now. I'm more interested in any statements which contain anything you've found suspicious and possibly incriminating.'

'Not just yet, Francisca, but it's early days and there is much piecing together and note taking to do. I'm basically looking for inconsistencies between what various people have said. That can often be a source of fruitful probing. As soon as I find something you should know about, I'll come around to The Mad Astronomer and tell you!'

I was delighted that Pedro was taking this re-investigation into Juan junior's death so seriously. He obviously felt happy doing this in the knowledge that he had the full backing of Professor Estrada. Who knew what this handsome young man would discover?

***

At about the same time that Baltasar left for Madrid, Sergeant Ortiz began an important stage of his investigation into the kidnapping.

'Mateo, could you go down to the cells with two of your colleagues and bring that woman up here? It's time we interviewed her. She's an odd one so I'd be surprised if she comes without a struggle.'

The same big gaoler unlocked and opened the door. The three of them went in.

'Señora, we would like to ask you about the events of the last few days, and other things. If we unlock those chains are you willing to come upstairs to the interview room?' said Mateo.

'I'm staying right here. You have no right to ask me anything and I'm not even going to tell you my name. So you can piss off. I'm going nowhere. You will have to take me by force.'

'That's no way to treat members of the king's Holy Brotherhood,' said Mateo.

'That's all you deserve and all you'll get from me.'

Mateo, his two assistants and the gaoler went into the cell. The two assistants grabbed the woman's arms and held them while the gaoler unchained her from the wall. She shouted obscenities at them while they did so. It took all four of them to carry her bodily up the stairs to the interview room where Sergeant Ortiz sat waiting behind the desk. They burst through the door half dragging and half carrying her.

'Would you like to sit in one of those chairs, señora?' said Sergeant Ortiz, nodding to the chairs which Baltasar, Inés and Francisca had occupied the day before and hoping that the woman would change her behaviour now that she was in the room.

She didn't answer.

'I'll repeat myself, in case you didn't take in what I said.'

She said nothing.

'Either you cooperate with me in interviewing you or I'll have to charge you with obstructing the course of a brotherhood investigation.'

'You can go to hell,' she snarled, her face red with rage and her eyes glowing anger. 'Charge me with what you like. You'll have to prove it in court.'

'I have four witnesses here that the courts regard as reliable. They've all been witnesses before. They will testify that you obstructed us.'

'They are just a bunch of thugs. I'll tell the court how brutal they were towards me.'

'I'm going to ask you some questions. You can decide whether to answer them. If you answer them reasonably, we will tell the court that you cooperated and your sentence will be more lenient. It will probably be more severe if you don't,' said the sergeant, coolly, not allowing himself to be provoked by this angry woman.

'Could you please tell me your name and your address?'

She struggled violently in the hands of the four men who were restraining her but she didn't utter a word.

'I have several other questions for you,' said Ortiz.

The woman glared at him.

'First who is the man who calls himself Sancho Mojaro?'

'Don't ask me,' she said, still struggling.

Ortiz continued. 'Where does he live and why did you kidnap Señora Francisca de Abaunza?

'How the hell do I know?'

Not to be deterred he asked her another question. 'Who organized the abduction of the señora?'

She said nothing.

'Fourthly, who was the woman to whom Señor Mojaro took Señora de Abaunza before the abduction?'

The struggling woman again said nothing and failed miserably in an attempt to attack the officers restraining her.

'Since you are not cooperating, I charge you with obstruction. It is unfortunate that you have chosen not to give us your name, otherwise I could have named you in the charge. Take her back to her cell please, gentlemen.'

Sergeant Ortiz stood up, paced around the room for a few moments, stepped towards the window and looked out onto the street, not paying attention to anything out there in particular. He had to solve this case. His future career depended on it. If he did not make quick progress, his senior colleagues would take it from him. He wanted to do well. This was one of the most serious offences that had been committed in Alcalá, certainly in the ten years since they accepted him in the brotherhood. The crimes committed here were mainly thefts from street traders, the odd break-in of a house and assaults, some with a sexual motive, but there hadn't been a murder for a long time and never before an abduction.

Sergeant Ortiz moved slowly away from the window and walked along the corridor back to his own office, not many paces away. He sat at his desk, clasped his hands behind his head and blankly looked into the distance. He remained puzzled. What was going on here? Who would want to treat an old lady like Señora de Abaunza the way these people did. Why? She could have died in that dungeon. It was a miracle that she survived there. She could literally have been scared to death. How courageous of her to hit that woman in the face with the chamber pot. And finish her off with the tray. It must have taken all her strength. What were these people trying to conceal? Were they in some way involved in her son's death, all those years ago? The crucial clue could be in the anonymous letter. He'd have to be patient and wait for its return.

Chapter 14

Baltasar had ridden only a *milla* or two from Alcalá when it started to rain, cold penetrating rain. Caesar, his black stallion, began to struggle and Baltasar had to think about finding shelter, at least for as long as it would take for the rain to ease off. In the distance, and through the driving wetness, he could just make out a building that could be a barn or a large shed, about three hundred *varas* to the left of the road. He gently kicked Caesar in the side, enough to make him canter, and off they headed towards the building they were to use as a refuge.

Not knowing whether the building would be occupied, he made sure his loaded flintlock was within easy reach. They rode on an uneven, stony path from the road and Caesar had no choice but to slow himself to a walk. The rain was getting harder as they approached the structure which still concealed its purpose. Baltasar thought it strange that there were no windows or doors on the side which they could see. The large sloping overhang of the roof looked to provide good shelter so Baltasar rode towards the roof underside and dismounted under its protection. Apart from those small drops that swirl about in the wind, he and Caesar were in the dry and on the downwind side of the building. The horse let out a grateful and appreciative neigh.

They both stood and waited. After about fifteen minutes, Baltasar was startled by a sound coming from the inside of the building. It was not the sound made by an animal and it could not be a human voice. He checked the position of his flintlock. A few minutes later, the sound occurred again but instead of a single burst, it repeated itself every few seconds. It struck Baltasar as similar to the noise of a saw cutting through wood but he knew it differed from that. It continued for five minutes or so and then stopped again. Someone was in that building doing something strange or at least something that Baltasar could not identify.

The wind became stronger and the driving rain turned to sleet, something not unknown near Madrid but still quite a rarity. The wind began to change direction so that shelter the roof overhang provided became less effective. Baltasar decided that he would investigate the other side of the building and find the door. The place was so isolated that there had to be part of it where horses could be tied up out of the weather. Surely, those who used the building, whatever its purpose, could not get there on foot. He took hold of Caesar's reins and walked him to the other side. The apparent lack of windows baffled him but, as he expected, quite a large door was positioned along that side. Mercifully, the large overhang also protected that side. As he reached the door, the strange sound started up again.

He tied Caesar to a post and stood there for a time. The sound continued. Curiosity took hold of him and he decided to try to enter. He wondered whether to knock or to go straight in. He knocked on the door but there was no reply. He decided to go in so turned the handle. The door was locked. He knocked again. Within a few moments a puzzled looking man in a large leather apron appeared at the door.

'What do you want?' the man said. With eyes wide open and eyebrows raised and twitching slightly, he looked puzzled and shocked, if not frightened.

'Just wondered if it was all right to shelter from the sleet. I'm on my way to Madrid but it's too bad to ride in.'

'You've already been sheltering here, señor. We heard the horse neigh as you stopped under the roof overhang. Tie him up in the stabling at the back and come in. I'll leave the door open. The least we can do is to give you a drink.'

Baltasar noticed the man change his expression to a weak smile. He walked quickly to the stables and was not surprised to see other horses there. He tied Caesar up out of the weather and walked back to the open door. He then realised what the noise was. A man, working on a wooden bench was shaping a metal container. He would pick it up, put it in an oven, take it out and look at it before delivering a series of hammer blows to create the shape he was making. In this case a large open bowl. So Baltasar had by an accident of the weather stumbled across a craft workshop. There were a number of other benches, a number of which were also in use by men working on various objects, some in metal others in wood and some in reeds for baskets. The mystery of the windows revealed itself. A good deal of light was coming in through some windows set in the south side of the roof, which he didn't see from outside.

The man who had let him in introduced himself to Baltasar. 'It's always good to help a passing traveller, especially if he's in need of shelter. My name is Andres and I am in charge here. Would you like a drink of something, maybe a beer?'

'Yes, a beer would be nice. I'm quite dry at the moment.'

'So you are on your way to Madrid? Do you work there?'

'Yes, I work there. I am a baker, so a craftsman like your men working here.' Baltasar had no intention of describing the exact reason for his return to Madrid. There were so many complicated factors in Francisca's kidnapping, he didn't want to give too much away. These people were strangers and who knew where their true interests lay.

'So you are running a workshop here. Very interesting. May I ask who gives you the work?'

'An interesting question, señor. Have you any connections with the brotherhood? In Alcalá de Henares, Madrid or anywhere else?'

Baltasar wondered where this discussion was leading. Surely these people hadn't stolen the materials they were working with. Could they be making forgeries of expensive works of art to sell at a profit? Were they some kind of fraternity which, if not illegal, operated on the edge of the law? Could it be that they were not quite legal but not quite illegal either.

'No, I have no connections at all with the brotherhood. I am just an ordinary baker, making bread and items of confection.'

'I can tell you a little more then. But first I must ask you to swear an oath that you will tell no one about our purpose. If you break the oath we will track you down and kill you.'

Baltasar could see no possible need to break such an oath. He had to admit, he was curious about the place. But he was no fool and could see no reason why this Andres would want him to know about what went on here, if it was supposed to be such a secret. Why would this man want to take the risk in telling him? He was puzzled so asked him directly.

'Why take the risk in telling me? I don't understand.'

'You don't get something for nothing and we may be able to make some use of you. You never know. A baker may want to make more money than he can earn by baking alone, so you may want to help us. And, what's more, even if you had reason to tell someone about us and we were closed down we would simply start up somewhere else. It might be inconvenient and that is why we would punish you heavily if you did!'

'All right, I swear I will tell no one about your operation here.'

'Are you quite sure?'

'Yes, I am.'

'Well, I'll tell you. These men you see working here are fugitives. Each of them is hiding from something or somebody. Some have committed criminal acts... others are hiding from civil authorities, shall we say. Each of them pays us to stay here.'

'Stay here? Where do they stay?'

'You will not realise that we have a basement here in which the men sleep...and a kitchen and wash area.'

'I don't understand why you are doing this craft work, in that case?'

'It is to occupy the men. And to give them some money.'

'I'm surprised the authorities haven't discovered you and shut you down,'

'It is because we are so careful in managing our business.'

'How many fugitives do you have at any one time?'

'No more than ten. That's all we can accommodate. There are nine at the moment.'

'So they are confined here...like a prison.'

'God, no. They can come and go as they please. At the risk of being caught. We have several who have jobs in Alcalá or Madrid. This is not a gaol! It's a refuge.'

'Are any of your lodgers women?'

'We had one once but it was a disaster. She became pregnant and had to leave.'

Like most who had lived a law abiding life, Baltasar had never heard of an operation like this before, and was still unsure of how it worked. He saw no danger from swearing this oath. He knew of no fugitives from the law or escapees from prisons. He finished the beer that Andres had given him and the two of them went to the door to examine the weather.

'Looks much better now. Down to a fine drizzle. I ought to mount up and go. I am aiming at a hotel in Torrejón de Ardoz for the night and I don't want to be caught in the weather again.'

'Let me take you around to the stabling,' said Andres.

Baltasar shook hands with the man and climbed up onto Caesar.

'Don't forget the oath you swore.'

'Don't worry,' said Baltasar, smiling generously. 'Thank you for sheltering me.'

***

He was luckier with the weather the rest of the way to Torrejón. The rain soon stopped completely so Caesar was able to take him at a steady canter all the way to the central square in the town. While riding there he was thinking about the strange refuge he had stumbled across, not far from the road. Some form of anonymity had to operate there. Otherwise, it would pay for any fugitive to report another of them to the authorities. But, none of them would surely want to go to the authorities in the first place. Still perplexed, his mind turned to his mission in Madrid.

He soon found a room in a hotel. It may have been the hotel that Inés and Francisca stayed in the first time they came through the town. He breakfasted early, settled his account and made off for Madrid and Francisca's house. Sitting astride Caesar and not more than a *milla* from the Alcalá gate, he had the uncomfortable feeling that he was being followed. At first, he could not imagine who would want to pursue him. It suddenly became obvious that there must be a connection between his pursuers and the anonymous letter. Whoever wrote it wanted it back. He would try to fool them. He nudged his foot into Caesar's side and loosened the reins. The stallion quickly and powerfully broke into a gallop and within a five minutes he was entering the city gate. Still unsure about whether he was out of sight of anyone chasing, he took a circuitous route to Francisca's house in the Madalena. He tied Caesar up and walked to the front door.

He unlocked it and walked in. He sensed that something was badly wrong. He walked into the drawing room. He was confronted by a scene of chaos. Someone or more than one had ransacked the room. Drawers were hanging out of the sideboard, their contents strewn across the floor. The mats and carpets had been lifted to reveal the bare floorboards. Every single ornament or other sentimental object had been swept from the shelves and mantelpiece. Many lay broken on the floor. Broken glasses and cups had been left there.

He looked into the other rooms on the ground floor. The second of the drawing rooms displayed an equal state of destruction, as did the dining room and kitchen. Poor Francisca would be devastated to see the state of ruination that had been inflicted on her house. He walked up the stairs. Scenes of incomparable disaster confronted him. The contents of the wardrobes and drawers had been strewn across the floors. Whoever had been there had taken the beds apart and turned the mattresses over. It would take ages to bring the house back to any kind of normality.

He went back down to the kitchen. A number of pewter pots were laying in the chaotic distribution of objects on the floor. He looked again at the shelf: only one of the pots was still in its place. He reached up to retrieve it. He looked in. There was a folded piece of paper nestling right at the bottom. It was the anonymous letter. He felt his heart beat faster. He had found it where others had failed to look!

It was far too late to begin the journey back to Alcalá de Henares. So he slipped the letter into his jacket pocket and rode Caesar the short distance to his house in the Calle Olivar. He spent an anxious night there having seen the devastation in Francisca's house. If he had been followed, he thought, did his pursuers, who surely knew of the ransacking of Francisca's house, know where he lived? If so, did they know he had found the letter? They couldn't know, surely.

While lying there, he couldn't help wondering what Francisca would think of the destruction brutally perpetrated on her house and its contents. She would feel repulsion at the thought of strangers not only invading her privacy but handling some of her most intimate and treasured possessions, many of which had belonged to her beloved Juan. He had no choice but to tell her about what he had seen. He dreaded her reaction.

After a tenuous sleep, he woke early and decided to leave just after daybreak. Neither Inés nor Baltasar had left food in the house. So he left on an empty stomach. He knew of a stall near the Alcalá gate where he could buy a breakfast. He had used it many times before.

'Baltasar, it's you,' cried the owner. 'We haven't had the pleasure of seeing you for weeks. Not going to the palace today? Pour him a glass of juice, Virginia. Want something to eat?'

He ignored the question about the palace. 'Yes, Paulo. Could you fry me a couple of eggs and a few tomatoes, maybe with some fried bread?'

'It will be there in a trice, young fellow!'

The sound of the eggs frying gave him an earnest appetite so he started to eat as soon as Virginia placed the tasty looking dish on the counter in front of him.

'So where are you heading today, my friend?'

Still wary about saying too much he gave a neutral answer. 'Up to Alcalá. My sister is there with a friend and I'm going to join them.'

'Some sort of holiday?'

'You could say that! So what do I owe you?'

'Call it nine *maravedís*.'

'Here's a *real*.'

'Here's some change.'

Inspired by the words of Sergeant Ortiz, who asked Baltasar to bring the letter back to Alcalá as soon as he could, he decided to push Caesar into completing the journey that day. It was less than six *leguas* and a strong stallion such as Caesar could easily manage it, given that they were starting early and would only stop for some short rest breaks. Shouting his farewells to Paulo, Baltasar put his foot in the stirrup and climbed up onto Caesar. The handsome black horse had been impatiently clomping its front hooves on the ground, as if expecting a speedy run. They set off at a gallop which became a steady canter after half a *milla* or so. He saw the odd wagon and a few lone horsemen but not much other traffic.

They reached Torrejón just after midday. Baltasar didn't want to stop there so he rode through and pulled off the road at an inn about a quarter of a *milla* past the town. He tied Caesar, not even showing a single drop of sweat from his exertions, to the rail outside and hooked a welcomed bag of hay around his neck. Three other horses were already tied there. Baltasar decided to go into the inn, not only for a drink and some food but also to give Caesar a rest.

'What can we do for you, señor?' said the pretty young lady in a maroon dress and a white bonnet standing behind the bar.

'Just a small beer and some bread and cheese, if that's all right.'

'Certainly, señor. It won't be a minute. Sit at a table and I'll bring it to you.'

Baltasar did as she suggested. He didn't feel comfortable sitting in the middle of a room like this, so sat at a table by a window which gave a view of the road. He had that strange feeling again. He felt that a group of three men sitting at a table on the back wall were paying him more attention than he deserved and definitely more than he wanted. Surely, they couldn't have been those whom he believed were following him the day before. It would be too much of a coincidence that they were there in this inn where he also had decided to stop. All three were in their forties, he thought, and dressed for riding. Each was wearing a round, firm brimmed, light brown hat. It was as if they had chanced upon a milliners and decided to buy one of this pattern each. Baltasar wondered if this headgear was part of a uniform. Maybe they belonged to some kind of secret organisation. He tried to think no more of them, even though they each gave him the occasional glance. While he was sitting, the three of them got up from the table and left. Baltasar still had that uneasy feeling about them even though they were no longer there.

Within five minutes or so, the good looking young girl brought him his plate of food and a drink. He didn't rush to finish but savoured the fresh bread and what seemed like a local cheese, sipping his drink as he did so. He sat there for a few minutes longer, took the last swig of the beer and went to the bar to pay. Moments later he was back on Caesar and they were on their way again.

Riding at a canter, he was surprised that by then there was more traffic on the road. It was not exactly busy but the steady stream of carriages, wagons and carts, especially coming toward Torrejón amazed him. He wondered if there was much trade between Torrejón and Alcalá de Henares. He could not imagine there was a great deal because each was only a small town.

While deliberating on the reasons for the increase in traffic, he could hear several horses approaching him from behind. He imagined that they wanted to overtake so he pulled over so they could do so. When the riders reached him, one of them turned towards him and shouted. It was one of the men at the inn with one of his compatriots by his side. The man was pointing a flintlock pistol at Baltasar's head.

'Turn off down that track, if you value your life. And follow us.'

Believing that it would be better to comply than to be shot there and then, he decided to do as instructed. A hundred *varas* off the main road and out of sight of the passing traffic, the two horsemen, each wearing the familiar brimmed hat, stopped and dismounted, leaving Baltasar astride Caesar. The one carrying the gun, still aiming it at Baltasar's head, came up to him.

'We have a simple request to make to you. We understand that you are carrying an unsigned letter written to a woman called Francisca de Abaunza. Just hand me the letter and you can go safely on your way.'

'What makes you think I have a letter?' said Baltasar.

'You went to the woman's house yesterday to find it and take it back to the brotherhood. We want to be sure the letter doesn't reach them.'

Baltasar quickly thought of a way through. 'You win. Here is the letter.'

He leant over and reached into his saddlebag. He quickly pulled out his flintlock, aimed at the man with the gun, fired it and hit him full in the face. Blood poured everywhere. The man collapsed in a heap on the ground. He accomplice climbed onto his horse and galloped off in fright. Baltasar followed but the man headed back down the road towards Torrejón.

Baltasar was elated. He had fooled his assailants and was now on his way to Alcalá. He even expressed his joy to Caesar. He should press on at speed. The last thing he needed was for the gunman's colleague to alert his other compatriots and for them to have another attempt at taking the letter.

***

For once there was no queue at the front desk in the brotherhood's office. He merely had to knock to alert the officer on duty there. The man appeared to be asleep.

'My name is Baltasar Martinéz del Mazo. I have a letter for Sergeant Ortiz.'

'Just a moment. I'll see if he's in.'

'Señor del Mazo, it's good to see you,' said Sergeant Ortiz, as soon as he set eyes on him. 'You look exhausted and worried. Come inside and I'll give you a drink.'

Sergeant Ortiz took Baltasar into the room in which he had interviewed the three of them.

'So, tell me the story. What happened?'

Baltasar told him everything from feeling he was being followed as he approached Madrid, the discovery of the ransacking of Francisca's house, through the chance sighting of three suspicious men at the inn, to being held up at gunpoint by two of these men. He told him he had almost certainly killed one of them by a single shot from his flintlock.

Sergeant Ortiz laughed and clapped his hands at the same time. 'Good work, señor. You have made a major contribution to our investigation Thank you! But I also owe you an apology.'

'Really?' said Baltasar. He wondered what he was about to hear. What had gone wrong while he had been away?

'Yes, definitely. I should have thought more about the possible dangers that could confront you before I sent you back to Madrid. I should have instructed Officer López to go with you and possibly another officer. But at that point I simply hadn't realised the significance of the letter which is much clearer now... because of what you have been through in getting it back to me!'

'Don't worry, sergeant,' said Baltasar, speaking to the officer as if they were old friends. 'As it happens, no harm has come to me and here is the letter.' He passed it over the desk to Sergeant Ortiz who unfolded it and read it.

'Hmm...interesting,' said Sergeant Ortiz.

The two of them parted with a handshake and Baltasar made his way by foot to The Mad Astronomer. Caesar walked by his side.

'You are back so quickly, Baltasar,' said Inés, planting a kiss on each cheek. 'Just three days for the whole journey!'

'And I have quite a story to tell. I'll just stable Caesar and go up for a wash and change my clothes. Let Francisca know I'm back and let's all meet in the dining room in...say, half an hour.'

'I can't wait to hear your story, Baltasar.'

***

We were already sitting at a table by the time Baltasar arrived. I immediately stood, walked the few paces towards him and kissed him on both cheeks. 'Thank you Baltasar. I am so grateful to you,' I said. 'You are a true friend, taking on a mission like that just for me!'

'You could put it that way, Francisca, but it was more for the brotherhood than for you. It was they who wanted the letter. The best thing you did was not to destroy it!'

'I was sorely tempted, several times! So you found it?' I said, still unsure.

'Of course, Francisca, and I have already given it to Sergeant Ortiz. It is already in good hands.'

'Did he look at it…examine it?'

'Yes, he opened it and read it.'

'Well, what did he say?' I said, just with a hint of impatience.

'He just said "interesting".'

'So he must have noticed something about it that formed some sort of clue,' I said hopefully and with some excitement.

'You are running ahead of yourself, Francisca,' said Inés, pulling me back to reality.

'I agree with Inés,' said Baltasar. 'They've now got the letter. It's up to them to make of it what they will.'

'So tell us, Baltasar, how did the trip go? Must have been fairly straightforward otherwise you wouldn't have got back in three days!' said Inés.

'It wasn't straightforward at all. To start with, I felt sure I was being followed by some riders as I got near Madrid. I kicked Caesar into a

193

gallop and shook them off. So I was certain that other people wanted that letter. I'm sorry to have to tell you, Francisca, that whoever wanted it had been into your house and ransacked it.'

Baltasar gave me a detailed account of what he saw. I cried waves of tears. I was utterly distraught. I could picture my treasured possessions scattered and broken on the floor. Juan and I and Juan junior had accumulated many objects of great sentimentality over the years we were together and the thought that some intruder had even touched them filled me with despondency and loathing. The thought that some were broken was unbearable.

'What about Juan's harp?' I said, through my tears.

'The harp is fine and still in its place in the drawing room.'

'Thank God for that. If that had been damaged I would have been even more upset. What am I to do? I must go back to put the house in order.' I cried again.

'Francisca, nothing is wrong that cannot be put right over time. Your place is here, being part of this investigation. The English professor and his wife are coming soon and you must meet them. Apart from that, Pedro has started to look at the case papers. If anyone should go, it should be me. But until the brotherhood have caught this so called Sancho Mojaro, I'm staying here with you. Is that understood? We can help you put the house in order when we are all back in Madrid.'

Inés's kind and helpful words, practical as ever, pulled me out of my misery and settled me.

'I think you are right, Inés. I'll stay here. One thing that puzzles me is how did these people get in? You used the key. Was there any sign of being broken into?'

'No. That surprised me, Francisca. The doors and windows were all intact. All I can think is that they must have had a skeleton key. But I haven't told you the rest of the story yet!'

194

He went on to tell us about being driven off the road at gunpoint and shooting dead the man who had demanded he hand over the letter.

'So it was kill or be killed?' said Inés.

'Exactly. I had no choice but to shoot him,' said Baltasar, looking down at the floor in shame. 'I still feel bad about it. I've never really hurt anyone before, let alone kill someone.'

He told us about Sergeant Ortiz's reaction over the killing.

'That must have made you feel better,' said Inés.

'Up to a point,' said Baltasar. 'Enough of me, what have you been doing while I've been away? Have you made any progress?'

Inés explained that we had been to see Pedro and that he had started to look at the case papers. She said he would call in here if he found anything important.

By then we had all but finished our dinner and were ready for our beds. It was such a relief that Baltasar had returned safely with the letter. I would be forever in his debt.

***

At breakfast the following morning we made another important decision. Baltasar volunteered to go back to Madrid to sort out my house. At first Inés and I were reluctant. We thought that, while Sancho Mojara was still at large, there was a danger that I could be kidnapped again. We soon concluded that Baltasar should return, especially since he had not reported to the palace for a few days, but that, assuming he was not needed there, he would return to Alcalá, once he had put my house in reasonable order.

'So we are wishing you farewell, once again, Baltasar. I just hope you are in no danger this time,' said Inés.

'I shall carry my gun and it's loaded,' he said. 'Those who wanted the letter and failed to get it from me must know by now that the brotherhood have it. I can't see any reason now for them bothering me.'

'Let's hope you are right,' I said.

Baltasar climbed on Caesar and having both kissed him, we waved him off.

Chapter 15

'There is nothing much we can do today,' said Inés, 'other than to sit here and wait for something to happen. Let's get out into the town again and see something interesting.'

I took Inés to visit the two convents, the Convent of Santa Catalina of Sienna and the Convent of the Agustinas, which I had been to on the day of my kidnapping. We were lucky to meet the kind nun who had shown me around the palatial Convent of Santa Catalina of Sienna. I was quite surprised that Inés enjoyed these buildings and their occupants so much. At about two in the afternoon, we arrived back at The Mad Astronomer to be greeted by a smiling Gonzalo.

'Señoras, there is a gentleman waiting to see you in the drinking area. He is sitting at a table by the window. He's been here for about an hour. I told him you were sure to be back soon.'

We went into the room to see an excited looking Pedro staring in our direction.

'Francisca and Inés! I promised you I would come here, if I had anything important to report and I have. Come and sit here and I'll tell you what I've found.'

Pedro hugged me and kissed me on both cheeks as Inés looked on. Surely, she wasn't jealous. He must have noticed her unhappy face so he then kissed her. We made ourselves comfortable at the table.

'Go on then,' said Inés, impatiently.

'I have now read most of the case papers on Juan junior. There are some other papers among them. They show there were two other cases of probable murder… a year after Juan junior died. The brotherhood investigated but never solved them. One was another student and the other was a member of the university staff. A junior lecturer in the law department, in fact. Each died in suspicious circumstances. I imagine that's why there are papers on the other two in the papers on Juan.'

'That definitely points to Juan being murdered rather than suicide,' I said, feeling elated. I could feel my heart beat faster at this exciting news. I also sympathised for the victims and their families. I hoped none of them had been through what I had suffered as a consequence of Juan junior's death.

'I agree,' said Pedro. 'But there are still things I don't understand. You didn't mention these other deaths so presumably you didn't know about them.'

'Not at all,' I said, 'and no one we've spoken to knows about them either. If they were part of the history of Juan's death, I'm sure the students we met the first time we went to the law department would have told us.'

'What do we do about it?' said Inés.

'I think we should tell the brotherhood, don't you, Pedro,' I said.

'Yes, that was what I was going to suggest. It's all part of your kidnapping, Francisca. And we don't know what Sergeant Ortiz knows about Juan junior's case because it all happened so long ago.'

'Let's go now,' I said. 'Let's get our coats.'

***

Sergeant Ortiz was a native of Ávila and moved with his family to Alcalá to be near his aging mother-in-law. For a Spaniard he was tall, five or six *pulgadas* above average, and quite a slim individual, clean shaven, smartly dressed and with his hair in a braid. He used to work for the Holy Brotherhood in Ávila so did not find it difficult to transfer to the one here, some ten years before.

He paced around his office for a few moments, as he generally did when deep in thought. He then sat back down again, pulled open a desk drawer and gently lifted out the file containing the letter to Francisca. He read it again:

'Señora de Abaunza, if you know what is good for you, you and your friend will pack your bags, mount your horses and return to Madrid. You are not welcomed here.'

Were there any clues in the text itself? It was a veiled, not a direct threat. The obvious implication was that something bad would happen to the señora, as indeed it had, if she and her friend didn't go back to Madrid. Perhaps the threat had not yet passed, despite her courageous escape. Whoever wrote it knew about the horses, so presumably knew they had ridden here. He or she knew there were two of them. He needed to question the señora again. He'd tell Mateo that he was going to see her now. He glanced down again at the letter. The handwriting looked odd. Had he seen it before somewhere?

***

Inés, Pedro and I were about to leave The Mad Astronomer and walk to the Office of the Brotherhood. Pedro opened the door only to be confronted by a face, not familiar to him, but well known to us. Sergeant Ortiz was about to enter the inn.

'What an interesting coincidence, Sergeant Ortiz. We were just about to go to see you!' I said.

'Quite amazing! We need to talk, Senõra de Abaunza. I'd prefer to use a private room. Is there one here, other than a bedroom?'

'I'll ask Gonzalo.'

The puzzled innkeeper let us around the back of the inn to a meeting room on the ground floor. All four of us went in and Pedro closed the door.

'Allow me to introduce you to Pedro Lobos de Pamplona,' I said. 'He is a lecturer in mathematics and is helping us investigate my son's death. He has some information you may find interesting.'

Pedro and Sergeant Ortiz shook hands. Pedro smiled generously but Sergeant Ortiz looked suspicious.

'May I start by asking you a few questions, señora? Señor Lobos de Pamplona and your friend may stay, if they wish.'

They welcomed the opportunity to stay and we all sat on the hard wooden chairs which we arranged in a circle. I didn't know what to make of this visit by Sergeant Ortiz but felt quite confident about dealing with this individual who seemed thorough and conscientious.

'I'm trying to resolve the problem of the letter: who wrote it? So I need information from you. It seems obvious but I am going to assume that it was someone who knew about your mission and knew you were here. When did you arrive here?'

'About a month ago. We can get the exact date from Gonzalo who will have a record of when he let the room.'

'We'll do that,' said Sergeant Ortiz. 'How long after that did you receive the letter?'

'The day after we arrived here. Late in the afternoon.'

'Exactly how did it get into your hands?'

'A lady on the reception desk gave it to me when Inés and I arrived back here from visiting some of the departments that my son attended at the university.'

'I don't suppose she told you when it arrived here and by whom it was delivered?'

'No.'

'I'll ask her. So tell me who you told about why you were here, in the order you told them.'

'On our first day we spoke to Gonzalo but I don't remember telling him why we were here. Then we went to the College of the King, just across the road from here, to look for the professor of law, the head of department. From meeting the friendly janitor, we joined in with a group of law students, celebrating the award of their degrees. They invited us for a drink and some food. We accepted and they told us where the head of department's office was. So we went there and it was closed so we went back and passed the students. We told them why we were here. In fact, there were three or four of them we spoke to about Juan. They said his death was part of the dark history of their department. We then came back here, had a meal and retired to bed. That's right isn't it, Inés?'

'Yes, as clear as I remember it.'

'The following day we went to the various colleges to see the professors. Again, we started with law. We explained to the professor's secretary why we were there and he went in the professor's office to arrange a meeting. The professor didn't want to or couldn't see us then so the secretary told us to come back at eleven in the morning on the Tuesday, which was one day later, almost to the hour.'

'So you saw him at about eleven, then?'

'About then,' I said.

'Then what?'

'We went to the Department of Astronomy, which is in natural sciences. We spoke to some students there about my son's death and then to the professor, Professor Lorenzo Ramos. We explained to him why we were there.'

'About what time was that?'

'About eleven thirty, I'd say, don't you think, Inés?'

201

'Yes, about then,' said Inés, seriously. In the meantime, Pedro just sat and looked on.

'Where then?'

'We went to the Department of Mathematics, which was closed and empty. Not a soul in sight. Outside we met an older man, actually about my age. He came to see his son Pedro. He introduced himself as Manuel Lobos de Pamplona. He is Pedro here's father.'

'Interesting coincidence,' said Sergeant Ortiz, serious faced and concentrating on what I said and analysing it carefully. 'What did you do next?'

Inés and I explained that we walked to the Iglesia Majestral and looked inside, and met Pedro Lobos de Pamplona there.

'How did you know it was him?'

'After we spoke to Señor Lobos de Pamplona, we walked to the cathedral because Francisca wanted to show me inside. We were surprised to find a service going on there. A priest came up to us and asked if we'd like to join the singing. He told us it was a thanksgiving by the mathematics department to show gratitude for their examination results. We asked him if a certain Pedro Lobos de Pamplona happened to be there. He explained that he was the faculty priest, so knew everyone in the department and that Pedro was in the cathedral. So that's how we met him! Right, Pedro?'

'Exactly!'

'What I don't understand is why Pedro is helping you look into your son's death. Why is he doing that?'

Not to be excluded from this discussion, Pedro answered for himself. 'When Francisca and Inés came to see my professor, Gregorio Estrada, to ask him about the death of Juan junior, Francisca's son, he first was unable to say that anyone with the name Juan Hidalgo de

Polanco had studied at the department so the two of them left disappointed. Francisca was certain that her son had studied there and returned a week or so later to confront the professor. He investigated further and confirmed that he had attended the mathematics department. He also offered my services to help in the investigation. I was delighted to be able to help these two charming ladies whom I had already met in the cathedral.'

'When I came in, you said you had something interesting to tell me. Is that so? And if so, what is it?' said Sergeant Ortiz bluntly, curling up his eyebrows in a frown, as if to disapprove of Pedro.

Pedro must have noticed his expression but paid no attention to it. 'Yes. What you may not know is that I have the case papers on the original brotherhood investigation into Juan junior's death. Studying them in some detail was part of my helping Francisca and Inés. What I've found among them are some papers relating to two other mysterious deaths, which occurred about a year after Juan junior died.'

'I'm not aware of these,' said Sergeant Ortiz. 'Mind you, I haven't been in the Alcalá brotherhood for that long. Were there any indications as to the causes of these deaths and who were the victims?'

'One was a junior lecturer in the law department. The other a student. I can't remember their names but they are spelt out in the file.'

'Apart from asking the señora the questions about whom she met, I was going to ask her for the report of the investigation on her son's death.'

'Obviously, I still have it, but I can get it for you. Now if you wish.'

'If you can bring it to my office tomorrow, preferably in the morning, that will be fine,' said Sergeant Ortiz, again looking disdainfully at Pedro.

'I'll be there by nine o'clock.'

Sergeant Ortiz had no more questions for us so thanked us all for the information we had given him, bid us all farewell and went, presumably via the reception desk to ask about the delivery of the anonymous letter. He said he would let us know how his investigation was progressing and tell us as soon as any important new facts emerged.

We three stayed in the meeting room to discuss our respective thoughts. We were surprised by the coincidence of Sergeant Ortiz's visit when we were about to visit the brotherhood. We wondered how long it would be before he would find the so called Sancho Mojaro and charge him with my abduction. We all felt confident with Sergeant Ortiz and that he would solve the mystery. Pedro had detected Sergeant Ortiz's unexpected attitude towards him but brushed it to one side. Sergeant Ortiz would, it seemed, be also looking at the case papers on Juan junior so who knew what new contribution he would make to that case, too? Then Pedro surprised both me and Inés.

'Francisca, I would like to invite you to my home for dinner tonight. If you agree, I'll meet you in reception here at, say, six o'clock by the church chimes.'

I didn't know what to say at first, I was so shocked. I could feel my face redden as I blushed! It's true that I harboured an attraction for this likeable, young and attractive man but could not see what he could see in me, a woman some thirty years, at least, older than him. But I also remember the tight and prolonged hug he gave me when Inés took me to his office to see him after I had escaped my kidnappers.

'Well, Pedro, that is so kind of you. I feel a bit awkward about the idea because I usually dine with Inés.'

'You go, Francisca. It will do us both good to have a change. Go and enjoy Pedro's company for the evening,' Inés said, responding with such selfless generosity.

'In which case, I accept your kind invitation,' I said. 'We'll meet in the reception area at six o'clock.'

'I'll go now,' said Pedro. 'There is much preparation to do!'

'That shocked you, didn't it,' said Inés, just after Pedro had closed the meeting room door behind him and presuming he was not listening outside. 'I said he had strong feelings towards you, Francisca.'

'I don't understand it. How can a young man in his thirties or early forties be attracted to an old lady like me?'

'The fact is, Francisca, you have a lovely personality and for a lady of your years are still good looking. You have a young attitude to life and a lot of men like that.'

'You are too kind, Inés! I don't believe a word of it! But it's good to hear and gives me confidence to enjoy the evening with Pedro.'

'Make the most of it, Francisca. You never know where it will lead!' she said, with a cheeky wink.

***

True to his word, Pedro met me at exactly six o'clock. He was wearing a heavy black overcoat that reached almost to the ground and a very wide, even brimmed, dark brown hat. His smile enveloped his whole face as his eyes met mine. I could feel a quiver of excitement pass through my whole body. He took off his hat to give me an affectionate hug and kissed me on both cheeks.

'I hope you don't mind a fairly long walk, Francisca…or should I ask Gonzalo to arrange a carriage?'

'Where do you live, then?'

'In the town, in the Calle Merced.'

'I don't know it.'

'It's not far from the Convent of Santa Catalina of Sienna which is where you took Inés this morning. Correct? And the Convent of the

Mercedarios Descalzos is in the street and opposite my house. Luckily, I'm on the sunny side of the street so it doesn't block out the sun!'

'I can walk it easily, Pedro, as long as you don't walk too fast!'

We walked there arm-in-arm, just like a mother being escorted by her young son. Pedro suggested linking this way so 'if he walked too fast, I could slow him down'. It couldn't have taken more than twenty minutes to arrive at Pedro's ornate front door. It was painted bright blue and a bell shaped, brass door knocker hung at its centre. The house looked cheerfully bright in its white wash and even in the fading autumn light seemed to attract me in. It was larger than I had imagined with a large double window on each side of the front door and, in the upper floor, a row of three windows, which looked down on the narrow street below. Substantial enough for a university lecturer who lived alone.

'What a lovely looking house,' I said, as Pedro unlocked the door.

'Yes, I am very pleased with it,' he said, putting out his arm to invite me to go in.

As I stepped over the threshold I was greeted by the delightful aromas of a hotpot or stew, gently cooking over a distant stove.

'So, the meal smells good… and as if it's well under control, Pedro!'

'Yes, it is a venison stew. Tell me if you don't like it. I also have some fresh vegetables and I can cook you a lamb chop if you prefer.'

'No, I love venison, Pedro. Sometimes my Juan and I used to have venison, after the king had been out hunting. Venison or boar… only if the hunt had been too successful and the palace kitchen couldn't cope with all the fresh meat!'

'That's marvellous, Francisca. Here…let me take your coat.'

I suddenly had that feeling of fear that occurs when what you are experiencing reminds you of something horrific that happened in the past, the more recent in the past, the stronger the fear. As Pedro uttered these words, I was reminded of Sancho Mojaro inviting me to dinner with that woman in Calle Ramon. I shuddered to a halt, frozen in my tracks.

'What's the matter, Francisca? You suddenly look pale.'

I told Pedro exactly what I was feeling and why.

'You have nothing to fear from me, Francisca, except my affection for you. You are a lovely woman and I am very fond of you. Please let me lead you into the drawing room. Come in and sit on a sofa.'

He took me along the hall into this beautifully furnished room. Unlike the hall, where the wooden floor glistened with the efforts of its polisher, a lightly patterned beige carpet completely covered the floor. A large two seated sofa stood against the wall furthest from the fireplace, next to the wall upon which hung a painting of a scene from a sea battle. Towards the centre of the room, stood two matching sofas, like two crouching seraphs, each facing and paying homage to the other. I sat in one of the sofas and Pedro sat in the other.

'Are you more settled now, Francisca?' he said, his eyes wide open and concerned.

'Yes, Pedro, indeed I am. It was one of those temporary moments which are soon overcome.'

'I'm so glad. I don't want you to feel uncomfortable here. Quite the opposite! Anyway, tell me a bit about yourself... Oh, spare me a moment while I check on the venison!' He stood and dashed out of the room only to return a minute or so later.

'It's fine. Almost ready. Shall we go into the kitchen and we can continue talking, as I cook the vegetables.'

The kitchen was a picture of order, just what you would expect from a mathematician. It reminded me of the kitchen in my house with a row of pots and pans suspended over a large, wood-fired stove. Pedro was cooking the venison in a pot so large, it appeared that he could feed a dozen, not just us two. He poured some water into a bowl and washed some tomatoes and some beans before putting them in pans on the hot stove.

'So tell me more about yourself, Francisca,' he smiled with curiosity. 'When we had dinner at The Mad Astronomer, we hardly had a chance to say anything about ourselves and it's now time we did!'

'I suppose you want me to start, as you are doing the cooking.'

'Correct, Francisca!'

'Where should I start? I'm sixty nine and you won't want an account of my whole life!'

'No, but just tell me what you want to! We can do this in stages. Not all at once!'

I told him about my family's move to Madrid after my father's business in Viscaya collapsed and how I met Juan my husband while the court painter, Diego Velázquez painted my portrait which he called, 'The Lady with a Fan'. I told him about Juan's incredible skills as a harpist and that he played for the king, nearly every day and how he became the Maestro of the court musicians; about the operas that Juan and Calderón de la Barca wrote, Juan the music and de la Barca the words.

'Could I stop there so you can tell me about yourself?'

He had just served the meal onto plates he had heated on the stove.

'I've set our places at the dining table, Francisca. Here's a cloth to hold the plate. Be careful, it's hot! You take yours and I'll take mine. Follow me!'

He led us into the most sumptuous dining room I had ever seen. A linen table cloth almost completely covered an oval, mahogany table decorated with a delicately contrasting inlay, probably in ash. Its legs were curved and supported the table from the middle. It could comfortably seat eight. It sat on a patterned Turkish carpet with the closest possible weave.

'This carpet is so beautiful, I feel I shouldn't walk on it!'

'Don't worry, it's been made to be walked on. Thank you, though, for appreciating it!'

We sat at the table, Pedro at the head and I next to him.

'The wine! I've forgotten the wine!' I was taken by surprise by his loud exclamation. Then he disappeared into the kitchen again, only to return with two large glasses and a bottle of *jumilla*.

'How did you know I liked *jumilla*?'

'I didn't but I like it myself. It's good that you like it, too!'

We started to eat the tasty looking meal that Pedro had prepared.

'What about you then, Pedro. Tell me about yourself!'

'I have been very lucky in my life but it's had its tragedies. My mother died when I was twelve and I was brought up by my father whom you met. We lived in Córdoba. We are converts from Islam to Christianity. It was the conversion which killed my mother. She just couldn't leave Islam. She died of a form of insanity which stopped her from eating. She starved to death and none of us could do anything about it. My sister is ten years older than me and is married to a lawyer. They live in Aranda de Duero.'

'Aranda? It's so small. Is there enough work for him?'

'Plenty. You'd be surprised. We moved to Alcalá when I was fifteen, just father and me. We lived together until I became a lecturer. Then I decided I'd like my own house. He was a banker in Córdoba and made a lot of money, mainly from usury, but not at illegal rates. So he gave me enough to buy this house and gave my sister and her husband the same amount exactly, just as any fair parent would. He loves his independence and I have to say, I value mine, too. I find it quite a strain sharing a house with him. But I won't elaborate on that. So here I am, a lecturer at the university.'

'So what do you do in that job other than teach?'

'I'll tell you but only after you've told me more about your life. I'm fascinated by what you've said so far. I think I've heard of your husband the composer. He was very famous! You must be very proud of him. Did he write the music for Diamante's Alpheus and Arethusa? I heard about the scandalous performance when Arethusa stripped off naked in front of the king! Everyone was talking about it for days!'

'Don't remind me! We all thought we'd have to appear before the Inquisition over that. But we never heard a word from them, much to our relief!'

'So more about you, please, Francisca!'

I told him more about Juan junior and his unexpected death, what effect it had on Juan and me, especially on my health. I told him about my stay in the asylum in the Casa de la Misericordia, about Inés's dream about how the light from the medal the Pope presented to her grandfather, Diego Velázquez, was going to bring me back to normality. And how, the very next, day it did.

'You have had a very interesting life so far, Francisca. As I've said before, I am very sorry about the death of Juan junior. I feel certain that some way or another we will solve the puzzle.'

By then we had finished the delightful meal that Pedro had prepared and were just sitting at the table talking.

'Would you like to see the rest of my house? I'd enjoy giving you a guided tour!'

'I'd love to, Pedro,' I said. We walked across the hall into the room opposite.

'This is the library and my study.'

It was the most elegant room with the same coloured carpet as in the drawing room, again completely covering the floor. His large mahogany desk, inlaid with gold embossed red leather, and with and matching swivel, red leather chair, faced the window. The most striking feature was the sheer number of books, carefully ordered and apparently catalogued, which lined the whole of the other three walls, right up to the ceiling.

'What an incredible library!' I said, truly astonished by the number of individual volumes. There must have been more than two thousand.

Yes, I am a bibliophile. I collect them. I've spent hundreds of *ducats* on them… and over the years I read nearly all of them. They are arranged in subjects but I've not labelled the shelves, just put these spacers between the topics.'

'That's one of the largest books I've ever seen,' I said, pointing to a colossal volume near the centre of the back wall.

'You've spotted an incredibly important book. It's called "New Astronomy" for short! Its actual title is longer but I can never get it right! It was written by an astronomer and mathematician called Johannes Kepler who was German and published it about seventy five years ago. It's about the motion of the planets around the sun. And, you could not know that my research is on the same topic. We in the mathematics department are working with the astronomers on it!'

'I'm amazed, Pedro. I remember Juan junior talking about understanding the motion of the planets and how mathematical it is.'

'I can explain it to you, if you wish! Maybe next time!'

211

A 'next time'! That was a good indication that we were getting on well. 'So you must know Professor Lorenzo Ramos, head of the department.'

'Yes, very well. He is one of my collaborators. He is as good at the mathematics as he is at the astronomy. And some of his graduate students are working with us, too.'

'Do you know a Professor Alan McDonnell, from a university in England? He is coming over with his wife and will be here very soon. I am to meet him because he probably taught Juan.'

'You know more about these people than I do, Francisca! Yes, I know Professor McDonnell. He is another of our collaborators. We will be discussing and exchanging our results when he is here. The English are well known for their work in this field. A scientist called Isaac Newton is writing a book that will revolutionize our understanding of gravity. This is the force which the sun exerts on the planets and holds us to the ground! Anyway, let me show you upstairs.'

I followed him up the sumptuous staircase. The banister was of oak and the stairs were laid in a rich red, plain but deep piled carpet, fit for a palace.

'This is my bedroom. It is one of four. My father often stays in that one,' he said, pointing to the one diagonally across the wide landing. He stepped in.

'So you sleep in a double bed!'

'Why not? I can spread out and take as much room as I want.'

I was sorely tempted to climb onto his bed but while I deeply wanted this handsome young man, I didn't want to make any moves that betrayed my true feelings for him. This was, after all, our first encounter in his house and he indicated a second invitation, only moments before. Then quite unexpectedly, he kicked off his shoes and jumped, like a tickled grasshopper, up onto the bed himself.

'See, Francisca, plenty of room for me!'

'I'm not sure what you are expecting me to do now,' I said, half smiling and saying exactly what I thought. Was this a prelude to our making love?

'Whatever you wish, Francisca. You can jump on with me if you wish or stay where you are. I promise I'll not press you into anything you don't wish to do. I just want you to feel comfortable with me and to trust me.'

I leant over the bed and planted a kiss on his lips. It was purely spontaneous and I still don't know why I did it.

'There, Pedro. Not quite a kiss goodnight!' I decided to take the lead. 'Now show me the other rooms up here!'

He flipped his legs around to the floor, put his shoes back on and showed me the other three bedrooms. They were so elegantly furnished I could hardly believe their beauty was conceived by a man, let alone a lecturer and mathematician. Back down stairs we returned to the drawing room.

'Perhaps it's time I went back to The Mad Astronomer, Pedro,' I said, feeling that I did not wish to inflict myself much longer on this generous man's hospitality.

'Let me escort you back, Francisca. It has been such a pleasure for me to entertain you, and especially to cook you a meal! And we know so much more about each other now. Please come here again, maybe in a few days' time? We won't arrange a date just yet.'

Pedro gave me one of classic hugs before he left me in the reception area of the inn. I don't know what the lady behind the desk made of it, but her eyes almost jumped from their sockets at the sight of us. With slightly raised eyebrows, she gave me a lit candle in a holder so I could safely see my way upstairs to my room. As I was about to unlock the door, I was surprised to hear Inés say goodnight to a man she was letting

213

out of her room. I hesitated so I could see him at closer range. It was none other than Professor Gregorio Estrada, the head of the mathematics department and Pedro's boss. I couldn't believe my eyes. I wondered whether to knock on her door to ask her about her meeting the professor. What was that about? Or should I leave it to the morning? I decided on the latter.

Chapter 16

'How did your meal go last night?' said Inés, as we met for breakfast at our usual table.

'Very well. He is such a nice man. I didn't realise that my feelings for him were so strong. He owns the most beautiful house, down at the southwest corner of the town in the Calle Merced, right opposite the Convent of the Mercedarios Descalzos.'

'Would I know it, Francisca?'

'Probably not. It's not far from the Convent of Santa Catalina of Sienna which we visited yesterday morning, remember?'

'Of course, those lovely nuns, living in a palace!'

'Well, Pedro's house is also like a palace.' I told her about the sumptuous furnishings in the drawing room, the huge library of books and the one I picked out that led him to tell me about his collaborators in the astronomy department. I told her he knew Professor Alan McDonnell and that he knew he was on his way from England to Alcalá.

You picked the right book, Francisca, by the sound of it.'

'Pure luck! He must have two thousand and more!'

I told her about the after dinner tour he gave me of the rest of the house, including showing me his bedroom.

'So you went into his bedroom, Francisca? You didn't... did you?'

'I didn't know what to do, Inés. He jumped onto the bed and looked up at me. It was a thought game. I think I could read his thoughts. He could read mine. He wanted to, I'm sure. Even though I'm a wrinkled old lady. And to be honest, so did I but I couldn't quite yield myself, not then and there. I don't know why, either way. No harm could have come of it. He couldn't make me pregnant at my age, so it might have done us both good. Maybe it was the thought of Juan, my beloved Juan. But I can't remember consciously thinking of Juan, not at that moment. So I leant over and kissed him on the lips but nothing else happened. But he did say we should meet for dinner again in a few days, but we didn't fix a date.'

'So you got quite close, my dear friend. And you are far from being a wrinkled old lady! You should have given in!' Was she feeling guilt at giving in to Professor Estrada, I thought, and hoping we might have shared the guilt of our actions?

'So what about you, Inés? Did you have a pleasant evening?' I wondered if she would admit to the professor being in her room or whether I would have to tease it out of her.

'Yes, I had a very nice meal, actually. After it, I went and sat in the drinking area for a time. Slightly to my embarrassment, apart from the lady behind the bar, the one I saw making love to Gonzalo, I was the only woman there.'

I gave her a frown, as if I knew something she wasn't telling me.

'That's an odd look, Francisca. Do you doubt what I'm saying?'

'No, not at all. Did you see anyone else you knew?' I was pleased with the question. She hesitated, not much but it was a moment before she replied.

'As a matter of fact, after I'd been there for about ten minutes, nursing a glass of wine, Professor Gregorio Estrada walked in. He recognised me immediately and walked over to the table. He said I was one of the women they were helping to investigate a death. He even remembered our names.'

'Did he buy you a drink?' I probed.

'Yes, he bought me another glass of wine. He sat with me for about half an hour, I suppose. I told him you'd gone with Pedro for dinner at his house. He really admires Pedro, you know. He was so complimentary about him. Then we talked about his work at the university. He's married but separated, you know. His situation is a bit like mine.'

'Then what?'

'I'm not sure how to put this, Francisca. He bought me another glass of wine. I felt quite merry but not drunk. He offered to take me to my room. We were both desperate to make love. As soon as we'd shut the door behind us, we each stripped off naked and jumped into my bed. Honestly, Francisca it was heaven! I have to admit, I feel quite ashamed now, now I'm sober again.'

'You should be, Inés. I just hope you're not pregnant. That's all I can say!' I saw no point in telling Inés that I recognised the professor when he left her room. He may of course have recognised me, but whether or not he would tell Inés was up to him: I gave him no clue that I knew it was him.

'I doubt it, Francisca. Unabashed as I was, I chose my time with care!'

***

'What do you make of this, Mateo,' said Sergeant Ortiz, looking at a page in the brotherhood's report on the death of Juan junior and holding the anonymous letter in his hand. It was about nine o'clock in the morning, about the same time as Inés confessed her enjoyable encounter with Professor Gregorio Estrada.

'Not sure what you're telling me, boss. What are you saying exactly?'

'See the writing on the letter. Now look at the writing on that page of the crime report.'

'By the blood of Jesus Christ! It's is the same!'

'You know what that means don't you?'

'If it is by the same person, he is or was a member of the Holy Brotherhood of Alcalá de Henares.'

'Dead right. Señor Sancho Mojaro, so called, is one of our own. He's signed his name here. He is Marcos Ribera. Do you recognise the name, Mateo?'

'I do. He retired about ten, maybe twelve years ago. I'd recognise him anywhere. He's tall and has sharp features. He's got the look of a university man which he's not. I can picture him now.'

'That explains why he convinced the señora he was trading with the universities. At least he looked the part. We need to arrest and charge him. Do you remember where he went when he retired? I think he went to Guadalajara.'

'Yes, I'm fairly sure. We must have his address as we will be paying him a pension.'

'Go there and arrest him, Mateo. Take some back-up.'

Mateo left Sergeant Ortiz at his desk, his brow furrowed in thought. It was obvious why this Marcos Ribera wanted to recover the letter. He was afraid that it would identify him as the kidnapper and possibly more. According to Baltasar, others were involved in trying to secure the letter's recovery. He detected some kind of complex conspiracy. But what was it about and why? It was even clearer that the death of Juan Hidalgo junior was neither an accident nor suicide. He had been murdered for some reason. He would find out by whom and why. He should tell the two women what he had discovered. He'd go now to The Mad Astronomer.

***

We were still chatting in the breakfast room when Gonzalo appeared. We couldn't agree what to do for the day and were in no rush to leave the room.

'Here is a letter for you, Señora Martínez del Mazo,' Gonzalo said, handing Inés a roughly sealed envelope. She recognised the writing as Baltasar's.

'I wonder what this is about,' she said, impatiently breaking the seal and opening it.

'Oh! He's on his way back to Alcalá. Hopes to be back tomorrow. Says he's done as much as he can to your house and that some of our family have helped him.'

'I can't say how grateful I am. He is so kind, Inés.'

'He must be on his way by now. Please don't tell him I bedded Estrada will you, Francisca.'

'Your secret is safe with me, Inés! Well, it's not exactly a secret, now you've told me!' We both laughed.

About twenty minutes later Gonzalo appeared again, this time escorting Sergeant Ortiz.

'I have some interesting news for you, señores. We are fairly certain we have identified the author of the anonymous letter. My colleague Mateo is going to arrest him.'

'Wonderful news, Sergeant. I feel safer already! Brilliant. You say Officer Lopez is going to arrest him. Where is he then, not in Alcalá?' I could have cried with relief. At least they knew that the man existed and that I was telling them the truth.

'No, but not far away, in Guadalajara. We will need you to confirm his identity once we have arrested him. We will ask you to pick him out from a line of men whom we will choose to look quite similar.'

'Very good news!' said Inés. 'I'm as thrilled as Francisca.'

'I'll let you know as soon as he's in our custody. Good bye for now.'

He left us staring at each other in disbelief. Inés came around to my side of the table and kissed me.

'We are nearly there, Francisca. We are going to solve Juan junior's case and your abduction!'

**

True to his word, Pedro invited me to dinner again, just two nights after we had dined together before. I detected his growing interest in me, which I found quite flattering and complementing to my increasing affection for him. Were we falling in love? Surely, he could not contemplate spending his life with a woman some thirty or more years older than him. Was he regarding me as a substitute for the mother he lost when he was twelve? The only way to find out was to follow his initiative and have dinner with him again. As before we agreed to meet in the reception area and we walked arm-in-arm to his gorgeous house.

'I have something different for you tonight, Francisca. Do you like fish?' he said, just as we entered the hall.

'I love it!'

'I bought a couple of hake fillets in the market this morning. I have a recipe for a chives and cream sauce that goes with them so well. And a bean salad.'

'It sounds perfect to me. I have some news for you which I didn't want to mention in the street, or in the hotel.'

'Well?'

The brotherhood have identified my abductor! They have gone to Guadalajara to arrest him,' I said, smiling with all of my face.

'I am thrilled, Francisca! I've been so concerned for your safety, even though Inés is with you again now.' He gave me a characteristic Pedro hug which lasted even longer than usual.

'Enough of this,' he said, disengaging. 'I must go into the kitchen or we'll not be eating tonight.' I followed him.

With a dexterity which surprised me, he skinned the hake fillets with a knife as sharp as a warrior's sword and put them into a pan to fry, adding a little olive oil and swirling them in it, so as to wet the underside.

'If you take over cooking the fish, Francisca, I'll prepare the cream and chives. It's cold tonight, so I've changed my mind about a salad. We'll fry some tomatoes and boil up some asparagus.'

Within fifteen minutes we were sitting at a curved end of the mahogany dining table, tucking into a tasty meal, jointly prepared. Then I asked him a question.

'Next time we dine here together, would you like me to prepare the meal? I'm almost as good a cook as you, Pedro.'

We both laughed at my question.

'Francisca, I would be utterly delighted. Just tell me what you want to cook and I'll buy the ingredients at the market. How about the night after next. I would suggest tomorrow but I'm giving a late tutorial and won't be finishing before nine o'clock. What are we going to talk about tonight?'

'Tell me more about your life in Córdoba,' I said, taking a sip of a white *rioja* he had poured and not quite knowing how he would respond.

'Córdoba was difficult. I told you about my mother. Very sad and it had a deep effect on me as a young boy. I loved her intensely because she was so gentle and kind to me and my older sister. I got on well with my father but there was always a kind of remoteness about him and he didn't like being challenged about anything, not by any of us. But he made a lot of money for a *mudejar* and kept us all in better conditions than most people enjoyed. Apart from mother's passing, the worst time was at school. The children were mainly born Christian so they bullied and generally harassed us *mujedars*. I hated it and focussed all my energies on learning as much as I could. Enough to come here to university. What about you, Francisca? Your early years?'

'Like you, my mother died when I was young, when I was sixteen. My father was utterly distraught. I don't know why but he found a priest to help me through my grief. I went to see him the first time and he did help, through prayer and reading from the Bible. We also sang hymns together. But the second time I saw him, he attempted to rape me. He didn't succeed. As he was about to enter me, I squeezed his testicles as hard as I could and twisted them round. He was in agony and had to let me go. I was still afraid so hit him on the head with a candelabrum. He collapsed on the floor and I thought I'd killed him but I hadn't. I can laugh about it now but it put me off men for a long time.'

'You must have recovered well, Francisca. Marrying and becoming a mother and I'm sure a wonderful one at that!'

'You flatter me, Pedro! But I enjoyed being a wife and mother!'

We continued in this vein for a full hour, telling each other about events in our respective lives, concentrating on the embarrassing and funny things from our past. I told him about some of the strange characters I used to serve at the Shod Carmelite soup kitchen and how I had to keep them from coming back for more helpings than they deserved. He told me about some of the errors he had made in his lectures which much amused his students. Then towards the end of this session, he posed an interesting question.

'Well, Francisca. Where do we go from here? You are an attractive woman and I am a single man. What do you think? How shall we spend the rest of the evening? I am in your hands entirely.'

222

I felt sure he was inviting some intimate physical contact. I remembered what Inés had said at breakfast the day before.

'Do you want me to be totally honest, Pedro?'

'Of course, and I don't want to go anywhere you'd prefer to stay away from.'

'Right. I'd like to revisit your bedroom. I want to make love to you.' To this day, I don't know how I came out with such an open display of need, for need it was. I really wanted this man. Whether it was love or just desire did not concern me but I seriously and urgently wanted him.

'Francisca, you have caught me unawares. I would like to make love to you, too. I promise I'll be gentle with you and we'll take our time. Shall we clear away the dinner things or would you prefer to go up now?'

'Let's go now. While I am so ready.'

'Let me lead the way, Francisca.'

We got up from the table, pushed our chairs back under it, picked up a lighted candle each from the sideboard and climbed up the stairs. He held the door of the bedroom open so I went in first. I made my way to the bed and lay on it, looking up at him. He joined me and we kissed and caressed each other. It was bliss for me and, from the yearning in his eyes, it pleasured him just as much. Whether he had made love to others before me was of no concern. We were in each other's arms and that was all that mattered. We caressed each other for a full ten minutes. Then he spoke.

'Shall we take our clothes off or keep them on, Francisca. Maybe you keep yours on, and I'll take off my pantaloons. Does that sound all right? I don't want to put my weight on you so I'll be behind you?'

'That sounds perfect, Pedro,' I smiled. I faced the window and lifted the back of my skirt. 'Am I in the right position, Pedro?'

'Exactly. I'm ready now!'

I could feel him youthfully and repeatedly pushing and prodding but he couldn't enter.

'I'm sorry, Francisca, but she doesn't want to take me in! I'm not sure what to do! I'm really afraid of hurting you.'

'I know just the solution! Go downstairs and bring up a little olive oil. That will make it easier for both of us.'

I stayed on the bed in the same position and relaxed while Pedro went quickly and, I imagined half naked, down the stairs. He soon returned.

'Here we are... an egg cup, half full and a small towel.'

'You think of everything, Pedro,' I said, still facing the window and away from him.

'Do you want to do it or shall I?'

'We both will. I'll help as best I can while you work in the oil with your fingers... Oh, it's cold!' I yelped.

'I'm sorry. I'll let it warm up in the palm of my hand for a moment.'

'That's better. You are being too gentle, Pedro. Push hard with your wet finger. It hasn't been used for a long time! I think you are making progress now,' I said, while doing my best to help him.

It was a nice sensation to have this man working on me. I wanted it to last but at the same time I wanted him to succeed.

'I think you are there now, Pedro. What do you think? Don't be afraid to go right inside!'

'Yes, I think that will be fine now. I'll just wipe you to take away the excess. You are beautiful there, Francisca.'

'What about the rest of me. You haven't mentioned that!'

'You are a beautiful woman, especially for your age. Your skin is smooth and pliable. It's a delight to look into your eyes.'

'Enough of that! Too much flattery isn't good for anyone! Put the egg cup on the side and we'll test out your efforts!'

I could have cried at the beautiful sensation of him making gentle love to me. It must have been eight to ten years since Juan and I had indulged ourselves and by then it was only partially successful but with this potent young man it reminded me of those heady days of our youth when we made love nearly every day and sometimes more than once.

I'm not hurting you, am I, Francisca.'

'Absolutely not. I'm enjoying this quite as much as one of your fabulous meals and, dare I say it, probably even more! You are a good lover, Pedro and are so gentle and considerate. You can keep going as long as you can. Good idea to use the olive oil, eh?'

'It worked perfectly. Where did that idea come from?'

'It's an interesting and amusing story. I'll tell you after we've finished. Assuming I haven't forgotten. You are doing so well. Young man.'

'So are you, young lady. Everything is working well.'

A few minutes later, Pedro shuddered to the perfect finish. I couldn't hold back my tears of joy. I felt renewed, as if I had regained my youth. My heart pumped with an energy that it had been denied for years. My skin tingled as if I was being touched on every part of my body at once. I took a few deep breaths to compose myself.

'Thank you, Francisca, those were the most ecstatic moments of my life. You are a marvel!'

'Only with the aid of the oil!'

225

'We must do that again. If only to see if we can recapture those wonderful moments!'

'What tonight?' I jested, pulling my skirt back down and sneaking a glance at him pulling on his pantaloons.

'No! What if I came to see you at The Mad Astronomer tomorrow? I could be just a social call if Inés was there, but if she was busy we could go to your room, but only if you wanted to. I am free in the afternoon, from about one o'clock and I have to return for the tutorial.'

'You can say you came to see if there was any news from the brotherhood. I'll make sure I'm in my room at one. You can ask Gonzalo to bring you up to me! I'm sure he will oblige. He'd never think we were about to make love!'

'Agreed,' he said, leaning over the bed and planting a moist kiss on my lips. 'So what is the story of the olive oil?'

I told him about Juan's brother Francisco's exceptionally wide manhood which his Aunt Catalina caught a glance of one morning when Francisco was young. It impressed her so much she had to make love to him. So she enticed him into her bed but he couldn't make it enter her, however hard he tried. I said that Aunt Catalina went to her kitchen, brought back a jug of greenish yellow liquid which she rubbed into herself and Francisco applied to himself and that they both enjoyed the happy result.

'Amazing, Francisca. What a nice story!'

Again, the charming Pedro escorted me back to the inn and left me in the reception after an even more intimate hug than usual.

'Until tomorrow!' he whispered in my ear.

'Until then! I'll be in my room alone from about twelve o'clock!'

***

226

I thought I'd go to my room via the drinking area. I could have gone straight to the stairs but something prompted me to use the longer route. Much to my surprise, Inés was there, chatting excitedly to Baltasar. I thought he wasn't going to arrive until the following day. Something was disturbing him and I wasn't sure what. I stepped over to him and gave him a kiss on both cheeks.

'I am so grateful to you, Baltasar. You are so kind going back to sort out my house. How did you get on?'

'Your house is in good order now, except for some damage to the sofas where they cut them underneath in search of the letter. It will take a woman's hand to repair them but I'm pleased with what we've done.'

'I really appreciate it. I can't tell you how much. You look worried about something,' I said, quite concerned.

'I am. I'm sure the same men who tried to take the letter from me last time followed me back here. I just couldn't shake them off. They must know I am staying here.'

'You must tell the brotherhood. Go now.'

'I'll leave it until tomorrow. In the meantime, I've loaded my flintlock and here it is.' He glanced around the room before pointing under his jacket.

'Have you told Baltasar our news, Inés?'

She gave me that puzzled look of hers before answering. I wasn't expecting her to confess to her love session with Gregorio Estrada but maybe she thought I was. 'Oh! Yes! Sergeant Ortiz has identified Francisca's kidnapper, the so called Sancho Mojaro. His real name is Marcos Ribera and he lives in Guadalajara. He was a member of the Holy Brotherhood. Officer Mateo has gone there to arrest him.'

227

'What great news. I'm so pleased, mainly for you, Francisca, but for each of us, including me! Does this mean we are near to solving the puzzle of Juan junior's death?'

'Let's hope so,' I said, smiling and hopeful.

'Apart from me being followed, I'm going to have to return to Madrid in the next two days. There are going to be several banquets at the palace. The first is in three days' time and I have to be back for it.'

'You may need a brotherhood escort, Baltasar. You must be concerned about those men who followed you. Why are they interested in you, now that the letter in in the hands of Sergeant Ortiz. There is nothing you can give them.'

'Could be revenge. I did kill one of theirs on the way back last time. Maybe they cannot accept it was in self-defence.'

'I'm tired,' I said. I'm going to my bed now. Shall we meet at breakfast at about nine o'clock by the cathedral chimes?'

The two of them agreed, we kissed each other and I went to my room.

***

The following day started badly. As I opened the door to the dining room, I could hear Inés and Baltasar arguing loudly. They were sitting facing each other. I wondered about going back to my room and leaving them until later but Baltasar had seen me and beckoned me in. I pretended I hadn't heard them. I went over, gave each a good morning kiss and sat down between them on the adjoining side of the table.

'How are you two, today?' I said, in all innocence.

'Things are not going well between us,' Inés said. Baltasar frowned.

'What can be the matter?'

'Inés wants to come back with me to Madrid,' said Baltasar, looking angry. 'But I've told her to stay here with you, at least until this Carlos is caught and locked up. She insists that he is already in the hands of the brotherhood because they've gone to Guadalajara to get him. But the one doesn't follow the other. He may escape them. He could have been tipped off about them. Who knows until the brotherhood tell us?'

'I don't want you to stay, Inés, if you want to go back. I feel much safer now that they are arresting this Carlos man, even if they haven't yet. I can't see him trying to kidnap me again.'

'Why don't we pay a visit to Sergeant Ortiz and ask him whether they've arrested your kidnapper or not. And you can tell them about the men who followed you here, Baltasar, if you still believe they did.'

'What a nerve, Inés. Do you think I've changed my mind?' These two were still arguing, even if the subject had changed.

'Not but you did say you thought they were following you. You weren't certain.'

'Wrong. I was certain I was being followed. I was unsure who they were.'

So after ten minutes frosty silence, we went to our rooms, put on our coats and walked to the Office of the Holy Brotherhood. There were two other people in the queue and once the man at the desk had dealt with them, he turned to us.

'You all together?'

Baltasar took the lead. 'Yes we are. We would like to see Sergeant Felipe Ortiz to ask about Señora de Abaunza's case. She was recently kidnapped but escaped.'

'Is she here?'

'Yes, I'm Señora de Abaunza.'

229

'I'm not sure if he's in. I'll check.'

The man disappeared for what seemed an age but returned with a smiling Sergeant Ortiz. We followed him into the interview room and sat opposite the desk in the same positions as we had before, after my escape.

'Let me speak first,' said Ortiz. 'I have some bad news. My colleague Mateo López went to Guadalajara to arrest Ribera but he's vanished. Not even his wife knows where he is. She says she hasn't seen him since the day you escaped. Better news is that after several more interviews we have identified the woman who held you in that basement. She is in the cells here. We've charged her with false imprisonment and conspiracy to kidnap. We hoped that she'd be tried at the same trial as Ribera. He is in hiding somewhere, in a safe house or some kind of refuge.'

'Did you say refuge?' said Baltasar, coolly. 'Only, when I returned to Madrid to get the letter, I stopped for shelter under the eaves of a building set back from the road.' He told Felipe the whole story finishing with the death threat he was given if he revealed its whereabouts to anyone else.

'That's one possibility, I suppose,' said Felipe. 'Would you be able to take us there?'

'What about the death threat? What if they saw me with you?'

'They wouldn't see you because you'd ride past or return. Whoever told you what it was must have told others. You can be sure of that. They'll never guess that it was you who told us!'

'I'm going back to Madrid today or tomorrow,' said Baltasar.

'The sooner the better for us,' said Sergeant Ortiz.

'I'm going back, too,' said Inés. Baltasar frowned at her so I intervened.

'Please don't worry about me, I feel perfectly safe here, now that Pedro is keen to keep in touch with me. He may even be coming to see me this afternoon to see if there is any news about Carlos Ribera.' While being grateful for all Baltasar and Inés had done for me, I could see advantage in them going back. The way would be clear to develop my friendship with Pedro.

'In which case we'll return today,' said Baltasar, 'and having an escort part of the way may overcome another problem. He told the sergeant he was sure he was being followed back to The Mad Astronomer when he returned the day before.

'You what?' said an apparently enraged Sergeant Ortiz. 'Do you mean to say you returned to Madrid without telling me?'

'Well, yes,' said a humbled Baltasar. 'I went to begin putting Francisca's house back in order.'

'I did ask you to tell me if you were to move. This was partly to give you protection, especially after your exchanges with the gunmen on your way back last time. You were asking for trouble going alone... and so soon after you'd killed one of them. This time we'll take you back to your front door!'

'What if we return here with our bags packed and on our horses at midday,' said Inés.

'Perfect,' said Felipe. 'I will accompany you at least to the so called refuge and I'll take Officer López who will be able to recognise Ribera, if we find him that is. We'll take other officers too. We'll all be armed.'

Chapter 17

As I lay on my bed at The Mad Astronomer, I heard a gentle knock on the door. I imagined it would be Gonzalo to tell me that Pedro was waiting for me downstairs. I slid off the bed, straightened my skirt, quickly put my hair in order and opened the door. How wrong could I be? It was Pedro standing there, on his own and smiling.

'Come in Pedro! I half expected to see Gonzalo, the landlord, telling me you were here!'

'I thought I'd find my own way up! You shouldn't have told me your room number.'

We had hardly closed the door when we began the most passionate embrace. Our tongues mingled in each other's mouths as we hugged intensely. It was simply wonderful for me to be in the loving embrace of this wonderful, caring man.

'Once again, Francisca, you should take the lead and if you'd rather just talk for now and not make love, I would be more than happy.'

'Don't lie,' I teased. 'You would be so disappointed if I said not now!'

'I suppose you are right, but honestly I would accept your decision and wait until you were willing.'

'I'm willing now, Pedro. Come on. I want to be naked this time. To show you all my wrinkles and my sagging breasts! And I want you naked, too!'

We couldn't undress quickly enough. I even helped him undo the braces holding up his pantaloons. They dropped to the floor revealing his nakedness. He placed his thumb and forefinger on the top button of my camisole and undid it. He then worked his way gently down until my breasts were completely exposed.

'They are lovely, Francisca. The breasts of a forty year old. You are in truly good shape. How old did you say you are?'

'I don't remember telling you. You can guess!'

'Let's have a change this time. I can't imagine we will need any oil. How embarrassing would it be to ask?'

We both laughed.

'I'll take my weight on my elbows and we'll face each other. Does that sound good?'

'Just perfect.'

We were soon interlocked in the most passionate lovemaking. I could smell the manly perspiration on his body. I hoped he was enjoying the perfume I had applied. I lifted my legs and wrapped them around his back, pulling him even closer to me. We kissed and dribbled into each other's mouths. We were about to reach a glorious climax when we were interrupted by a knock on the door.

'What shall we do, Francisca?'

'Stop for now and I'll get dressed. You do the same!'

'Won't be a minute,' I shouted. 'Who is it?'

'Gonzalo. I have some visitors for you!'

'Tell them I'll be down soon!'

'They are outside with me!'

'Just a minute!' I called out. 'Hide under the bed, Pedro,' I said, my voice diminished to a whisper, 'I'll pretend to lock the door. I won't be more than half an hour. Do you want to wait?'

'Yes, I'll be here when you come back.'

***

To my astonishment, Gonzalo was accompanied by three people, two of whom I recognised. One was Professor Lorenzo Ramos, the Head of the Astronomy Department, the other was a woman I couldn't quite place but felt confident I had seen before. She was about thirty five or so, plainly dressed and with her hair tied in braids which fell over her shoulders, almost to her waist. I didn't recognise the third person at all. He was a fairly round, bald headed individual of about forty five to fifty. Gonzalo slipped away and left them standing at the threshold of my room.

'Señora de Abaunza, it is a pleasure for me to introduce you to Professor Alan McDonnell and his wife, Constanza. They arrived here yesterday after an arduous journey from England.'

It suddenly struck me that I'd met this woman sixteen or so years before, when Juan junior had introduced Juan and me to three of his college friends. Constanza was one of them. She dressed plainly then but the long braids of hair were new.

'I'm so pleased to meet you, Professor McDonnell and you, Mrs McDonnell. I think we met while my son Juan was at university here, at the College of the King.'

'I don't remember, señora. Maybe we did. I don't know,' she said.

From her slight hesitation and the straight look she gave me, I felt sure she was lying.

'But I do remember your son, Juan. We were good friends and he had many here.'

Suddenly remembering Pedro's plight, I suggested we go downstairs and continue our discussion there. I pretended to lock my room door.

'I also remember Juan well. He was an enthusiastic and talented student,' said Professor McDonnell, as we sat in the meeting room we used when Sergeant Ortiz wanted to talk to us. It thrilled me to hear him

234

say it, so much I could feel the tears welling in my eyes. 'We were all devastated to hear of his death. Professor Ramos has brought us here because we knew Juan and I've told him we will do all we can to help solve the case.'

'I'm not sure what we can do,' said Constanza, taking a different view. 'It was all so long ago. We've not been here for twelve years.'

Her comments irritated me and made me suspicious. I clearly remembered her vigorously defending Juan junior against being attacked by two other students who accused him of being a 'royalist'. It was as if it was yesterday. There was something wrong here.

'I shall put my mind to those events of sixteen years ago,' said Professor McDonnell and let you know what I come up with. Constanza and I are staying at Professor Ramos's house. Maybe we could all meet for dinner here at your hotel. How about tomorrow night, say seven o'clock.'

'I'd love that, Professor. Do you mind if I bring a friend from the Mathematics Department?'

'Not at all. Would you like to come, Lorenzo?'

'Of course. I'd be delighted'

***

Having said my goodbyes, I dashed back upstairs to see Pedro. He lay naked, curled up and sound asleep on my bed. I wondered about leaving him. I knew he had a busy evening ahead and it seemed wrong to wake him, purely for selfish reasons. While I was wondering about what the English professor could possibly do to help and why Constanza reacted the way she did, he stirred.

'You're back, Francisca! What was that about?'

'I'll tell you afterwards' I said, took my clothes off and joined him on the bed.

235

'So tell me,' he said, once our mutual pleasure had reached its natural conclusion.

I explained.

'So you've met McDonnell, so you are a step ahead of me! You say he knew Juan junior?'

'Yes! I almost cried when the professor said what he did about Juan. I don't know what he can do to add to the investigation. He may just remember something important. I think his wife knows more than she's saying. They've invited us to dinner with them tomorrow. I'd love you to come, Pedro. Here at seven o'clock.'

'I really want to, Francisca, if only to support you.'

'You are kind!'

'Do you mind if I go now, Francisca. I have some work to do before my tutorial tonight. Shall we meet here tomorrow for breakfast? We could then go to the brotherhood to see if they've arrested Ribera. You'll feel even safer if they have.'

Let's do that, Pedro. At nine?'

We kissed and he hugged me with undiminished passion.

***

The band of armed brotherhood officers, headed by Sergeant Ortiz and accompanied by Baltasar and Inés, approached the point where Baltasar had sheltered at the refuge. At Sergeant Ortiz's signal, they stopped.

'What we are going to do is this,' he said. 'Officer López, myself and two other officers are going to the refuge. You, Baltasar and Inés will not stop but carry on to Madrid. My other officer will be with you all the way. Is that clear?'

'Yes,' said Inés and Baltasar in unison.

The four brotherhood officers gingerly approached the refuge and Sergeant Ortiz knocked on the door. Each had their pistols concealed and at the ready. No one answered so he knocked again. The door opened and a man with a leather apron opened it. Unbeknown to Sergeant Ortiz, it was the same person who had let in Baltasar.

'Good afternoon. My name is Sergeant Ortiz of the Alcalá Holy Brotherhood. I understand you run a craft workshop here. Tell me, is a certain Carlos Ribera one of your employees?' Shrewdly, he didn't use the word 'refuge'.

'No officer, we have no one of that name working here.'

'In that case, would you object to us meeting each of those who work here, just in case he is using another name?'

'What's this man done, officer… for such a large number of you to want to see him?'

'May I say that is none of your concern? Are you going to let us in or do we force our way?'

'Come in,' the man said, resigned to having no choice.

Officer López took the lead in working his way around the benches and looking at the men attending them. He was sure he would recognise Ribera, whether he had grown a beard or long hair or whatever disguise he may be hiding behind. After all, he had worked closely with him, even though it was ten or twelve years before.

'No he's not here, boss, unless he's hiding somewhere.'

'We'll soon see.'

The four of them searched every room in the place until they had convinced themselves he was not there.

'Thank you,' said Sergeant Ortiz to the man who had let them in. 'He's not one of yours, it seems.'

Disappointed but not altogether surprised, the four of them picked their way back to the main road and turned towards Alcalá de Henares. Apart from the occasional cart which came towards them and a rider or two, there was little traffic so they made speedy progress. The weather was ideal, even if the cold wind was blowing in their faces.

'That's him!' shouted Officer Lopéz, as a lone horseman coming in the opposite direction passed them.

'Stop in the name of the law!' shouted Sergeant Ortiz. The man ignored him. Sergeant Ortiz aimed his flintlock in the air and fired. The man kept riding.

'Let's go,' said Sergeant Ortiz. 'We must catch him, uninjured if we can. As we get closer, fire in turn over his head. Don't spare the horses!'

They loosened the reins, jabbed their heels into their horses' sides and rode at full gallop. The man kept going, passed the turn-off for the refuge and was leaving them trailing. Lopéz's powerful young stallion thrived on the chase so he soon led the other three in the pursuit. The man looked round, placed a gun on his elbow and fired. The shot flew above their heads. He kept riding for at least half a *milla* and again looked round to see how much he had gained on them. One of the constables fired his gun in the air. At that moment, the man lost control of his mount and fell onto the road in a heap.

'Faster!' said Sergeant Ortiz. 'Let's get to him before he can remount.'

The man tried to stand up but fell to the ground again as if injured. In a cloud of dust the four heaved their horses to a halt.

'Sure that's him, Mateo?' said Sergeant Ortiz.

Officer Lopéz jumped off his horse and approached the fallen rider. He grabbed him by the hair and stared him in the face. 'Good afternoon, Carlos. It's a real pleasure to see you after so many years! I arrest you for kidnap, false imprisonment and attempted murder. You will accompany us back to the Office of the Holy Brotherhood in Alcalá de Henares where you will be held in custody until tried.'

The four of them helped the bruised Ribera back onto his horse. Sergeant Ortiz tied his hands behind his back and a rope to his horse's bridle. They trotted back to Alcalá with Ribera in tow.

***

Pedro and I were sitting in the dining area of The Mad Astronomer enjoying a fried egg breakfast and grape juice.

'Francisca, I have an interesting idea which I'd like you to think carefully about. Now that Inés and Baltasar have gone back to Madrid, why go to the expense of staying at this inn? I'd love you to come and stay with me. You would be my guest.'

'Goodness, Pedro. You've made me think now.'

'There are few things I should say. I would not expect you to help me with the cooking or looking after the house. You would have a separate bedroom. And I have to say, I am really fond of you, Francisca. I really want to ensure you are well cared for in Alcalá. This is the best I can do. You don't have to decide now.'

My mind went into an uncontrolled spin, just like a child's wobbling toy top. I didn't know what to do. The offer shocked me but at the same time it seemed totally natural. We had become intimate friends. There was nothing I would hide from Pedro and nothing I would not discuss with him. I would talk to him about my friends, my family, my views and anything I wanted to test on another close person, even about my faltering body. I wondered what Juan would think. Somehow, perhaps influenced by my prejudices, I thought Juan would strongly approve. I felt certain he would want me protected, wherever I might be, here, in Madrid or anywhere else. I only wished I could ask him.

My mind's state of indecision was broken by the appearance of Sergeant Ortiz at the dining room door. He came over to our table.

239

'Good morning, you two! I can see I'm interrupting a serious discussion. Should I go and come back later?'

'No, Sergeant Ortiz, of course not!' I said. 'I am just discussing with Pedro whether I should stay here or not.'

'If you do move, please let me know where. It is important that I know your address.'

'I will, naturally.'

'I've come to you with some news and a request, Señora Abaunza. Señor Carlos Ribera is under arrest. We captured him yesterday. He was riding back to the refuge your friend Baltasar discovered. We have interviewed him and he denies anything to do with kidnapping and imprisoning you. So we have organised an identification parade. It will take place at the Office of the Holy Brotherhood at eleven o'clock this morning. I would be grateful if you could attend please. We will simply ask you to point to the man who assaulted and kidnapped you. Would you be available?'

'Yes. I'd be delighted to help, Sergeant Ortiz.'

'May I come, too?' said Pedro. 'I will provide support to the señora.'

'Of course you may. Until eleven by the cathedral clock, then.'

Sergeant Ortiz left us to continue our discussion.

'Please don't misread my intentions, Francisca. We have enjoyed the most satisfying and enjoyable physical contact twice now but I am not asking you to stay in my house to make it easier. If we decided never to make love again, I would still ask you. I hold you in great respect and admiration. I am deeply fond of you and I want to provide you with protection as well as my company. We would be good for each other. We have so much in common that we can share.'

'What can I say, Pedro? I'd love to stay at your beautiful house and will willingly do my share of the cooking and housework.' I went around the table and kissed him full on the lips. 'I am fond of you, too, and long may it continue!'

'I can't say how pleased I am, Francisca. We will be wonderful for each other, I'm sure. Shall we move you this afternoon? Or would you like a day or two more at The Mad Astronomer?'

I hesitated at the suddenness of all this but not for long.

'I agree, Pedro. Let's get the identification parade over with and move this afternoon!' I smiled at the thought of Inés's reaction. Although I knew about her dalliance with Professor Lorenzo Ramos, I had never confessed to her that I had made love to Pedro. She might even be shocked!

***

Pedro had ridden to The Mad Astronomer and by way of a change, and to exercise my neglected young mare, Matilda, we rode at a trot to the Office of the Holy Brotherhood. Sergeant Ortiz welcomed me as if I had come to identify a corpse rather than a live human being.

'Are you sure about this?' he asked, as Pedro and I were ushered into his office. 'I only ask because seeing your kidnapper again may upset you.'

'It may,' I said. 'But it will be worth it to know this evil man will never do anything like it again.'

He and Officer Lopéz escorted us to a room at the rear of the building. Lopéz went in and left me, Pedro and Sergeant Ortiz outside.

'They are all in there. There are twelve of them. Most similar in appearance to Ribera. When Officer Lopéz tells us he's ready, he will ask you in. You go in with him and look along the line. Start from the left and look carefully at each. Officer Lopéz will stand next to you.

241

Point to the man you believe is the so called Sancho Mojaro, if he's there. Officer Lopéz will ask him to step forward so you can confirm. Once you've done it, Officer Lopéz will bring you out. Is that all right?'

'That will be fine.'

Moments later, Officer Lopéz emerged and held out his arm to invite me in. My heart leapt when I saw him. There could be no doubt. He was fifth from the left. I pointed to him and he looked straight into my eyes. His expression remained neutral.

'Step forward, fifth from the right.' (His right, of course.) He stepped forward. Two of Sergeant Ortiz's men appeared, took him by the arms and led him away. I was surprised at what effect it had on me. I could see why Sergeant Ortiz had treated me so gently when he spoke in his office. It felt like I imagined identifying a corpse would feel.

Sergeant Ortiz took us back to his office.

'Well done, Señora Abaunza. This has gone very well. Now we are absolutely sure this is the man who abducted you, we can interview him in detail. He has a lot to explain. The next time I speak to you, it will be about the death of your son. I believe we could be close to solving the case.'

'That would be wonderful news, Sergeant Ortiz. We wish you good luck. I should tell you before we leave, that I am moving from the inn. As from this afternoon, I shall be the house guest of Pedro Lobos de Pamplona.'

'Please give me your address, señor.'

'I live in Calle Merced, the third house on the left going east.'

'Opposite the Convent of the Mercedarios Descalzos?'

'Yes.'

'I know the road. Thank you for telling me, señora.'

'Well done, Francisca,' said Pedro as we climbed back on our horses. 'That must have been quite an ordeal, seeing your kidnapper again.'

'It was. It surprised me!'

We went back to the hotel. I packed my saddlebags and settled my account. I had to remind Gonzalo that he had agreed that the stabling of my horse would be at no charge. While still harbouring doubts about him, I thanked him for looking after me, Inés and Baltasar so well. I scribbled a note to Inés telling her I was about to become Pedro's guest and told her where he lived. I smiled as I wrote it, wondering how she would react. I also told her I had positively identified Carlos Ribera as my kidnapper and that I'd write with any more news. I gave the letter to Gonzalo who offered to post it and reminded him that five of us would be dining there that evening. Pedro and I remounted our horses and made our way to his house.

'Welcome to your new residence, Francisca,' he said, smiling.

'I am really looking forward to this,' I said. 'I still have certain reservations but I'm sure it will work out.'

'Please tell me, Francisca. Let's sit in the drawing room and chat things over. First, let's stable the horses around the back.'

We were soon sitting on the settee.

'What's worrying you, Francisca? Please don't feel obliged to spend every minute with me. You are an independent person. You can spend as much or as little time with me as you wish. Obviously, I'd like to spend a good part of my time with you!'

'The problem is, Pedro, I have no friends in Alcalá other than you... I don't want to be lonely or a burden on you... and I'll be going back to Madrid before long. I still have a life there.'

243

'Let me be open with you, Francisca. I know there is a big age difference between us but I think I am falling in love with you. I'm not sure how you feel towards me.'

'I'm very fond of you, Pedro, and I may be falling for you. I'm just not sure about living in Alcalá. Let's see how things develop between us over the coming days.'

Pedro helped me take my things upstairs. I chose the bedroom next to his. He showed me the cupboard and wardrobe space I could use and left me to unpack. While I did so, I felt I had been ungrateful, expressing doubts about staying in Alcalá and talking about loneliness. I dreamed up a plan. If our relationship blossomed into a full commitment to each other, I would sell my house in Madrid and find some work here, similar to what I'd done at the Shod Carmen soup kitchen. I peered out of the bedroom window. The Mercedarios Descalzos were just across the road and surely they wouldn't refuse me as a volunteer. I shouldn't get too far ahead of myself but I did feel good after having these thoughts. Then I had another idea. I went downstairs and peered into the drawing room. Pedro was sitting there reading some papers.

'I have a good idea, Pedro. I'd like to celebrate my arrival in your house. Would you please make love to me?'

'I think I could manage that! My room or yours?'

***

The meal with the professors got away to an awkward start. The three of them, the two professors and Constanza, arrived half an hour late. Constanza had made no effort to look her best and frowned at me and Pedro as she came in, seemingly not wanting to be there. She wore the same plain skirt and camisole top she wore when I met them the day before. The two professors gave us a friendly smile as they came into the dining room.

'We are so sorry to be late,' said Alan McDonnell. 'We mistook the time we agreed yesterday. Only Constanza got it right! We humbly apologise.'

Pedro glanced at me and I looked at him. There was nothing we could do but accept their explanation. We were, after all, their guests.

'That is not a problem, Professor McDonnell. Please allow me to introduce you to Pedro who is a lecturer in the Department of Mathematics. He is helping me with my investigation into my son's death.'

'We already know each other, of course,' said Professor Lorenzo Ramos. 'We are collaborating on a project about planetary movement. In fact, Professor McDonnell is working on it too, but, as far as I know, he hasn't met Pedro.'

'I am so pleased to meet you, Professor McDonnell. We have been writing to each other for a few years now.'

'And to meet you, Dr Lobos de Pamplona. Please allow me to introduce you to my wife, Constanza.'

Pedro stood and shook hands with her. Still in a frosty mood, she said nothing.

'Enough of this formality, let's call each other by our first names,' said Professor Ramos.

We all agreed and, from that moment, the conversation became more relaxed, even if Constanza was reluctant to join in. Gonzalo entered the room a few moments after the introductions, told us what we could chose for dinner and asked what we wanted to drink. Professor Ramos asked him to make out the bill to him and invited us to choose from whatever Gonzalo had available.

'We won't bore you ladies with the results of our research,' said Alan McDonnell. 'But we can talk about anything else!'

During the meal, we talked about the McDonnells' difficult journey from England and how they thought their ship was going to capsize in the high seas of the Bay of Viscaya. They told us about the bad weather in England and how people died of cold in the worst of their winters. Pedro and I had discussed beforehand whether to say anything about my moving into his house and had decided against it. So it was to his amusement, that, in answer to a question, I told them how nice it was to stay at the hotel and how well Gonzalo and his staff were looking after me, Inés and Baltasar.

'I have been thinking hard about the case of your poor son but, I'm sorry to say, I haven't come up with anything that I didn't discuss with the brotherhood at the time. How is their investigation going? And yours?'

Between us, Pedro and I brought them up-to-date with the kidnapping, the capture of the former constable, Carlos Ribera, and my identification of him at the identification parade.'

'Did you say, Ribera?'

'Yes.'

'He was the constable who interviewed me over your son's case,' said McDonnell. 'I was very surprised when he told me that his wife was studying chemistry in the Natural Sciences Department. I remember it well. It was, and probably still is, unheard of for a woman to be studying that subject.'

'Interesting question,' I said. 'Very unusual subject for a woman to study.'

At that point, Constanza complained of pains in her stomach and asked if we could bring this pleasant occasion to a conclusion.

'I hope it's not something you've eaten here,' said Lorenzo, half in jest.

'I don't know but I feel quite sick.'

'Let me take you outside,' I said. 'We'll leave the men here for a moment.'

As soon as we were struck by the cold air outside, Constanza leant over and was sick at the roadside. I put my arm round her shoulder to comfort her but she pushed me away. I tried again but she still rejected my help. I rushed inside to tell Alan McDonnell what had happened. He went out to help his wife while Lorenzo Ramos settled the account with Gonzalo. Lorenzo soon returned and apologised for the sudden conclusion of the dinner. Pedro and I thanked him for his hospitality and asked him to pass our wishes to Constanza to recover soon. We stood to give our farewells to Lorenzo and sat back down at the table.

'Time for us to go back to my house,' said Pedro. 'But let's wait until they've gone!'

'I'm not sure I told you this, Pedro, but Juan died of arsenic poisoning, almost certainly. He suffered from the identical symptoms and at the post mortem, some fluids taken from his stomach were fed to mice and killed them. I just wonder...'

Pedro interrupted me. 'Francisca, you've just struck gold! I now remember the mention of arsenic in the case files. Are you asking whether Ribera's wife had access to arsenic? And whether she killed Juan junior?'

'Just that, Pedro!'

'We must tell Sergeant Ortiz!'

***

By nine o'clock the following morning, we were standing in a tiny queue at the Office of the Holy Brotherhood. A lone woman of about my age, dressed to keep out the cold, waited in front of us. She turned around to greet us.

'What's a mother and her son doing here, this time of day?'

'Probably the same as you,' I said, before Pedro had a chance to utter a word and seeing no point in disabusing her. 'We've come to report a crime.'

'No, I'm here because I lost my purse yesterday and I want to ask if anyone has handed it in.'

An official unlocked the door and we entered. We all stood at the counter, with the woman in front of us. We waited several minutes before anyone appeared to deal with us. Then an officer with a blue shirt and a familiar face appeared.

'Yes, señora. What can we do for you this morning?' She explained her loss. He asked her about where she had been the day before, whether she could have dropped her purse in a shop or at the market. Then he went back into an office and appeared again, shrugging his shoulders. They didn't have it so she left, disappointed.

'And you, señores? I recognise you, don't I?'

'Yes, we've been here several times in connection with my kidnapping and my son's unexplained death.'

'Of course. You've been dealing with Sergeant Ortiz. I'll see if he's in.'

Sergeant Ortiz appeared with his characteristic smile. 'I wasn't expecting to see you two today! Good morning!'

'We've come with some information,' I said. I told him about the dinner the night before and what Professor McDonnell had told us about Ribera's wife studying chemistry.

'That could be very important, señora. Especially if she had access to the chemical which killed your son. Arsenic, if I remember correctly.'

'Correct,' said Pedro, feeling well qualified, having read the case papers.

'That is new information. I wasn't even aware she had been a student. As a matter of interest, did anyone else at the dinner party see any connection between the subject she studied and your son's death?'

'I don't think so, do you Pedro?'

'I don't think so either, not that we could see. It seemed odd that Professor McDonnell's wife was sick almost immediately after the professor had said it.'

'Probably a coincidence or something she had eaten. Leave it with me and I'll follow it up,' said Sergeant Ortiz, before shaking our hands and leading us back to the outer office desk. 'I'll let you know about any further developments and the date for the trial.'

'I wonder what Sergeant Ortiz and his men will do, Francisca?' said Pedro, as we walked, holding our horses' bridles, back to his house in the Calle Merced.

'I imagine he'll go to the Ribera's house and interview her. He may even search it. Other than that, I don't know. I feel good about the arsenic connection. There is something in it, I feel sure.'

'I really hope you won't be disappointed, Francisca.'

Chapter 18

One bright, fresh morning, about five days later, when Pedro was at the university lecturing, I was standing in the kitchen, preparing myself a drink when I heard a knock at the door. I shook slightly, not expecting a visitor and I was alone. I wondered whether to ignore it so I did for a minute. Whoever it was knocked again. I decided I'd go to the door and ask who was there before I opened it.

'It's Sergeant Ortiz, señora. I have some news for you. Officer Mateo López is with me!'

What a relief. I still lacked confidence after the hideous experience of the kidnap. I simply felt vulnerable when, now that Ribera had been arrested, I suppose I should not.

'I'll let you in!'

I opened the door to the ever smiling Sergeant Ortiz and his colleague.

'Good to see you, Sergeant Ortiz!'

'Equally, it's good to see you, señora. May we come in?'

'Of course. Follow me.'

I led them into Pedro's drawing room and invited them to sit on the settee as I sat on a sofa. I offered them a drink but they declined.

'Go ahead, Sergeant Ortiz,' I said.

'We have organised the trial. You may be surprised to hear it will be held in the Royal Courts of Law in Madrid in three weeks' time, beginning on the 14th of December. There is simply no court room in Alcalá large enough to accommodate the case. There will be five accused persons, Ribera and his wife, the woman to whom Ribera took you for dinner, the woman who held you prisoner and another person you have already met, the janitor at the College of the King. Ribera, his wife and the janitor are accused of conspiracy to murder your son. Ribera is also accused of abduction and false imprisonment and the other two women are accused respectively of colluding in an abduction and false imprisonment. Ribera is also charged with perverting the course of justice.'

I immediately burst into tears. 'I'm sorry, Sergeant Ortiz. I am overjoyed and sad at the same time,' I said, wiping my eyes in my handkerchief.

'I can fully understand, señora,' he said and came over to put a comforting arm around my shoulder. 'You, of course, will be the principal witness. I trust that will be all right.'

'Of course, Sergeant Ortiz,' I said, having just about regained my composure.

'The not such good news is that although we are certain that your son was deliberately poisoned, we do not know who actually administered it. So none of them is directly charged with your son's murder. This may or may not come out at the trial. Who knows? We will continue our questioning of these people, which is our right, so we may find out more before the trial. In the meantime, do you have any questions, señora?'

'I feel apprehensive about being a witness but I am fairly confident I'll manage. May I bring my friend Pedro along, and Inés and Baltasar?'

'Of course. They will sit in the public gallery but you will be close to them.'

'What about those men who followed my friend Baltasar to Madrid and back. Who are they, and have you arrested them? They may yet take revenge on Baltasar for killing one of their comrades.'

'We are still investigating that part of the case, señora. We are sure Ribera sent them for the letter, knowing where you lived in Madrid.'

'How could he know?'

'We think he noted it from the case papers. Your address in Madrid and that of your son in the Puerta Cerrada are in the file. So are the addresses of the other two victims. We are sure these men know that we have the letter. We think Ribera contracted them to follow Baltasar and now he's out of action, we are confident they won't cause more trouble. This won't stop us from finding them and we have a few lines to pursue.'

'Thank you for telling me. I have no more questions for now, Sergeant Ortiz.'

'In which case we will leave. If you think of anything else you'd like to ask, please let me or Officer Lopéz know.'

I saw them to the door and they went.

So they still didn't know who actually killed Juan junior. Surely it must have been Ribera, his wife or the doorman. I was totally surprised at his arrest. He seemed such a nice man when Inés and I spoke to him. It proves that you can never tell what someone has done or what they are really like merely by talking briefly to them or from their appearance, especially if they have something to hide.

I was dying to tell Pedro the news about the trial and burst into tears again as soon as he came in.

'Whatever is the matter, Francisca? I've not seen you like this before. What has happened?' he said, wondering, I'm sure, whether something had broken in our relationship and I was about to tell him I was leaving.

'Sergeant Ortiz has been here with Mateo. They told me the date for the trial. It's in three weeks, on the 14th of December. I'm sorry, Pedro, it is an emotional shock for me. I am happy and sad at the same time. Juan

252

junior's death was fading into the past but now it is part of the present and the future. I am being irrational aren't I?'

'No, Francisca. It is perfectly understandable and you will have more to suffer at the trial. The details of Juan junior's death will be spelt out in court and you will have to live through it, I fear. You will be one of the main witnesses.'

Having dried my eyes, I told him who had been charged, what the charges were and that the trial would be held in Madrid at the Royal Courts of Law.

'Why can't it be held here?'

'The court is too small for a trial this big. You will come with me won't you, Pedro?'

'Of course I will, Francisca. I'd hate you to have to go through it alone,' he said. Then in a lighter vein, 'Could I stay at your house? You can give me a conducted tour!'

I sat down that night and wrote a letter to Inés, telling her about the trial and the accused.

***

The following three weeks passed surprisingly quickly, despite my feeling apprehensive about appearing in court. Pedro was my main distraction. We both thought we were falling more and more deeply in love. We spent every spare moment together and, dare I admit it, we even slept in the same bed, either my bed or Pedro's. Our lovemaking was sublime. We enjoyed our couplings in every room in the house, except the room Pedro's father used. Our inhibitions surfaced only on the weekend that Pedro's father came to stay.

I still couldn't really understand why Pedro was falling in love with me, a woman so much older than him, thirty five years in fact. But love is a strange thing and we had so much in common. We both loved music, reading, art, eating well and, most of all, being together. Pedro played the violin and often played for me, especially after dinner. He reminded me so much of Juan my husband with his willingness to entertain and please me. Sometimes Pedro and I would read to each other, he from one of the classics and me from one of those plays by Tirso Molino or a story by Cervantes, usually from the immodestly entitled 'Exemplary Novels'.

To make the most of my time while Pedro worked at the university, I helped the nuns at the Convent of Santa Catalina of Sienna. I simply walked the hundred *varas* or so to the convent, walked in and told them I could help them, if they wanted me to. The first nun I saw was the one I first met outside and who asked me in to look around. She smiled and hugged me as soon as she recognised me. I told her why I had come and she took me in to meet the Mother Superior who was equally pleased with my offer. I could not have been more surprised when they took me into the kitchen and asked me to wash the breakfast dishes! There must have been upwards of fifty nuns living there so it took me almost two hours to complete this initiation task, if that is what it was, including drying them and putting them all in their wooden racks. The situation greatly improved when they asked me to join them at the soup kitchen in the Iglesia Magistral. I felt quite at home there doing an almost identical job to the one at the Shod Carmelites in Madrid, while married to Juan. They could see I enjoyed it and gave me regular work there.

These three weeks gave me time to think seriously about the future. Could I bear to leave Madrid and move to Alcalá to live with Pedro? Should I discourage him from being so much in love with me? Would he be prepared to move to Madrid to live with me? While the distance between Madrid and Alcalá was small, an easy two day ride, to make a permanent move one way or another would seriously change the life of whoever moved. I could not settle these issues alone so one night, after about two weeks, I opened discussion on these sensitive topics with Pedro while we were sitting together on the settee.

'Well, my dear young man, what are we going to do in the future? Let's face up to it, I am not a young woman. Death could strike at me at any time. If I lived to be an ancient eighty five, that would only give us sixteen years together. I am past child bearing by many years and you would make a wonderful father. I don't know what to think, Pedro.'

'You have surprised me, Francisca, raising these subjects. The one thing is certain: we are in love, Francisca. What do you mean, "I don't know what to think".'

'You would be better off with a younger woman is what I am trying to say,' I said, as unemotionally as I could. 'Do you remember the woman in the queue in front of us at the Office of the Brotherhood? She thought I was your mother!'

'I am glad we are having this conversation, Francisca, because I too have been putting some thought into these topics. This is my conclusion. You will not die at any time. Even if you died in a year's time, as long as I spent that year with you, my life would have been fulfilled. As for children, I have no real interest in having any. What we don't have we won't miss. So, as long as you are prepared to have me living with you, I will.'

At that point I moved closer to him and kissed him on the lips. 'That settles it, Pedro. All we have to decide is where we are going to live.'

'Not just that,' he said. 'Will you marry me?'

I could not help shedding a tear, a tear of pure joy. 'Yes, I will marry you, Pedro!' I had never felt happier since the day Juan and I moved into our house in the Calle de la Madalena.

'There are other things to settle,' I said. 'We need to work out where we will live. Here in Alcalá, in Madrid or somewhere else? The best solution would be for me to sell up in Madrid and move into your house. I love it here and, now I have a job with the Convent of Santa Catalina, both our lives would be fulfilled. The alternative is for us to live together in Madrid but you don't have a job there.'

'I'm sure I could find well-paid work in Madrid, Francisca. It seems a shame to take you from your friends. Inés and Baltasar would really miss you if you moved here with me.'

'They will have to miss me. I'm going to move in with you! Inés will always be my friend, but my place is here with you!' I said, snuggling even closer into him.

'What will you do with your house, Francisca?'

'Probably sell it, but I could rent it for a time. We don't have to decide yet. What we do need to do is to decide where we should marry. I met you in the Iglesia Magistral and would love to get married there!'

'Then we are agreed, Francisca!'

'Come on then, let's slip into a bed and celebrate our future. My turn to say it: yours or mine?'

***

The trial was only three days away when we packed our saddlebags and set off for my house in Madrid. One of the first tasks I had to complete was to return the post mortem report to the palace. Pedro kindly accompanied me. The palace returned the security payment in full and Pedro carried it back to my house. True to her word, Inés had kept it clean and tidy since she and Baltasar had returned. She had even repaired the settees and beds that the intruders had damaged while looking for the letter. There was nothing she could do to replace what they had broken but disguised the damage as best she could by filling the shelves with some pots and trinkets she'd bought from the Plazuela de Selenque market. Her kindness was boundless and made me feel guilty, to a degree, about moving to Alcalá.

Pedro was impressed when I showed him around. Just as he'd done for me, I showed him each room, one by one, starting downstairs. He even strummed the strings on Juan's harp which stood like an odd shaped sentry in the corner in the drawing room.

It seemed strange to have a man, other than Juan, sharing my bed but my love for Pedro was no different. Others might think I was wrong to treat him this way but this was my life and I felt confident I was right. I needed a strong and sensitive man at this difficult and challenging time in my life. I felt sure Juan would encourage my love of this young, gentle person who clearly loved me. He would bless our union. But we were here for the trial and that had to take precedence over everything else.

The Royal Courts of Law cast a forbidding spell over Pedro and me as we walked into this temple of justice. I felt nervous and inhibited. Pedro encouraged me to be relaxed. I felt better after seeing Sergeant Ortiz who, while we were walking along a dark corridor to the room which he said was to be used for the trial, came over to greet us.

'It is good to see you, señora! You are the most important person here, as far as I'm concerned,' he said with his usual beaming smile. 'I have arranged for you and Señor Lobos de Pamplona to sit together, as you are friends!'

'I was feeling nervous until we saw you, Sergeant Ortiz. Now I feel a lot better...not perfect but nearly so!'

'Thank you for being so considerate, sergeant,' said Pedro.

Sergeant Ortiz showed us into the court room. It was cavernous. I wondered how people would 'see justice done' when so much of the front was obscured by massive stone pillars.

'If you sit here, señora, you will be right next to the witness box. So you won't have far to walk under the public gaze!'

'But I don't want to be near the accused!'

'You're fine here... they will be over there,' he said, pointing to a raised area on the other side of the room. 'You can relax for now. The trial will start in about fifteen minutes. You can see there are already people in the public gallery and there are still some coming in.'

By ten o'clock, the court room was almost completely full. Some in the audience were dressed in the finest clothes, as if they were going to a theatre which I suppose this was, of a type. Many chatted and joked with each other. At the last minute, Inés and Baltasar walked in, scanned the unfamiliar room and waved at me and Pedro before squeezing onto a bench to sit. The noise died down to some degree as a constable whom I recognised brought in the accused and lined them up in the box. Ribera took the lead, followed by his wife, then by the woman whose house he took me to for the supposed meal, and then the one who kept me imprisoned in that awful basement. They were followed by the doorman.

An usher in a well-worn black jacket appeared from a side door and shouted, 'Silence in court!' His instruction achieved only a patchy result so he shouted again, this time at the very top of his voice, 'Silence in court!' This time, silence spread right across the room. The presiding judge entered: a slim, stern, senior figure. I expected him to be in formal dress but his only concession to formality was his long, blond wig. It was as if he'd just got off his horse and put on the headdress immediately before entering court.

'Please rise,' shouted the usher. All but a lame few stood. The judge bowed and sat in his elevated chair, the back of which was decorated by a large regal crown. He wordlessly signalled us all to sit.

'Read out the charges,' he said, loudly enough for the whole court to hear.

An official read them out.

'And what do they plead?' said the judge.

The official invited each in turn. Each said not guilty.

'That means we'll have to hear all the evidence, every shred,' whispered Pedro.

'Who is prosecuting this case?' said the judge.

258

A large, round, moustachioed individual wearing a black gown stood up from a bench in front of the judge. 'I am, Your Honour.'

'Then please proceed.'

'Could Carlos Ribera step forward in the dock?' said the prosecutor.

Ribera stood forward. The prosecutor asked him to confirm his name and his pleas of not guilty which he duly did. He showed no sign of emotion.

The prosecutor then invited Sergeant Ortiz into the witness box and invited him to swear the oath. He asked him to give the evidence against Ribera. Sergeant Ortiz gave a professionally convincing account. He began with a brief statement about Juan junior's death, quoting from some notes he had taken from the post mortem report. He then moved on to the kidnapping and the chance discovery of Ribera's handwriting, both in the papers on Juan junior's case, for which Ribera was the chief investigator, and on the anonymous letter. He explained that Ribera, having conspired in Juan junior's death, ensured the investigation failed to find his killer. This evidence proved the connection between Juan junior's killing and my abduction.

'Rubbish!' shouted Ribera from the dock. 'Total nonsense.'

'Silence, Señor Ribera,' said the judge, almost inaudibly as if to invite silence by example. 'Or you'll be charged with contempt of court.'

'Please continue, Sergeant,' invited the prosecutor.

Sergeant Ortiz reported the deaths of the student and lecturer at the College of the King, both of which happened about a year after the death of Juan junior and for which no charges had been preferred. He explained that the connection was that all three victims were ardent supporters of the monarchy. He gave evidence that all those in the dock were members of a republican faction, based in Alcalá de Henares. It met regularly in a rented room in the college. The group was named 'Fighters for the Republic' in some duplicate receipts Sergeant Ortiz offered the court.

'Forgeries,' shouted Ribera.

'One more exclamation and the trial will proceed without you,' said the judge, in an even lower but more emphatic voice than before.

'May I now call, Señora Francisca Paula de Abaunza to the witness box, Your Honour?' said the prosecutor.

'You may,' said the judge, impassively.

For a second I could not move. Then I knew I had to. Pedro steadied me as I rose from my seat. I stepped into the witness box. After giving my name and swearing the oath, the prosecutor began.

'Do you recognise the gentleman who stepped forward in the dock, whom we have been referring to as Señor Ribera?'

'I do, Your Honour,' I said, hesitatingly.

'No need to give me a title, señora. Only the judge is called Your Honour,' said the prosecutor, his thumbs engaged in the collar of his gown. A ripple of laughter from the public gallery greeted his pronouncement. I glanced at Pedro who shook his head to disapprove of the gallery's mirth.

'Tell me about when you saw him before and all the circumstances.'

I told him about meeting him at dinner in The Mad Astronomer, his eventual invitation to dinner at the house of a lady friend of his called Carmella, about him hitting me hard on the head in Carmella's house and, that this was the last I saw of him before I picked him out in the identification parade.

'Strange that you remembered the woman's name,' said the prosecutor. 'It is an unusual one, don't you think?'

'It is, sir. That's how I remembered it.'

Pedro glanced up smiling as if to compliment me.

'Do you recognise her in this court?'

'Yes, she is the third on the left in the dock.'

'But that señora's name isn't Carmella. She gave a different name when she pleaded.'

'As you say, sir, but that is the woman whose house I went to for the supposed dinner. Señor Ribera used that name when he introduced me to her.'

The woman visibly flinched at my words and looked towards the back of the room.

'Do you recognise any of the other women in the dock?'

'Yes, I recognise the one next to her to the right.'

'Who is she?'

'She's the one who held me captive after I'd been kidnapped.'

'How can you be so sure? According to the case depositions, the woman who came to see you in that basement wore a mask all the time she was with you.'

'She took it off to wipe blood from her face after I'd hit her with the chamber pot. Also, I recognised her voice when she spoke when I identified her after her arrest,' I said, staying calm while feeling vulnerable and nervous.

'Can you tell the court about your confinement in the basement of the warehouse you were taken to after being abducted?'

I gave a fairly lengthy account of those horrible four days. I managed it without a tear falling but I could feel the dampness in my eyes. I concluded by saying I had hit the masked woman in the face with the pot, which smashed to pieces, and then escaped after tying her up and locking her in the room. People cheered, whistled and applauded.

The judge intervened surprisingly loudly. 'Silence or I'll have you all thrown out!' The exaggerated threat sufficed.

'Do you recognise anyone else in the dock?' continued the prosecutor.

'Yes, I recognise the doorman at the College of the King. He is standing next to the right.'

'When did you last see him?'

'The last time I went to the College of the King, about two months or so ago.'

'Did you tell him about the death of your son and if so when?'

'Yes, the first time we met him. That is, my friend Inés and I. It was on our first day in Alcalá at about two in the afternoon. We saw him again on the second day at about ten o'clock in the morning.'

'Thank you, señora. I have no more questions. You may now go back to your seat.'

I can't say I'd ever felt more relieved. It wasn't so much giving my version of events but the sheer number of people in the court. There must have been two hundred packed in there like sheep in a pen. And I could not be sure how they might react to what I was saying. While high up in the box I noticed a few more people there whom I did not expect to see: Professor Alan McDonnell and his wife, Constanza, both looking very serious. I could not acknowledge them but did look their way with a half-smile.

At that point, the judge called out again. 'Who is defending?'

'I, Sir,' said a short, well-dressed man with braided hair. He wore a brown jacket rather than a gown.

'May I call Sergeant Ortiz, My Lord?'

'Go ahead,' said the judge, fidgeting his fingers impatiently.

'You have, of course told this court a pack of lies about Señor Rivera who, as he has stated is innocent of all charges. He protests that someone other than him, knocked Señora de Abaunza unconscious and took her away from the dinner party. The similarity between his handwriting and that on the so called anonymous letter is merely coincidental. Who is to say the señora didn't write the letter to herself, to draw attention to her plight? He was, as you say, the officer responsible for her son's case but like many others, it remained unsolved. What do you say to all that?'

Sergeant Ortiz smiled confidently. He drew on Ribera's membership of the Fighters for the Republic; that Juan junior's case and those of the other two murders were the only outstanding cases of their kind; that I had positively identified Ribera as the man who struck me; that he was the only other guest at the party; and evidence he would be giving about the involvement of Ribera's wife and the doorman at the College of the King would provide further evidence linking Ribera to Juan junior's murder.

'No further questions,' said the defence counsel, his head lowered in defeat or shame.

'Who do you want to call next?' said the judge.

'Sergeant Ortiz again,' said the prosecutor. 'So what is your evidence against the doorman, Señor Caballo?

'It is that Señor Caballo is also a member of the Fighters for the Republic. So, knowing that Juan junior was an ardent Royalist, he hated him and wanted him destroyed. He escaped prosecution sixteen years ago because the investigating officer, Carlos Ribera was part of the conspiracy. My evidence against him began when Señora de Abaunza told me about the delivery of the anonymous letter. She received it on her second day at The Mad Astronomer. In fact, a receptionist at the inn told me it was delivered to the inn on the evening of the señora's first day there. At that time, the only person she and her friend, Inés Martínez del Mazo, had told about the death of her son and of her intention to investigate it…apart from a few students…was Señor Caballo. He feared that the señora could be successful in her mission so he immediately went to see Ribera who was then staying at the home of his mistress in the Calle Ramón where the señora was invited at the pretence of a dinner. Ribera decided to write the anonymous letter which he did there and then, in the presence of Caballo. That was Ribera's biggest mistake. Had he asked Caballo or his mistress to write it, we may never have connected him with the murder. Caballo took the letter and gave it to an assistant to deliver that day to The Mad Astronomer. It remained in a pigeon hole until a receptionist gave it to Señora de Abaunza the following day.'

'Really, Sergeant? Do you have any other evidence to support that?'

'A partial confession, señor.'

'Partial? What do you mean?'

'We interviewed both Señor Caballo and his assistant. The assistant told us that, in all innocence, he delivered the letter to The Mad Astronomer on his boss's instruction. Clearly, Caballo asked his assistant to run the errand to avoid anyone at the inn recognising him. When we confronted Caballo with what the assistant told us he admitted asking the assistant to deliver the letter and that Ribera had given it to him to be delivered to the inn.'

'I have no more questions, sergeant.'

'Presumably you'd like Señor Caballo to step forward in the dock,' said the judge.

'Indeed I would, Your Honour,' said the prosecutor.

The prosecutor asked Caballo what he had to say in response to the sergeant's statement. Remarkably, and looking to the floor, Caballo said, 'I have no comment.'

'Then step back,' said the judge. 'Whom do we call next?'

'I'm afraid we need to speak to the sergeant again,' said the prosecutor. A ripple of laughter passed through the court. I couldn't really see why. The sergeant gave the court the evidence he had against Ribera's mistress and the woman who had held me prisoner. Only the mistress said anything in her defence: she complained that Ribera had demanded that I should be invited to her house, otherwise Ribera would disfigure her for life.

'The God hating liar!' shouted Ribera, as soon as she came out with it.

'May we now discuss the case against Señora Ribera, My Lord?' said the prosecutor.

'Of course,' said the judge. 'Please step forward señora.'

Sergeant Ortiz was still in the witness box when the prosecutor addressed him. 'Perhaps you could describe the evidence against Señora Ribera who is charged with conspiracy to murder.'

'There is not a great deal of evidence, señor but it is profound. To begin with, the señora is also a member of the Fighters for the Republic and has been since its inception some seventeen or eighteen years ago. At the time of Juan junior's murder, she was one of only two women studying at the University of Alcalá de Henares. She was studying chemistry, apparently with the aim of becoming a dispenser of medicines. She therefore had access to a large range of chemicals including arsenic, which is presumed to have killed Señor Hidalgo. Some three weeks or so ago, my colleagues and I conducted a detailed search of the Riberas' house in Guadalajara. Hidden in a cupboard

265

within a concealed cupboard in the kitchen we discovered two jars containing a whitish grey powder. The powder smelt vaguely of garlic. When we asked her what the substance in the jars could be she said it was a pigment she used in her pastime of painting. She could not explain why it was hidden in this secret cupboard. We took the jars to the Department of Chemistry at the university who identified their content as arsenic. They said it could not be used as a pigment because of its properties as a poison. We then confronted the señora with this evidence. She then admitted that she had been part of a conspiracy to kill Señor Hidalgo but said she had not been the person who killed him.'

The judge invited Señora Ribera to step forward in the dock.

'Why did you plead not guilty when you admitted your part in the conspiracy to officers of the Holy Brotherhood?

'I didn't. The officers are not telling the truth. The brotherhood are better known as fixers of evidence than they are as solvers of crime.'

The sergeant has produced highly damning evidence against you, señora. Have you anything to say in your defence?'

'My husband asked me to obtain the arsenic, My Lord. I had no idea what he wanted it for. After all, he was a constable and, as far as I knew, an upright man. He told me he wanted it to poison rats,' she said, calmly, looking the judge straight in the eye.

A moment after Señora Ribera spoke, Mrs Constanza McDonnell stood up from her bench in the audience and, speaking through her tears and red in the face, spoke loudly to the court. 'That woman is a liar,' she said. 'She gave the poison to me. I poisoned Juan Hidalgo. It was me!'

I didn't know how to react. She stunned me. Here I sat confronting the murderer of my son. I cried tears of mixed emotion. I had accomplished my mission in Alcalá, almost totally by the efforts of others, including my beloved Pedro.

'Arrest her, now!' shouted the judge. 'Put her with the other accused!'

The two Madrid constables who had stood in front of the public area barged past others, including Professor McDonnell, who was white with shock, and bodily dragged the crying Constanza to the dock.

'You are charged with the murder at some date in 1669 of Juan Hidalgo, the son of Señora de Abaunza who is present in this court. Do you have anything to say in your defence?' the judge said, calmly but just as surprised as everyone else.

'Nothing,' she stuttered.

'Is there anyone who is prepared to act in this woman's defence?'

There was no reply.

'In which case I will question her myself,' said the judge. 'What is your name and where do you live?'

'Why do I have to answer these stupid questions?' screamed Constanza.

'Because I cannot give my verdict on someone in the absence of knowing who they are or where they live,' said the judge, almost inaudibly.

She said her name and that she lived in Oxford, England.

'That's better. Now tell me why you killed the said Juan Hidalgo. What was your motive?'

'I was at the time a member of the Fighters for the Republic. We hated Royalists and Juan Hidalgo junior was one of the fiercest defenders of the monarchy you could meet. His father worked for the king. We hated Hidalgo. He had to die. So I poisoned him with the arsenic Señora Ribera gave me.'

'How did you do that?'

'I pretended we were friends and when we met I put a small drop of arsenic in his drink. I did that about eight times, I suppose. The last time I put in more than I had before, because I knew he was going from Alcalá to his home to Madrid and I wanted him to die there. That would remove suspicion from us in Alcalá.'

'What a poor motive for a murder, señora. To take a life simply because of a person's beliefs is a grave act of inhumanity.'

'I am now nearly seventeen years older now and it has preyed on my conscience since. I would never do such a terrible thing again. I feel worse now that I have seen Señora de Abaunza which I did only a month or so ago, after first seeing her when her son was studying at the university. She is a charming lady and didn't deserve to lose her son at my hands.' She collapsed in tears. An officer of the court lifted her back to her feet.

'I have no further questions, other than to repeat the one I first addressed to you. Do you have anything to say in your defence?'

'No,' she said, tears running down her contorted face.

The judge, half reading from his notes and half improvising, then summarised the case against the now six accused. He then delivered his verdict.

I find Señor Ribera, Senora Ribera and Señor Caballo guilty of conspiracy to murder Juan Hidalgo. I find Mrs Constanza McDonnell guilty of the murder of Juan Hidalgo, son of...'

Before the judge had time to finish, four gunshots shattered the calm of the court. Four of the accused collapsed in the dock. Two men standing were each holding two smoking pistols. People screamed. Many dived under the benches. Many fell on top of those already under. Others stampeded toward the doors. A crowd at the entrance were climbing over each other to get out. Order became chaos. Pedro looked at me with wide open eyes. I returned a stupefied gaze.

'Get on the floor,' he said. We both did.

I was terrified. I looked at the judge. He was getting back on his feet and straightening his wig. He did his best to regain control. 'Arrest the gunmen. Now!'

Four constables appeared from nowhere, climbed over the benches and grabbed the gunmen who shouted out as they were dragged from the court.

From the younger one: 'They killed my son!' From the older: 'They killed my son, too. Now they've got what they deserve!'

Order was half restored as the constables took the protesting gunmen out. Court attendants rushed to the four who were shot: Ribera and his wife, Caballo and Constanza. They helped them to their feet. Each had been shot in the shoulder or chest. While badly injured each was still alive. Blood covered the floor.

The judge stood. 'I sentence all four of you to death by hanging. Now get them to the hospital!'

Ribera and his wife were taken on stretchers; Constanza and Caballo walked, clutching their bleeding shoulders.

He then sentenced the two uninjured women, 'Carmella' and the one who had held me prisoner. 'I sentence you two to three years in prison for conspiracy to kidnap. I now declare these proceedings closed.'

'Stand up in court,' said the usher.

Many stood as the judge, his wig still at an odd angle, stepped down and left the court. Those still in the audience spoke to each other in urgent conversation. None had seen anything like this before. None had recovered from the state of shock.

Pedro and I hugged each other and made our way out of the court to be greeted by Inés and Baltasar who both hugged me at the same time.

'Congratulations, Francisca. It's all over now,' said Inés smiling as I'd never seen before.

'A brilliant result!' said Baltasar.

***

The sentencing of Ribera and his wife, Constanza, Señor Caballo and the women active in abducting me, concluded an important chapter in my life. I could now start the next one. Pedro and I could begin our new lives together.

The End

Afterword

You, the reader, may wish to know about some of the factual background to this novel.

Francisca Paula de Abaunza, the main character, was the wife of Juan Hidalgo de Polanco (28 September, 1614 - 30 March, 1685), probably the most famous composer of 17th century Spain. He was appointed in 1629 to the position of Harpist in the Royal Chapel of King Philip IV. He was a prolific composer of secular and religious music and wrote the music to the first two Spanish operas. Juan Hidalgo is the protagonist in my first novel, 'The Harpist of Madrid', of which this novel is the sequel.

Juan Hidalgo almost certainly knew Diego Velázquez, the court painter and world renowned artist, because they worked in the court of the king at the same time. The period of overlap of their service was about twenty five years.

Francisca and Juan Hidalgo were the parents of a son, their only child, also called Juan Hidalgo, who became a student at the College of the King at the university in Alcalá de Henares, a town about 20 miles to the east of Madrid. He entered the university on 11 September, 1664 after a special request from His Majesty. Such was the influence of his father. He died on 11 July 1669 in mysterious circumstances while still a student at the university. No record exists of the cause of death. He was buried in the parish of San Ginés.

Diego Velázquez's successor as court portrait painter to the king was Juan Bautista Martinez del Mazo. Del Mazo married the famous painter's only surviving daughter, Francisca de Silva Velázquez y Pacheco. Among their offspring was Inés Manuela Martinez del Mazo who in this novel is a friend of Francisca de Abaunza. Inés was therefore a granddaughter of Diego Velázquez. It is possible that Inés and

Francisca knew each other but I have no evidence to support that. Inés had a brother called Baltasar who was a few years younger than her.

Except for some of the historical characters mentioned in discussions between Francisca, Inés and Baltasar, all the other characters are fictional. Any resemblance between them and actual characters who lived in Spain at that time is purely coincidental.

All the locations in Alcalá de Henares and Madrid existed as do many of them to this day. All the street names are authentic.

Gordon L. Thomas